On with the Story

Other Books by John Barth

The Floating Opera

The End of the Road

The Sot-Weed Factor

Giles Goat-Boy

Lost in the Funhouse

Chimera

LETTERS

Sabbatical
A Romance

The Friday Book
Essays and Other Nonfiction

The Tidewater Tales
A Novel

The Last Voyage of Somebody the Sailor

Once Upon a Time
A Floating Opera

Further Fridays
Essays, Lectures, and Other Nonfiction, 1984–1994

On with the Story

STORIES

John Barth

Little, Brown and Company

BOSTON   NEW YORK   TORONTO   LONDON

Originally published in hardcover by Little, Brown and Company, 1996
First Back Bay paperback edition, 1997

The characters and events in this book are fictitious.
Any similarity to real persons, living or dead,
is coincidental and not intended by the author.

Most of these stories first appeared in periodicals:
"The End: An Introduction" in *Paris Review*;
"Ad Infinitum: A Short Story" in *Harper's*; "And Then One Day,"
"Preparing for the Storm," and "Good-bye to the Fruits" in *Conjunctions*;
"On with the Story" in *TriQuarterly*; "Love Explained" in *Yale Review*;
" 'Waves,' by Amien Richard" in *Trafika*;
"Stories of Our Lives" and "Ever After" in *Atlantic*;
"Closing Out the Visit" in *Iowa Review*; and
"Countdown: Once Upon a Time" in *Mississippi Review*.

Library of Congress Cataloging-in-Publication Data

Barth, John.
    On with the story : stories / John Barth. — 1st ed.
        p.   cm.
    ISBN 0-316-08263-5 (hc)   0-316-08359-3 (pb)
    1. United States — Social life and customs — 20th century — Fiction.
    2. Married people — United States — Fiction.   I. Title.
    PS3552.A7505   1996
    813'.54 — dc20   95-45790

10 9 8 7 6 5 4 3 2 1

MV-NY

*Published simultaneously in Canada
by Little, Brown & Company (Canada) Limited*

Printed in the United States of America

for Shelly

"$\Delta p \Delta q \geq \dfrac{\hbar}{2}$."

— Werner Heisenberg

". . . the laws of narrative . . . are as inexorable
as the laws of physics, though less precisely ascertainable."

— Scholes and Kellogg, *The Nature
of Narrative*

On with the Story

On with the Story

Check-in

So: After an extended and exhausting though exhilarating trip (all too short for those of us in no hurry to get where we're going), they check in, as they've been privileged to do at a fair number of pleasant-to-splendid stopping-places over the years. Accommodations clean, attractive, comfortable but not luxurious — just right for their purposes. King-size bed, well-stocked minifridge, good pressure in the shower even when everybody in the resort is changing for dinner. Fine view of the grounds, the beach, and the ocean from their top-floor low-rise balcony, high enough for perspective and privacy but not for vertigo, and open to the balmy tradewinds. All more than suitable; just what they had in mind for what they have in mind.

Although they're understandably pulled both ways, per prior agreement they don't get right down to their business. There's afternoon enough left for them to stroll the handsome spread — generic, they decide, but one of their favorite genres: Tropical Paradise. It was no easy call, if far from their toughest, whether to go this route or to choose instead from among some "realer" scenes they've loved — Iberia, say, or Umbria, rugged Alaska or the tranquil Chesapeake — or for that matter simply to stay at home, where they've worked and played and loved for so many/few years, and there be done with it.

"Are they sorry they've come?"

Not yet, anyhow; sorry only that things have come to this.

"She's not up for a dip in Mother Ocean out there; I can tell you that."

Therefore neither is he, he supposes.

"What *are* they up for?"

Good question. Despite the risk of mood-crash, they go back up to their room, already welcomingly familiar; they finish unpacking and settling in and presently decide, although neither has much appetite, to have their first night's dinner in the buffet-style main restaurant rather than in one of the several "specialty" annexes, in order to get the feel of that aspect of the place and some sense of their fellow guests — all innocent vacationers, presumably, as once upon a time were they themselves.

"Here's to the presumption of innocence."

Likewise to once-upon times. While the couple undress to shower to change to go down to dine, an early-evening rain-squall rolls in from the green hills behind their "last resort" and out to sea. As now and then happens in such cozied circumstances (witness Dr. Freud on the aphrodisial sound of falling water, Dido and Aeneas storm-snug in their Carthaginian cave, lovers among Rome's fountains or in motel shower stalls, honeymooners at Niagara), they find themselves for the how-manyeth time making king-size love — love, anyhow, on that king-size, no longer unrumpled bed — chuckling, knuckling back tears, soon enough murmuring and sighing, now gratifyingly spent and sweat-wet, skin to skin.

Presently: "Wrong order of events. Now they have to shower again."

Now they *get* to shower again, as their narrator sees it — and so, presently, they do. Although not meaningless, their order of events isn't important, anyhow not crucial, up to the final agenda-item.

"Agreed."

Take a sentence like his last one there, for example — *Although not meaningless,* et cetera — and rearrange its members through their other possible permutations, beginning it with *Up to the final agenda-item,* for example, or *Their order of events isn't important*; she'll see what he means.

Fondly, even nostalgically: "He does like to 'take a sentence,' doesn't he."

Yes, well. How's her appetite?

"Better now."

To dinner then, more pensive than festive, where indeed they address the formidable buffet with more gusto than one would have predicted, and chat amiably with their random tablemates (a seating-custom of the establishment) as if they were in fact fellow innocent vacationers. They even put away a carafe of the house red, which their narrator here pronounces quite acceptable.

"Good omen."

A misstep, they realize at once: not their wine consumption, but that casual-ironic remark of hers, made as they leave the great airy informal dining hall. Numerous other guests, those presumably innocent tablemates included, have adjourned earlier to stroll the beach or dance off their dinners in the outdoor disco-plaza or secure good seats for the nightly cabaret-style "animation" to follow; but our couple are in no hurry, no hurry at all, and so we've let them linger over the last of the not-bad beaujolais. At the word *omen,* however, their spirits plummet. Let's get them out of here.

"She's ready."

All too. Not back to the room yet, though, if he can help it: *There be dragons*, as the old maps used to say. They attempt the beach-promenade, among casuarinas and clacking coconut palms, but one of them hasn't the strength for it, let's say. Well before its end, she stops at a water-facing bench, sits, draws him after, kisses his hand, smiles.

"It really *was* a good sign, the wine and their enjoyment of it. Their ending is off to a good start."

Can't speak. Nuzzles the back of *her* hand in reply.

Presently: "Maybe tell her a story or something?"

Oh, sure. Right.

"A promise is a promise."

Is a promise. If he tells her a story, then . . . ?

"No promises."

That's as good a deal as he's likely to cut just now, he supposes. A temporizer to the end, however, he persuades her to go back with him through the fragrant oleanders and the fragranceless but indispensable bougainvilleas and hibiscuses — hibisci?

"*Hibiscus* does it."

— to their "village," their villa, their floor, their room, their balcony or bed (her call), if she wants a story. He's no Homer, he reminds her en route, nor even an Uncle Remus; if she wants a story, he'll read her one — Haven't they always read stories to each other? — but that's as close to the oral tradition as his job description comes.

"She's too pooped to argue."

Amen.

Presently: "So here they are."

And here we go. The storyteller, we agree —

"*They* agree."

The teller, they agree, is allowed to nod off at any point in the tale. His buns are truly dragging.

"Not as she sees them. And while we're looking, look at that moon."

Also the next, and the next, and the next.

"Don't."

Sorry.

"The listener, too, we agree . . ."

They. Goes without saying.

"Say on, then, dearest best friend: *Once upon*, et cetera."

First of a series?

"Don't count on it. Count on nothing. On with the story, okay?"

I.

The End: *An Introduction*

. . . As I was saying, ladies and gentlemen, before that little unpleasantness: I have just been assured, by those in position to know, that this evening's eminent "mystery guest" has arrived, and should be with us any time now.

Did I say "arrived"? In the literary sense and on the literary scene, our distinguished visitor "arrived," of course, with her first collection of poems, or at latest with her prizewinning second. On the international political scene, as the whole world knows, she arrived with a vengeance — excuse the poor joke, not intended — upon the publication of that more recent, truly epical poetic satire of hers whose very title it is dangerous to mention favorably in some quarters, though thank heaven not here. At least I *hope* not here; that unbecoming ruckus just now makes me wonder. And as of just a short time ago, I'm delighted to announce, she has arrived in our city. Even as I stretch out these introductory remarks — introducing my introduction, I suppose we might say, while we await together the main event — the most controversial poet of our dying century (*politically* controversial, it's important to remember, not artistically controversial, for better or worse) is in mid-whisk from the airport to our campus, to honor us by inaugurating this new lecture series. In that final sense, she should arrive here in the flesh —

the all too mortal, all too vulnerable flesh — within the quarter-hour.

In that meantime, I thank again the overwhelming majority of you for your patience with this unavoidable delay. It is owing, let me repeat, neither to any dilatoriness whatever on our visitor's part nor to transoceanic air-traffic problems, but solely to the extraordinary security measures that, alas, necessarily attend and not infrequently impede the woman's every movement. Who could have imagined that, at this hour of the world, a mere book, a mere *poem*, could provoke so dreadful a stir?

Well. As some of you may know, I myself am a writer, not of verse but of fiction: one whose "controversiality," such as it is, is fortunately of the aesthetic rather than the political variety. And I must acknowledge that although it is my professional line of work to imagine myself into other people's situations, I cannot for the life of me imagine what it must be like for such a free, proud, articulate, sensitive, gregarious, impassioned, and altogether high-spirited spirit as our impending visitor's to endure and even to go on making art under her constricted circumstances — not to mention courageously putting herself in harm's way by accepting from time to time such invitations as ours (whose absence of advance publicity I'm sure you appreciate, although your numbers suggest that word somehow got out despite our precautions). I shake my head; I am awed, truly humbled. It was my good fortune to first meet and enjoy the company of our eminent/imminent guest some years ago, before the present storm of political controversy broke upon her, back when she and I were happily just representative scribblers from two different countries sharing a lecture platform in a third — and I heartily do not envy her present celebrity! At the same time, for her sake if not for my own, I much wish that some Arabian-Nights genie could put me and every one of us who treasure artistic freedom and deplore murderous zealotry into our guest's skin, each of us for just a single day, and she in ours, to give us the chastening, attention-focusing taste of terrorism and to give her, who must surely crave it, a bit of respite therefrom: a souvenir of the artist's more usual condition of being blissfully ignored by the world at large.

But I was speaking of meantimes, was I not — indeed, both of meantimes and of mean times, and of introductions to introductions. For some decades, as it happens, I have belonged to that peculiarly American species, the writer in the university. Indeed, it has been my pleasure and privilege for many years now to be a full-time teacher at this institution as well as a full-time writer of fiction. As, again, some few of you may have heard, at the end of the current semester I'll be retiring from that agreeable association (my replacement has yet to be named, but I don't mind confiding to you that we're taking advantage of this new lecture series to look over a roster of likely candidates — not including tonight's visitor, alas — to any one of whom I would confidently entrust the baton of my professorship). There is an appropriate irony, therefore, in its having devolved upon me, as perhaps my final public action as a member of our faculty, to introduce not only tonight's extraordinary guest speaker but also this newly endowed "Last Lecture" series that her visit will so auspiciously inaugurate.

Valediction, benediction: I see therein no contradiction — and while I'm in the nervously improvised doggerel-verse mode, let me pray that to my valedictory *introduction* there may be no further *interruption*. . . .

So. Well. Until our guest materializes, kindly indulge me now an impromptu brief digression on the subject of . . . introductions.

The purpose of introductions, I have somewhere read, is normally threefold: first, to give late-arriving members of the audience time to be seated, as I notice a few in process of doing even now; second, to test and if necessary adjust the public address system for the principal speaker; and at the same time (third) to give her or him a few moments to size up the house and perhaps make appropriate program modifications. Introductions, therefore, should go on for longer than one sentence — but not much longer. And may Apollo spare us the introducer who either in the length of his/her introduction presumes upon the speaker's allotted time or in its manner attempts to upstage the introducee!

But tonight, it goes without saying, is another story. We need not ask of it the traditional Passover question — "How is this night different from all other nights?" — although that is the question that I urge apprentice storytellers in my "workshop" to put to the main action of their stories. Why is it that Irma decides to terminate Fred *today*, rather than two weeks ago or next semester? What was it about *this* satirical verse-epic of our visitor's that provoked so astonishing and lamentable a reaction, which her scarcely less provocative earlier works did not? You get the idea. I trust you'll appreciate, however, that in all my years of introducing our visiting writers to their audiences, this is my maiden experience of being not so much an introducer as a warm-up act for "him who shall come after me," as John the Baptist put it (in this instance, *her* who shall etc.). The bona fide introduction that I had prepared — short, short, I assure you, and not badly turned, if I do say so myself — I am thus obliged to expand ad libitum like one of those talking heads on public-television fund-raisers, either until there's mutiny in the ranks (but let it be more orderly, in that event, than that uncivilized earlier disruption) or else until our eagerly awaited guest . . .

One moment, please.

She is? Allah be praised for that! (No disrespect to that deity intended.)

My friends: I'm perfectly delighted to announce that the limousine of our so-patiently-awaited leadoff lecturer-du-soir, together with its attendant security convoy, *has reached the campus*, and that therefore it should be a matter of mere minutes — another ten or fifteen tops, I estimate and profoundly hope — before I happily yield this podium to the Godot for whom we've all been waiting. May that news update appease you while I now go straight to the matter of this series:

The anonymous benefactress who endowed "Last Lectures" (she was, like our guest, a she; that much I can tell you. Perhaps the muse?) throughout her long and prosperous lifetime was a perennial student, by her own description, and an inveterate "cultural attender," ever present on occasions like these. In her advanced age, she came to realize and even to derive some critical zest from the circumstance that, for all she knew, any given lecture or similar cultural occasion that she happened to be attending could feasibly be her last. It was her whimsical but quite serious inspiration, therefore, to endow handsomely a series of public lectures at this institution, with the stipulation that each speaker would be asked to imagine that this will be his or her valedictory presentation, or "last lecture" — as, for all any of us knows, any given utterance of ours might well turn out to be. Thus would we hear our visitors' "bottom-line" sentiments, their summings up; and thus by the way would the situation of the guest approximate that of the hostess — who, I'm sorry to report, went to her reward shortly after rewarding *us* with her philanthropy, and so cannot attend, at least in the flesh, this first Last Lecture, nor any of those to follow (the interest on our muse's endowment being generous, we expect this series to extend ad infinitum).

Do I dare point out — indeed, I do so dare, for I knew this lady and her mordant wit well enough, once upon a time, to believe that she would enjoy the irony if she were with us — that tonight's circumstances have matched donor and donee even more aptly than intended, inasmuch as both are now ... forgive me ... *late?*

Well.

What?

Aha. Gentlemen and ladies, ladies and gentlemen: *She is in the building!*

Excuse me? Okay; sorry there: Our distinguished visitor and her security entourage are *approaching* the building, it seems, although for several reasons I would prefer to say that she is "in the building" — for aren't we all, come to that, in the process of building and of being built every moment of our active lives: a-building and a-building until the end, whereafter our building, we may hope, will survive its builder?

Hum.

The end, I've said, and now say again: *the end.* And having so said, with those words *I* end, not my introduction — for our guest's custody, as it were, has yet to be officially transferred from the state and municipal security people to our own, I'm told, or to some combination of the two, or the three: a transfer now in progress elsewhere in this building even as I end, not my introduction of our visitor, whom I've yet to *begin* to introduce, but my introduction to that introduction. No fitter way to do that, I hope you'll agree, than with a few words about ... endings.

Endings, endings: Where to begin? I myself am not among the number of those Last Lecturers whose distinguished names you've seen on our posters and other advertisements (all except that of this surprise inaugurator, for good and obvious reasons). I don't mind declaring, however, that I could readily deliver a last lecture myself on the subject of endings. Further, that had I been invited so to do, I could not have done better than to begin with the opening exclamation of our Mystery Guest's world-challenging verse-epic, which exclamation I shall take the liberty of Englishing thus: "An end to endings! Let us rebegin!"

As we wind up our century and our millennium — this is Yours Truly speaking now, not our impending visitor, and you have my word of honor that the moment she enters this auditorium I shall break off my spiel in midsentence, if need be, as Scheherazade so often breaks off her nightly narratives, and go straight to the very brief business of introducing her — as we end our century and millennium, I was saying, it is no surprise that the "terminary malady" afflicts us. Of the End of Art we have been hearing ever since this century's beginning, when Modernism arrived on the stage of Western Civ. Picasso, Pound, Stravinsky — all felt themselves to be as much terminators as pioneers, and where they themselves did not, their critics often so regarded them: groundbreakers, yes, but perhaps gravediggers as well, for the artistic tradition that preceded and produced them. By midcentury we were hearing not only of the Death of the Novel — that magnificent old genre that was born a-dying, like all of us; that has gone on vigorously dying ever since, and that bids to do so for some while yet — but likewise of the Death of Print Culture and the End of Modernism, supplanted by the electronic visual media and by so-called Postmodernism. And not long ago, believe it or not, there was an international symposium on "The End of *Post*modernism" — just when we thought we might be beginning to understand what that term describes! In other jurisdictions, we have Professor Whatsisname on the End of History, and Professor So-and-So on the End of Physics (indeed, the End of Nature), and Professor Everybody-and-Her-Brother on the End of the Old World Order with the collapse of the Soviet Union and of international Communism.

In short and in sum, endings, endings everywhere; apocalypses large and small. Good-bye to the tropical rainforests; good-bye to the whales; good-bye to the mountain gorillas and the giant pandas and the rhinoceri; good-bye even to the humble frogs, one is beginning to hear, as our deteriorating ozone layer exposes their eggs to harmful radiation. Good-bye to the oldest continuous culture on the planet: the Marsh Arabs of southern Iraq, in process of extermination by Saddam Hussein even as I speak. Good-bye to once-so-cosmopolitan Beirut and once-so-hospitable Sarajevo, as we who never had the chance to know them knew those excellent cities. The end of this, the end of that; little wonder we grow weary of "endism," as I have heard it called.

And yet, my patient-beyond-patient friends, things do end. Even this introductory introduction will end, take my word for it — and I wish I could add "the better the sooner," as one might sigh at the end of splendid meals, splendid sessions of love, splendid lives, even splendid long novels: those life-absorbing, life-enriching, almost life-displacing alternative worlds that we lovers of literature find ourselves wishing might *never* end, yet savor the more for knowing that they must. Yea, verily, I declare, things end: our late muse/benefactress's enviable life, our own productive lifetimes, and soon enough our biological lives as well — happily or haplessly, all end. As I like to tell my students . . .

Excuse me?

Very well, and hallelujah: *She is proceeding at this very moment with her security escort through the several checkpoints between our improvised safe-reception area below-*

stairs and our final staging area, just . . . offstage, excuse that feeble wordplay — and will you gentlemen in the rear of the hall *kindly* return to your seats pronto and spare us all the indignity of once again marshaling our marshals, so to speak — who, as that earlier demonstration demonstrated, are standing by. I thank you in advance. I thank you. Now, please . . .

As I was saying: I advise my student apprentices to read biographies of the great writers they admire, in order to be encouraged by and take comfort in the trials and discouragements that attended *their* apprenticeship — but I recommend they skip the final chapters of those biographies. For a writer, after all, the alternative "last-chapter" scenarios are almost equally distressing, quite apart from the critical reception of one's works during one's mortal span: Either the end comes before one has had one's entire say (we recall John Keats's fears that he might cease to be before his pen had gleaned his teeming brain) — What an unspeakable pity, so to speak! — or else one goes on being and being *after* one's pen has gleaned et cetera: not so much a pity as simply pathetic. Therefore, say I to my coachees: Skip the endings.

The biographical endings, I mean: the endings of the great authors' life-stories. To the endings of those authors' great *stories,* on the other hand, I urge and enjoin apprentice writers to pay the most scrupulous and repeated attention, for at least two reasons, of which it won't at all surprise or distress me if I have time to share with you only the first before this endless introduction happily ends — its happiest imaginable ending being that it never gets there, if you follow my meaning.

Reason One is that it's in a story's Ending that its author pays (or fails to pay) his narrative/dramatic bills. Through Beginning and Middle the writer's credit is good, so long as we're entertained enough to keep turning the pages. But when the story's action has built to its climax and started down the steep and slippery slope of denouement, every line counts, every word, and ever more so as we approach the final words. All the pistols hung on the wall in Act One, as Chekhov famously puts it, must be fired in Act Three. Images, motives, minor characters — every card played must be duly picked up, the dramaturgical creditors paid off, or else we properly feel shortchanged on our investment of time and sympathy, the willing suspension of our disbelief.

There are, to be sure, ways of paying one's bills by brilliantly defaulting on them: apparent non-endings that are in fact the best of endings, anyhow the most appropriate. We might instance the alternative and therefore inconclusive endings of Dickens's *David Copperfield* and John Fowles's *French Lieutenant's Woman*; the roller-towel ending/rebeginning of James Joyce's *Finnegans Wake*; the recombinatory "replay" ending of Julio Cortázar's *Hopscotch*, to name only a few examples; likewise the more immediately contemporary phenomenon of "hypertext" fiction: those open-endedly labyrinthine computer novels that may be entered, transited, and exited at any of many possible points and waypoints. Such non-endings, I repeat, if managed brilliantly (and a mighty *if* that is), can be the most apt imaginable, and ipso facto the most satisfying.

And the reason for *that*, my friends (Reason Two of two, which I, for one, never imagined or wished that I would find myself giving voice to here tonight), is this: that every aspect of a masterfully crafted story, from its narrative viewpoint through its cast of characters, its choice of scene, its choreography, tone of voice, and narrative procedure, its sequences of images and of actions, things said and things left unsaid, details noticed and details ignored — everything about it, in short, from its title to its ending, may be (nay, *will* be) a sign of its sense, until sign and sense become, if not indistinguishable, anyhow inextricable.

Of this ground-truth, no apter demonstration can be cited, I trust you will agree, than our first Last Lecturer's —

Will you *please*, you people there in the back! . . . What? *What?*

Oh my. I say, there!

As . . . Dear me! What now? . . .

As I . . . As I was

Pillow Talk: "That's a story?"

Well, it's a beginning. As he warned her —

"And that's the end?"

In a manner of speaking. Figured we'd get endgames on the table early.

Presently: "Isn't it a touch close to —"

Home? I suppose so, but —

"Not what she meant. Now that he mentions it, however . . ."

He didn't mention it. Forget he mentioned it.

"The Unmentionable."

Old Unspeakable.

Presently: What else is there to talk about?

"If he loves her, he'll think of something. No threat intended, and thanks for the story, really."

He just thought of something.

"Let's hear it."

Mañana, okay? It's a long day's night.

"Well . . ."

If she loves him.

"Goes without saying, like some other things."

Sleep now, then. Hasta mañana.

"One night at a time, we guess. Mañana's another story."

And so it was. To wit (at some still-jet-lagging siesta-time next day, let's say):

2.

Ad Infinitum: *A Short Story*

At the far end of their lawn, down by the large pond or small marshy lake, he is at work in "his" daylily garden — weeding, feeding, clearing out dead growth to make room for new — when the ring of the telephone bell begins this story. They spend so much of their day outdoors, in the season, that years ago they installed an outside phone bell under the porch roof overhang. As a rule, they bring a cordless phone out with them, too, onto the sundeck or the patio, where they can usually reach it before the answering machine takes over. It is too early in the season, however, for them to have resumed that convenient habit. Anyhow, this is a weekday midmorning; she's indoors still, in her studio. She'll take the call.

The telephone rings a second time, but not a third. On his knees in the daylily garden, he has paused, trowel in hand, and straightened his back. He returns to his homely work, which he always finds mildly agreeable but now suddenly relishes: simple physical work with clean soil in fine air and sunlight. The call could be routine: some bit of business, some service person. In the season, he's the one who normally takes weekday morning calls, not to interrupt her concentration in the studio; but it's not quite the season yet. The caller could be a friend — although their friends generally don't call them before noon. It could be a telephone solicitor: There seem to be more of those every year, enough to lead them to consider unlisting their number, but not quite yet to unlist it. It could be a misdial.

If presently she steps out onto the sundeck, looking for him, whether to bring him the cordless phone if the call is for him or to report some news, this story's beginning will have ended, its middle begun.

Presently she steps out onto the sundeck, overlooking their lawn and the large pond or small lake beyond it. She had been at her big old drafting-table, working — trying to work, anyhow; pretending to work; maybe actually almost really working — when that phone call began this story. From her upholstered swivel chair, through one of the water-facing windows of her studio, she could see him on hands and knees down in his daylily garden along the water's edge. Indeed, she had been more or less watching him, preoccupied in his old jeans and sweatshirt and gardening gloves, while she worked or tried or pretended to work at her worktable. At the first ring, she saw him straighten his back and square his shoulders, his trowel-hand resting on his thigh-top, and at the second (which she had waited for before picking up the receiver) look houseward and remove one glove. At the non–third ring, as she said hello to the caller, he pushed back his eyeglasses with his ungloved hand. She had continued then to watch him — returning to his task, his left hand still ungloved for picking out the weeds troweled up with his right — as she received the caller's news.

The news is bad indeed. Not quite so bad, perhaps, as her very-worst-case scenario, but considerably worse than her average-feared scenarios, and enormously worse than her best-case, hoped-against-hope scenarios. The news is of the sort that in one stroke eliminates all agreeable plans and expectations — indeed, all prospect of real pleasure from the moment of its communication. In effect, the news puts a period to this pair's prevailingly happy though certainly not carefree life; there cannot imaginably be further delight in it, of the sort that they have been amply blessed with through their years together. All that is over now: for her already; for him and for them as soon as she relays the news to him — which, of course, she must and promptly will.

Gone. Finished. Done with.

Meanwhile, *she* knows the news, but he does not, yet. From her worktable she sees him poke at the lily-bed mulch with the point of his trowel and pinch out by the roots, with his ungloved other hand, a bit of chickweed, wire grass, or ground ivy. She accepts the caller's terse expression of sympathy and duly expresses in return her appreciation for that unenviable bit of message-bearing. She has asked only a few questions — there aren't many to be asked — and has attended the courteous, pained, terrible but unsurprising replies. Presently she replaces the cordless telephone on its base and leans back for a moment in her comfortable desk chair to watch her mate at his ordinary, satisfying work and to assimilate what she has just been told.

There is, however, no assimilating what she has just been told — or, if there is, that assimilation is to be measured in years, even decades, not in moments, days, weeks, months, seasons. She must now get up from her chair, walk through their modest, pleasant house to the sundeck, cross the lawn to the daylily garden down by the lake or pond, and tell him the news. She regards him for some moments longer, aware that as he proceeds with his gardening, his mind is almost certainly on the phone call. He will be wondering whether she's still speaking with the caller or has already hung up the telephone and is en route to tell him the news. Perhaps the call was merely a routine bit of business, not worth reporting until their paths recross at coffee break or lunchtime. A wrong number, even, it might have been, or another pesky telephone solicitor. He may perhaps be half-deciding by now that it was, after all, one of those innocuous possibilities.

She compresses her lips, closes and reopens her eyes, exhales, rises, and goes to tell him the news.

He sees her, presently, step out onto the sundeck, and signals his whereabouts with a wave of his trowel in case she hasn't yet spotted him down on his knees in the daylily garden. At that distance, he can read nothing in her expression or carriage, but he notes that she isn't bringing with her the cordless telephone. Not impossibly, of course, she could be simply taking a break from her studio work to stretch her muscles, refill her coffee mug, use the toilet, enjoy a breath of fresh springtime air, and report to him that the phone call was nothing — a misdial, or one more canvasser. She has stepped from the deck and begun to cross the lawn, himward, unurgently. He resumes weeding out the wire grass that perennially invades their flower beds, its rhizomes spreading under the mulch, secretly reticulating the clean soil and choking the lily bulbs. A weed, he would agree, is not an organism wicked in itself; it's simply one of nature's creatures going vigorously about its natural business in a place where one wishes that it would not. He finds something impressive, even awesome, in the intricacy and tenacity of those rhizomes and their countless interconnections; uproot one carefully and it seems to network the whole bed — the whole lawn, probably. Break it off at any point and it redoubles like the monster Whatsitsname in Greek mythology. The Hydra. So it's terrible, too, in its way, as well as splendid, that blind tenacity, that evolved persistence and virtual ineradicability, heedless of the daylilies that it competes with and vitiates, indifferent to everything except its mindless self-proliferation.

It occurs to him that, on the other hand, that same persistence is exactly what he cultivates in their flowers, pinching back the rhododendrons and dead-heading yesterday's lilies to encourage multiple blooms. An asset here, a liability there, from the gardener's point of view, while Nature shrugs its nonjudgmental shoulders. Unquestionably, however, it would be easier to raise a healthy crop of wire grass by weeding out the daylilies than vice versa.

With such reflections he distracts himself, or tries or pretends to distract himself, as she steps unhurriedly from the sundeck and begins to cross the lawn, himward.

She is, decidedly, in no hurry to cross the lawn and say what she must say. There is her partner, lover, best friend and companion, at his innocent, agreeable work: half chore, half hobby, a respite from his own busy professional life. Apprehensive as he will have been since the telephone call, he is still *as if* all right; she, too, and their life and foreseeable future — *as if* still all right. In order to report to him the dreadful news, she must cross the entire lawn, with its central Kwanzan cherry tree: a magnificently spreading, fully mature specimen, just now at the absolute pink peak of its glorious bloom. About halfway between the sundeck and that Kwanzan cherry stands a younger and smaller, but equally vigorous, Zumi crab apple that they themselves put in a few seasons past to replace a storm-damaged predecessor. It, too, is a near-perfect specimen of its kind, and likewise at or just past the peak of its flowering, the new green leaves thrusting already through the white clustered petals. To reach her husband with the news, she must pass under that Kwanzan cherry — the centerpiece of their property, really, whose great widespread limbs they fear for in summer thunder squalls. For her to reach that cherry tree will take a certain small time: perhaps twenty seconds, as she's in no hurry. To stroll leisurely even to the Zumi crab apple takes ten or a dozen seconds — about as long as it takes to read this sentence aloud. Walking past that perfect crab apple, passing under that resplendent cherry, crossing the remaining half of the lawn down to the lily garden and telling him the news — these sequential actions will comprise the middle of this story, already in progress.

In the third of a minute required for her to amble from sundeck to cherry tree — even in the dozen seconds from deck to crab apple (she's passing that crab apple now) — her companion will have weeded his way perhaps one trowels-length farther through his lily bed, which borders that particular stretch of pond- or lakeside for several yards, to the far corner of their lot, where the woods begin. Musing upon this circumstance — a reflex of insulation, perhaps, from the devastating news — puts her in mind of Zeno's famous paradox of Achilles and the tortoise. Swift Achilles, Zeno teases, can never catch the tortoise, for in whatever short time required for him to close half the hundred yards between them, the sluggish animal will have moved perhaps a few inches; and in the very short time required to halve that remaining distance, an inch or two more, et cetera — ad infinitum, inasmuch as finite distances, however small, can be halved forever. It occurs to her, indeed — although she is neither philosopher nor mathematician — that her husband needn't even necessarily be moving away from her, so to speak, as she passes now under the incredibly full-blossomed canopy of the Kwanzan cherry and pauses to be quietly reastonished, if scarcely soothed, by its splendor. He (likewise Zeno's tortoise) could remain fixed in the same spot; he could even rise and stroll to meet her, *run* to meet her under that flowered canopy; in every case and at whatever clip, the intervening distances must be halved, re-halved, and re-re-halved forever, ad infinitum. Like the figured lovers in Keats's "Ode on a

Grecian Urn" (another image from her college days), she and he will never touch, although unlike those, these are living people en route to the how-many-thousandth tête-á-tête of their years together — when, alas, she must convey to him her happiness-ending news. In John Keats's words and by the terms of Zeno's paradox, *forever* will he love, and she be fair. Forever they'll go on closing the distance between them — as they have in effect been doing, like any well-bonded pair, since Day One of their connection — yet never close it altogether: asymptotic curves that eternally approach, but never meet.

But of course they will meet, very shortly, and before even then they'll come within hailing distance, speaking distance, murmuring distance. Here in the middle of the middle of the story, as she re-emerges from under the bridal-like canopy of cherry blossoms into the tender midmorning sunlight, an osprey suddenly plummets from the sky to snatch a small fish from the shallows. They both turn to look. He, the nearer, can see the fish flip vainly in the raptor's talons; the osprey aligns its prey adroitly fore-and-aft, head to wind, to minimize drag, and flaps off with it toward its rickety tree-top nest across the pond or lake.

The fish is dying. The fish is dying. The fish is dead.

When he was a small boy being driven in his parents' car to something he feared — a piano recital for which he felt unready, a medical procedure that might hurt, some new town or neighborhood that the family was moving to — he used to tell himself that as long as the car-ride lasted, all would be well, and wish it would last forever. The condemned en route to execution must feel the same, he supposes, while at the same time wanting the dread thing done with: The tumbril has not yet arrived at the guillotine; until it does, we are immortal, and here meanwhile is this once pleasing avenue, this handsome small park with its central fountain, this plane-tree-shaded corner where, in happier times . . .

A gruesome image occurs to him, from his reading of Dante's *Inferno* back in college days: The Simoniacs, traffickers in sacraments and holy offices, are punished in hell by being thrust head-downward for all eternity into holes in the infernal rock. Kneeling to speak with them in that miserable position, Dante is reminded of the similar fate of convicted assassins in his native Florence, executed by being bound hand and foot and buried alive head-down in a hole. Before that hole is filled, the officiating priest bends down as the poet is doing, to hear the condemned man's last confession — which, in desperation, the poor wretch no doubt prolongs, perhaps adding fictitious sins to his factual ones in order to postpone the end — and in so doing (it occurs to him now, turning another trowelsworth of soil as his wife approaches from the cherry tree) appending one more real though venial sin, the sin of lying, to the list yet to be confessed.

Distracted, he breaks off a wire-grass root.

"Time," declares the Russian critic Mikhail Bakhtin, "is the true hero of every feast." It is also the final dramaturge of every story. History is a Mandelbrot set, as infinitely subdivisible as is space in Zeno's paradox. No interval past or future but can be partitioned and sub-partitioned, articulated down through ever finer, self-similar scales like the infinitely indented coastlines of fractal geometry. This intelligent, as-if-still-happy couple in late mid-story — what are they doing with such reflections as these but attempting unsuccessfully to kill time, as Time is unhurriedly but surely killing them? In narrated life, even here (halfway between cherry tree and daylily garden) we could suspend and protract the remaining action indefinitely, without "freeze-framing" it as on Keats's urn; we need only slow it, delay it, atomize it, flash back in time as the woman strolls forward in space with her terrible news. Where exactly on our planet are these people, for example? What pond or lake is that beyond their pleasant lawn, its olive surface just now marbled with springtime yellow pollen? Other than one osprey nest in a dead but still-standing oak, what is the prospect of its farther shore? We have mentioned the man's jeans, sweatshirt, gloves, and eyeglasses, but nothing further of his appearance, age, ethnicity, character, temperament, and history (other than that he once attended college), and (but for that same detail) nothing whatever of hers; nor anything, really, of their life together, its gratifications and tribulations, adventures large or small, careers, corner-turnings. Have they children? Grandchildren, even? What sort of telephone solicitors disturb their evidently rural peace? What of their house's architecture and furnishings, its past owners, if any, and the history of the land on which it sits — back to the last glaciation, say, which configured "their" pond or lake and its topographical surround? Without our woman's pausing for an instant in her hasteless but steady course across those few remaining yards of lawn, the narrative of her final steps might suspend indefinitely their completion. What variety of grasses does that lawn comprise, interspersed with what weeds, habitating what insecta and visited by what birds? How, exactly, does the spring air feel on her sober-visaged face? Are his muscles sore from gardening, and, if so, is that degree of soreness, from that source, agreeable to him or otherwise? What is the relevance, if any, of their uncertainty whether that water beyond their lawn is properly to be denominated a large pond or a small lake, and has that uncertainty been a running levity through their years there? Is yonder osprey's nest truly rickety, or only apparently so? The middle of this story nears its end, but has not reached it yet, not yet. There's time still, still world enough and time. There are narrative possibilities still unforeclosed. If our lives are stories, and if this story is three-fourths told, it is not yet four-fifths told; if four-fifths, not yet five-sixths, et cetera, et cetera — and meanwhile, meanwhile it is *as if* all were still well.

In non-narrated life, alas, it is a different story, as in the world of actual tortoises, times, and coastlines. It might appear that in Time's infinite sub-segmentation, 11:00 A.M. can never reach 11:30, far less noon; it might appear that Achilles can never reach the tortoise, nor any story its end, nor any news its destined hearer — yet reach it they do, in the world we know. Stories attain their denouement by selective omission, as do real-world coastline measurements; Achilles swiftly overtakes the tortoise by ignoring the terms of Zeno's paradox. Time, however, more wonderful than these, omits nothing, ignores nothing, yet moves inexorably from hour to hour in just five dozen minutes.

The story of our life is not our life; it is our story. Soon she must tell him the news.

Our lives are not stories. Now she must tell him the news.

This story will never end. This story ends.

"That's more like it."

Thanks.

"Thank you."

Him.

"Whoever. *Whom*ever. But there is no Him."

Just a manner of speaking.

"Pillow talk."

Why not?

Presently: "Why not: I guess because the world's full of *really* miserable people: refugees and political prisoners, brutalized and starving, or just people in dreadful pain from whatever cause, to whom the situation of that couple in that story would seem unimaginably luxurious. Not to mention *our* situation."

Theirs. Notwithstanding which . . .

"Notwithstanding which, Q.E.D., 'This story ends,' alas but amen. Are they up for tennis?"

Can he believe his ears?

"Why not? It's not exactly what they came here for, but here's where they came, after all, where there happen to be tennis courts and sailboards and snorkeling-reefs and discos. Let's run them through all of it, one more time."

A thousand and one more times!

"One time at a time, and count on nothing. Does he have the heart for it?"

Does she?

"No."

Likewise. You're on.

"Let's go."

They go and, having gone and bittersweetly done, in time return.

Presently (or, as might be said):

3.

And Then One Day . . .

Her professional knack and penchant for storytelling, Elizabeth liked to believe, had descended to her from her father, an inveterate raconteur who even in the terminal delirium of old age and uremic poisoning had entertained his hospital-bedside audience with detailed anecdotes of bygone days. The decade of his dying had been the century's next-to-last; in his mind, however, the year was often mid-1930ish, and the anecdotes themselves might be from the century's teens and twenties, which had been his own. The bedside audience was principally Elizabeth herself (or, sometimes, the night-shift nurse), although the anecdotist mistook her variously for her long-dead mother and for sundry women-friends of his youth and middle age, whereto deliriant memory from time to time returned him.

"Shirley?" he would say (or "Gladys?" "Irma?" "Jane?"), with the half-rising inflection that signals impending narrative: "D'you remember that Saturday morning five years back — no, six, it was: summer before the Black Friday crash — when I borrowed Lee Bowman's saddle-brown Bearcat to drive you and Eileen Fenster down to Dorset Station, and just as we were crossing the old Town Creek drawbridge . . ." Or, "Frieda, honey, run these damn affidavits over to Amos Creighton 'fore the courthouse closes, or there'll be no trial till after Armistice Day. Young Lucille Creighton told me once . . ."

What his actual last words were, Elizabeth didn't know; her father had died at night, in the county hospital, while she was in a distant city promoting her latest novel. The proximate cause of his death had been a fall in the corridor whereinto he'd managed deliriously to wander (despite his doctor's orders for bed-restraints when the patient was unattended), believing himself en route down High Street to fetch certain files from his little law office on Courthouse Row — which had in fact been torched during the black civil-rights ruckus of the 1960s. The final cause, however, was general systems wear-out in the ninth decade of a prevailingly healthy life, and so his daughter and sole heir had chosen not to press the matter of that possibly negligent non-restraint. The last words that she herself had heard him speak he had addressed to an imagined listener (Frieda again, his devoted secretary through most of Elizabeth's childhood) the day before the night of his fatal fall, just as Elizabeth, relieved by the hired nurse, was leaving his hospital room at the close of afternoon visiting hours to drive to the airport across the Bay. Once again back in the Prohibition era, he had been retailing to long-deceased Frieda the escapades of a legendary moonshiner down in the marshes of Maryland's lower Eastern Shore, whose whiskey-still successfully evaded detection by one federal "revenuer" after another. "And then one day," she'd heard her father's voice declare from the bed behind her as she stepped out into the tiled hallway . . .

And then he was beyond her hearing range, and not long thereafter she likewise his, alas, forever.

Retrospectively, it struck her that those words were (strictly speaking, *would have been*) an altogether apt though paradoxical exit line for a born storyteller like her dad — as also, come to that, for herself, somewhere down the road:

the story just kicking into gear as the teller kicks the bucket (she didn't know, in fact, whether her father had tripped over something in that hallway or slipped on the polished tiles or merely collapsed). At his funeral services — well attended, as he had been something of a civic leader and a popular "character" in their little hometown — she had told "the anecdote of the anecdote," as she called it, and it had been appreciatively received. No surprise: She was, after all, a professional. To friends and well-wishers over in the city, where she kept a small apartment, she found herself retelling it from time to time thereafter, no doubt sprucing it up a bit for narrative effectiveness as I've done here (her dad would understand): Who could know, for example, where the old ex-counselor had imagined himself to be as he wandered unattended down that fell hallway, or whether he'd even been delirious?

One of those city-friends happened to be not only a fellow wordsmith but a professor of wordsmithery at Elizabeth's graduate-school alma mater and, in fact, the coach of her advanced literary apprenticeship some years since. Over lunch at his faculty club, he remarked to his star ex-coachee that in the jargon of narrative theory, as opposed to the hunch-and-feel of actual storymaking, the formulation *and then one day,* or any of its numerous equivalents, has a characteristic function, aptly suggested by her phrase "the story just kicking into gear": It marks the crucial shift from the generalized, "customary" time of the dramaturgical "ground situation" to the focused, dramatized time of the story's "present" action, and thus in effect ends the plot's beginning and begins its middle.

"We're back in school! Come again, please?"

He topped up her Chardonnay and reminded her, between wedges of club sandwich, that every conventional story-plot comprises what she ought to remember his calling a Ground Situation and a Dramatic Vehicle. The GS is some state of affairs pre-existing the story's present action and marked by an overt or latent dramatic voltage, like an electrical potential: *Once upon a time there was a beautiful young princess, the crown jewel of the realm, who however for some mysterious reason would neither speak nor laugh,* et cetera. In the language of systems analysis (if Elizabeth could stomach yet more jargon), this state of affairs constitutes an "unstable homeostatic system," which may be elaborated at some length before the story's real action gets under way: The king and queen try every expedient that they can come up with; likewise their ministers, lords and ladies, physicians, and court jesters, as well as sages summoned from the farthest reaches of the realm — all to no avail, et cetera.

He cited other examples, from Elizabeth's own published work.

"I remember, I remember. But for years now I've just *written* the damn stuff, you know?"

You have indeed. Anyhow, this princess is as gracious and accomplished as she is comely, wouldn't you agree? A model daughter as well as a knockout heir to the throne — but nothing can induce her to so much as crack a smile or utter a syllable. In royal-parental desperation, her father proclaims that any man who —

"Always a man."

Not infrequently a man, especially in the case of problem princesses. Any man who can dispel the spell that the king is convinced has been laid on his daughter by some antiroyalist witch can have half the kingdom and the young lady's hand in marriage. If the guy tries and fails, however . . .

"No free lunch."

And mind you, this is still just the Ground Situation. Many are the gallants who rally to the king's challenge; likewise wizards of repute, renowned fools, and assorted creeps and nobodies. The princess attends their stunts and stratagems with mien complaisant —

"Mien . . . ?"

Complaisant. But be damned if she'll either laugh or speak. And so it goes, Zapsville for all contenders, year after year — and the story proper hasn't even started yet. You're not enthralled, Liz.

"Enough that *she* is. I can't stop thinking of poor Dad, that last night in the hospital, while I was off book-touring in Atlanta. Where was the goddamn nurse?"

And then one day . . .

"The handsome stranger. What else is new?"

Well. Sometimes it's the lad next door, whom the princess had never thought of in *those* terms. In any case, it's the screw-turning interloper in his saddle-brown Stutz Bearcat of a Dramatic Vehicle, come to precipitate a *story* out of the Ground Situation. The Beginning has ended, dear Liz; the Middle's begun.

"Maybe, maybe not." Unlike certain princesses, she smiled a bona fide, perhaps even half-mischievous, smile. "Thanks for lunch and lecture, anyhow."

Disinclined as she was to theorizing, once her erstwhile teacher and subsequent friend had glossed her late sire's "last words" in that particular way, Elizabeth came increasingly to regard them as talismanic. She remained appreciative of her father's role as her narrative model (*narrational* would be the more accurate adjective, in my opinion, but it smacks of the jargon that our protagonist disdains) — perhaps even more appreciative than before, as those incantatory words resonated through her sensibility. In time, however, she found herself rethinking not only the origins of her vocation but indeed the story of her life in the light of that fateful, though trite, formulation.

For some months immediately following her mother's early death, for example, young Elizabeth and her elderly father had continued the family's agreeable custom of Wednesday-night movies at the town's one theater. Thirty years later, the successful novelist still remembered clearly her pleasure in the idyllic state of affairs established in the opening sequences of many of those old films (although she'd quite forgotten the "ground situations" themselves and was less than certain that they had inevitably been marked by some "overt or latent dramatic voltage"): a pleasure doubtless sharpened by her unarticulated foreknowledge that trouble must ensue — otherwise, no story.

In our actual lives, of course, she recognized, there is no "and then one day" — although in the *stories* of our lives there may very well be; indeed, there *must* be, she supposed . . . otherwise no story. The story of her life as a storyteller, for instance, she could now imagine as having begun not with the more or less enthralled osmosis of her father's anecdotes (which, it belatedly occurred to her, had been merely that: anecdotes, not stories), but rather with her apprehensive recognition, in those childhood Wednesday-night movies, of the necessary impending disruption of those so-idyllic opening scenes.

In the draft of an extended thank-you note to her friend somewhere after their "end-of-the-Beginning" lunch, she declared experimentally as much to herself as to him, *Since time out of mind I'd been absorbing stories — told and read to me by Mom and Dad (Mom especially: Dad told anecdotes about down-county moonshiners and his courthouse cronies); read for myself in storybooks; witnessed in Stein's Avalon Theater, which we-all attended en famille on Wednesday nights more faithfully than church on Sundays. And then one day — watching some now-nameless G-rated production that happened to open with a particularly en-*

gaging family scene shot in Glorious Technicolor, as they still called it in the late Fifties (this will have been while Mom was sick in Dorset General, I suddenly remember, but hadn't died yet, and so I'd've been about 10 — and you, dear friend, were 30-something already, long married, with a kid my age . . .), I see up on the screen a pair of handsome, good-humored, obviously loving parents; two or three appealing youngsters of appropriately distributed age and sex; no doubt a pet dog, mischievous or soul-eyed or both, gamboling about the sunny ménage. . . . Note how I draw this introductory construction out, not wanting to come to its closing dash and the sentence proper — and then one day, *with a vividness that still impresses me three decades later, I understood that that "unstable homeostatic system"* must be disrupted — *for the worse, in this instance if not in all such instances, as it could not imaginably be made happier than it was* — must be disrupted for the worse, *and very soon at that, or there'd be no story, and we'd all start to fidget, bored and baffled, and presently make catcalls at the screen or the projection booth and even leave the theater, feeling as cheated of our 25 cents as if nothing had appeared on-screen at all* — since from the dramaturgical *point of view (as some people I care about would put it) nothing had.*

How's that for a Faulknersworth of syntax, Coach-o'-my-heart, and an Emily Dickinsonsworth of dashes from your quondam protégée?

In fact, of course [she went on, more to herself now than to him], *the unconsciously anticipated threat (never again unconsciously for this member of the audience) duly materialized: The family's happiness was, if not shattered, properly jeopardized by some Screw-Turning Interloper or Ante-Raising Happenstance* — *the MGM equivalent of Mom's galloping cancer* — *that potentiated the conflict already latent if not overt in the Ground Situation, then escalated that*

conflict through the rising action of the plot to some excit-
ing climax, and ultimately restored the familial harmony in
some significantly and permanently (however subtly) altered
wise, if I've got your seminary lingo right. It was exactly to
spectate and share this disruption and its sea-changed reso-
lution that we'd coughed up our two bits and set aside our
two hours; I understood *that, consciously now, and under-*
stood further (though not yet quite consciously) that what I
was understanding was one difference between life and art,
or between our lives and the stories of our lives.

For the language wherewith to conceptualize and reflect
upon that understanding, friend, deponent 'umbly thanketh
her ex-and-ongoing teacher. Her turn to take him *to lunch,*
next time she's in town, and to discuss, maybe, Middles?
Wednesday next?

And then one day (it occurred to her just after she had
redrafted and mailed a much-abridged version of this mis-
sive) — one Wednesday P.M., it was, to be precise, maybe
half a year after her mother's death — her father had restored
their cozy Avalon twosome to a threesome by including in
it faithful Frieda. Not long thereafter, Elizabeth had returned
it to a twosome by deciding that she preferred Saturday mati-
nees with her junior-high girlfriends to Wednesday evenings
en famille, if that term still applied.

In the jargon of systems analysis [word came back
promptly from across the Bay], *the unstable homeostatic sys-*
tem is incrementally perturbed by the you-know-whom and
anon catastrophically restored to a complexified, negentropic
equilibrium. Next Wed's bespoke, dear L, but Thurs's clear,
tête-à-têtewise.

Very well, Miz Liz, said she to herself: You're not his only
star ex-coachee, and/or he's not as ready to do Middles yet
as you mistakenly inferred him to be — at least not in *your*
story. And so with a professionally calibrated mix of mild

disappointment, continuing interest, cordial affection, and ultimate shrug-shoulderedness, she replied that Thursday next, alas, was bespoken for *her*, but that either the Wednesday or the Thursday following was (currently) free.

How things went or did not go with this pair, Middlewise, we'll consider presently. In the interim, Elizabeth found herself ever more intrigued, bemused, very nearly possessed by the paradigmatic aspect of her father's "exit line" (the line his, in the first instance, the exit hers, from his hospital room; then the exit his, from her life and his own, the line hers to ponder) and of the sundry Ground Situations in her life — sorry there: in her life-*story* — that that line could be said to have ended, for better or worse. She had innocently audited a thousand stories — *and then one day* in Stein's Avalon she had experienced what amounted to an enlightenment as to the nature of dramatic narrative, and this first had led to others, and after certain further crucial corner-turnings she had matured into a successful working novelist. Her girlhood had been prevailingly sunny and lovingly parented (she had come late and welcomely into her parents' lives), *and then one day* her mother manifested alarming symptoms, and was shockingly soon after dead. Father and daughter had proceeded as best they could with their life together and its attendant rituals — not unsuccessfully, in her young judgment — *and then one* (Wednes)*day* there sat plump Frieda at her dad's other side (Elizabeth's mother had been slender even before her illness, as was her healthy daughter now approaching middle age), and after Frieda, Shirley — or was it Irma — and after Irma et cetera; and far be it from Elizabeth to begrudge her father, either at the time or in retrospect, consolatory adult female company in his bereavement, but she and he had never thereafter been as close as she felt them to have been theretofore. Through her subsequent small-town public-school years she had been increasingly restless and irritable, though not truly unhappy — *and then one day* (thanks to the joint beneficence of her father and a childless aunt) she had been offered matriculation at a first-rate private girls' boarding school across the Bay for the last three of her high-school years, and that splendid institution had transformed her — had anyhow guided and abetted her transformation — from one more amorphous and unsophisticated though not unintelligent American teenage mediocrity into a really quite poised, knowledgeable, firm-principled and self-possessed young woman, if she did say so herself, looking forward eagerly to the increased responsibilities, challenges, and freedoms of college undergraduate life — in particular to the serious study of great literature, which she had come ardently to love, and the serious pursuit of "creative writing," for which she had discovered herself blessed with an undeniable flair and, just possibly, a genuine talent.

I am sorry to report that her baccalaureate years proved a time of pedagogical disappointment and considerable personal disorientation — all later turned to good account in Elizabeth's fiction, but scarifying to work through. Short of funds (that beneficent aunt had believed secondary education more crucial than undergraduate education), she attended a not-bad university on scholarship and found her underclass "professors" — many of them first-time teaching assistants only perfunctorily supervised — almost uniformly inferior to her experienced, knowledgeable, demanding, and enormously attentive prep-school teachers. The time here will have been the early 1970s: The grade inflation and à la carte curricula of the countercultural Sixties had made a near-mockery of academic standards on many American campuses, including Elizabeth's, at least in the liberal arts. LSD, marijuana, and hashish (but not yet cocaine and "designer drugs") were in almost as common use as alcohol; sexual promiscuity, like a straight-A average, had become so nearly the norm as to lose its meaning. For two years, to her own dismay, this promising young woman goofed off, slept around, abused substances and herself, managed a B average that she and her former high-school advisor agreed should have been a D at best, scarcely communicated with her father, very nearly lost her scholarship (which she knew she no longer deserved), likewise her life (stoned passenger in a car piled up by a stoned roommate who had introduced but not converted her to lesbian sex) and all sense of herself — not to mention of her notional vocation.

And then one day — one semester, actually, the second of her junior year — she found herself, in at least two senses of that phrase, in a fiction-writing "workshop" presided over by a visiting "writer in residence": a mid-thirtyish short-storier of modest fame, leather-jacketed charisma, and a truculent intensity that numerous apprentices, Elizabeth included, found appealing. Preoccupied with his own writing and career ambitions, to his and the university's shame (say I) he paid scant attention to his students' manuscripts but considerable attention to the authors themselves, in particular the two or three who happened to be physically attractive as well as somewhat talented young women. Of these, our Elizabeth was easily the most of both. Although the campus disruptions by anti–Vietnam War protesters in the preceding decade had frightened U.S. college administrators into shortening the academic semester from its traditional fifteen weeks down to thirteen, in that abbreviated period this writer-in-residence managed serial "skin tutorials," as he frankly called them, with all three of his talented/attractive protégées as well as with another rather less so but jealous of her classmates' special coaching. In short, of the seven female students in his workshop he bedded four, and in those sexually unpolitical though luxuriant days the only protest (made petulantly to the writer himself) came from a fifth who felt herself pedagogically shortchanged.

Among these four, unsurprisingly, his favorite and the most frequently thus tutored was Elizabeth; and it must be said for the unprincipled bastard that while he was an aggressive sexual imperialist, a shameless exploiter of the student/teacher relationship (which ought ever to be inviolate), an indifferent coach who did no line-editing whatever of his apprentices' manuscripts, and in my judgment not even a particularly gifted writer himself, he nevertheless knew a bright turn of phrase when he saw one, a false note when he heard one, a praiseworthy plot-foreshadowing or blameworthy red herring when one swam into his ken. What's more, in the perspiratory intervals between skin tutorials he did not scruple to remark such of those as he recollected from his tutees' prose. A genuine artist-in-the-making, if I may so put it, recognizes and takes to heart such nuggets of authentic professional feedback, praise and blame alike, regardless of the circumstances of their proffering; if it can be argued that a talent like Elizabeth's would have found its voice sooner or later in any case from accumulated practice and experience of literature, of the world, and of herself, it can also be argued that she found hers rather sooner thanks to the intercopulatory editorializings of her first real writer/coach — whose literary reputation her own would far outshine by when she reached his then age.

Now: The muses, it goes without saying, care nothing for university degrees or such distinctions as graduate versus undergraduate students, only for transcendent gifts disciplined one way or another into mastery. Our institutions being organized as they are, however, and our Elizabeth knowing, upon receipt of her baccalaureate, that she was possessed of ability and ambition but not of means to support herself through the next stage of her apprenticeship (commonly the most serious, arduous, and discouraging), she applied to several of the more prestigious of our republic's abundant graduate writing programs, was accepted at two of them, and chose the one that offered the larger stipend plus tuition-waiver. (It was also rumored that her erstwhile "skin tutor," an academic gypsy, was scheduled to visit the other program, and the memory of *her* exploitation of *him*, as she had almost come to think of it, embarrassed her. She had been, she told herself, no starry-eyed naïf, but an unformed talent craving professional direction the way a wintertime raccoon craves salt and determined to take it wherever she could find it.) In that new venue she had the good fortune to practice intensely for the next two years in the company of similarly able and ambitious peers, with and against whom to hone her skills under the benevolent supervision of a writer/coach more accomplished in both areas than had been his forerunner in her apprenticeship. This one kept his hands scrupulously off his charges — indeed, he had less social connection with them than in my opinion such coaches ideally should have — but very much on their manuscripts, which he took time to read more than once, to line-edit judiciously, and to review with their authors both in conference and in seminar. So did the young woman's art flourish in these circumstances (and her physical and moral well-being likewise, for she had exchanged substance abuse for a glass of table wine with dinner and perhaps an after-class beer with her comrades-in-arms, and sexual promiscuity for near-abstinence until, as soon enough happened, she found a coeval lover suited to her maturing tastes), by MFA-time she had placed short stories in three respectable literary periodicals and had sufficiently impressed her mentor with her maiden novel-in-progress that he felt he could show it to his own agent without compromising his credibility.

And then one day, therefore, she found herself possessed of a better-than-entry-level book contract, and some months thereafter of a favorable front-page notice in the *New York Times Book Review* — shared, to be sure, with a brace of other promising first novelists (that had been the reviewer's handle), but hers the most glowingly praised. Her debut paid out its advance on royalties and earned its publisher a modest profit as well as enjoying a *succès d'estime*, with the consequence that for its sequel her agent negotiated a handsome contract indeed, given that Elizabeth was and remains an essentially "literary" author. By age thirty-five, after a brief and unsatisfying marriage, she was supporting herself comfortably on her royalty income alone.

No, dear Liz (her ex-second coach, ongoing friend, and still-occasional mentor will object if she reviews her life-story with him in these terms, as I rather fancy her doing at their next lunchtime get-together): Those book contracts and that *Times* review don't qualify as Screw-Turning, Ante-Raising Interlopers on the order of Plump Frieda and Comrade Leatherjacket.

"May herpes simplex rot his predatory crotch. But he did call a spade a spade, you know, when he bothered to call anything at all. Why *don't* they qualify, prithee?"

You tell me.

Because, she would suppose, she has uncharacteristically lost track of precisely which story-of-her-life she's in process of telling, and a fortiori of what constitutes its GS as distinct from its DV, or its Beginning from its Middle. In the story of her literary apprenticeship (*one* story of it, anyhow, she imagines her friend mildly correcting her), those egregious skin tutorials had most certainly been an eye-opener, let's say, that initiated her serious application to the craft of fiction. "Viewed another way, however, that clown was just one more court jester, right? An unusually aggressive one, coming closer than most to getting a rise out of Princess Pokerface but still not succeeding, so off to Zapsville he goes, and good riddance. It was *you* who made the difference, dear friend."

No plausible tribute declined by the management. We both suspect, however, that what "made the difference" — as in most such real-life processes, if not in fiction — was some small quantitative increment precipitating a significant qualitative change. The girl sits through ninety-seven Hollywood movies in Stein's Avalon, and then one day, in midst of the ninety-eighth, she rather suddenly grasps some things about basic dramaturgy. So she writes ten yearsworth of practice-fiction without making noteworthy progress except in language-mechanics and the range of her vocabulary, meanwhile accumulating mileage on her experiential odometer, and then one day . . .

"Or it happens," Elizabeth hears herself declaring as if to her Chardonnay, "that two people who first knew each other in some uneven professional connection, like lawyer/client or doctor/patient, maintain a more or less attenuated friendship when that connection has run its course. They're still not quite peers, but their paths cross from time to time on officially equal footing at campus arts festivals or over lunch maybe once per season, with occasional letters or phone talks between, usually one of them congratulating the other on some new publication. . . ."

Very literary lawyers, these guys.

"Very. This goes on for years and years, while their professional lives exfoliate more or less in parallel and their personal lives turn whatever separate corners they turn."

Objection, counselor: In the matter of their personal lives you've got it right, but the curve of *her* career is steadily upward (as was his at her age), while his, as is to be expected, has leveled off and even begun its decline, fortunately gentle.

"So he declares."

Likewise, N.B., his physical capacities.

"So he sees fit to declare. In any event, almost without their noticing it —"

They notice it. But they both have good reasons for not acknowledging it.

"Excellent reasons. All the same, little by little, with neither of them especially leading it, or maybe each half-consciously leading it more or less by turns, their cordial and sporadic connection subtly changes character."

At least it pleases them to believe that the change has been subtle.

"Each has a failed marriage under his/her belt by this time, no? Hers of short duration, to a fellow former coachee of Sir Leatherjacket, as it happens, of whom she came to suspect her spouse terminally jealous. Anyhow, on the basis of considerable experience she'd begun to infer that she didn't particularly *like* men her own age. An ill-starred match, this one, but the split was prevailingly amicable."

I had gathered as much, Liz, but am gratified to hear it said. Not likewise in her friend's case, alas: a *well*-starred match, whereof the end was sore indeed. More community property to hassle over, for one thing, plus a few decadesworth of shared history, plus that daughter somewhere aforementioned. . . .

"A daughter *her age*, which datum gives the woman of this pair due pause. The mildly troubling truth appears to be that just as *she* seems most naturally attracted, other things equal, to men nearly old enough to be her father, *he* seems most drawn, in an egregious male-stereotypical way, to women nearly young enough et cetera."

Not bloody often, as Apollo is his witness. And when are things ever equal?

"Things never are. On with the story?"

On with it, by all means: This pair does lunch here and there from time to time for years and years, while the plate tectonics of their Ground Situation goes about its virtually imperceptible though nonetheless seismic business.

"And then one day . . . ?"

If any such conversation actually took place between these two, we may be confident that it was by no means so formal and narratively tidy as the foregoing. In fact, however, no such conversation did take place, and even had it so taken — untidily, inefficiently, marked by blurts, irrelevancies, unstrategic hesitations — it would not likely have led to anything of dramaturgical interest, inasmuch as the "senior" conversant had long since remarried and was not about to jeopardize that happy connection with infidelity; and the "junior" conversant, truth to tell — having grown up as a motherless only child and been taught emotional self-reliance both by life and by that excellent girls' boarding school — was disinclined to grand passions, sustained intimacy, even for that matter to an unselfishly shared life, though not to the occasional adventure. After the amicable dissolution of her short-lived marriage, Elizabeth had moved back across the Bay into her father's house to oversee his last age; when upon his death that house became hers, she continued to live and work therein contentedly (between her frequent travels) with a large Chesapeake Bay retriever as her chief companion: a more than ordinarily handsome, talented, and successful woman with numerous friends, infrequent casual lovers, no further interest in marriage and none in motherhood, and for that matter no very considerable sexual appetite — although she quite enjoyed occasional lovemaking the way she enjoyed the occasional lobster-feast, gallery opening, or night at the opera.

But even if their situations and temperaments had been otherwise, such that their affectionate casual friendship developed into an *amitié amoureuse* and thence one day or year into a full-scale May/September love affair (June/October, I suppose, even July/November, given their unhurried pace thus far), with whatever consequences to their lives and careers — so what? Reinvigorated by his new "young" companion (although in fact he hadn't been feeling *de*vigorated as things stood), the aging wordsmith closes out his oeuvre with a sprightly final item or two before ill health or senility caps his pen for keeps; alternatively, he so loses himself in the distractions of a new life at his age that he writes nothing further of more than clinical or biographical interest; or an automobile crash, whether his fault or the other driver's, kills him before either of those scenarios can unfold. Inspired by the first truly mature sexual/emotional relationship of her life, Elizabeth in her forties develops from a quite successful though not extraordinary novelist into one of the memorable voices of her generation; her works are everywhere acclaimed by that minuscule fraction of Earth's human population who take pleasure in the art of written literature, and although death claims her mentor/lover all too soon, she manages to remain vigorously productive even after receipt of her Nobel Prize. Or it turns out that their connection doesn't turn out; both parties soon enough recognize (he the more painfully, given the cost of his misstep) that things between them had better remained at the *amitié amoureuse* stage, better yet at the cordial occasional-lunch stage. Or it does work out, anyhow looks to be working out, when alas the MD-80 ferrying them to St. Bart's on holiday is blown out of the Caribbean sky by Islamic-fundamentalist terrorists; or perhaps Elizabeth, attending to some urban business, is shot dead by an irked carjacker when she resists his heist of her saddle-brown Jaguar.

In each and any case, so what? One more short or not-so-short story of bourgeois romance, domestic tribulation, personal and vocational fulfillment or frustration, while the world grinds on. Even were it one more narrative of aspiration and struggle in some worthy, impersonal cause, perhaps of fundamental decency versus self-deception, the seductions of language, and the human inclination to see our lives as stories — So what?

The world grinds on; the world grinds on.

So what?

That's a mighty *so what*, she imagines her friend responding with some concern. Does Miz Liz not remember his distinguishing, back in her advanced-apprentice days, between the readerly reactions *So what?* and *Ah, so!* — the former indicating that the author's narrative/dramatic bills remain unpaid, the latter that her dramaturgical bookkeeping is in good order?

"Sure she remembers, now that he mentions it. Okay, so she remembers: So what, when all's said and done?"

Ah, so: Our Elizabeth appears to have written herself into a proper corner. She has understood all along, more or less, that neither her life nor her father's nor any soul else's is a *story*, while at the same time wryly viewing and reviewing hers, at least, as if it were. And then one day, some imperceptible "quantitative incrementation" . . .

On this particular telling, the story of her life thus far (more accurately, I must point out, the story thus far of her life) — its four decadesworth of sundry ups and downs, consequential waypoints and corner-turnings — amounts after all not to a Middle-in-progress, as she has habitually supposed; nor (on this telling) will it so amount four further decades hence, should she live so long, quite regardless of how things go. On this telling she imagines herself then, an old woman at a writing-table in her father's house or some other, having in the course of her long and by-no-means-uneventful life done this and this and this but not that, or that and that but never this, with such-and-such consequences — the whole catalogue of actions, reactions, and happenstances amounting to no more than an interminable Beginning: a procession of jester/gallants acting out before a complaisant-miened but ultimately impassive princess.

At her feet, her loll-tongued, curly-furred, saddle-brown Chesapeake Bay retriever stirs, makes a small deep wuffing sound, and without lifting his great head from his forepaws, opens his pink-white eyes and shifts his muzzle half-interestedly doorward, as if perhaps sensing something there-beyond, perhaps not. Elizabeth registers subliminally the animal's tentative curiosity but is, as usual, preoccupied with, even lost in, her story-in-progress, if that adjective can be said to apply:

And then one day . . .

"Dot dot dot? . . ."

Suspension points; couldn't manage without them. Things left unsaid . . .

Presently: "Real people don't do it this way."

Really? How do Real People do it?

"They just *do* it, for pity's sake. No running halfway round the world to some resort-chain Paradise. Real people just up and do it and be done with it and that's that."

No fuss no muss no bother?

"No suspension points."

Presently: We're not RPs; we're us.

"Them."

They're who they are, not some other couple.

"Bad luck for them."

Bad and good don't come into it. They've loved each other. . . .

"Still do."

Absolutely.

"Bad luck for them. If anything, that makes things harder."

Well, dot dot dot.

"They're playing our song."

We're playing theirs. Care to dance?

Eventually: Never mind Real People. We'll all be Real next time around.

"They wish."

Meanwhile, they're stuck with being us, and vice versa. There're worse fates.

"For sure. Look at that sunset."

Wind's breezing up. He could tell her a story about that, while they're killing time.

"Dot dot dot. Not funny."

Kiss.

Presently: "Tell."

4.

Preparing for the Storm

Weather the storm that you can't avoid, the old sailors' proverb advises, *and avoid the storm that you can't weather.* No way our waterside neighborhood can avoid *this* character; for days now she's been on our "event horizon": a one-eyed giantess lumbering first more or less our way, then more and more our way, now unequivocally our way. Unless her track unexpectedly changes, Hurricane Dashika will juggernaut in from our literal horizon at this story's end, and no doubt end this story.

In times past, such seasonal slam-bangers took all but the canniest by surprise and exacted a toll much higher for their victims' nonpreparation. Nowadays the new technology gives all hands ample, anyhow reasonable notice. There are, of course, surprises still, such as the rare blaster of such intensity as to overwhelm any amount of accurate forecasting and prudent preparation. In the face of those (which we hereabouts have so far been spared), some throw up their hands and make no preparation whatever; they only wait, stoically or otherwise, for the worst. Wiser heads, however, do their best even in such desperate circumstances, mercifully not knowing in advance that their best will prove futile — for who's to say, before the fact, that it will? — and meanwhile taking some comfort in having done everything they could.

Contrariwise, there is undeniably a "Cry Wolf" effect, especially late in the season after a number of false alarms (a misnomer: The alarms aren't invalidated by the fact that more often than not the worst doesn't happen). Reluctant to address yet again the labors of preparation and subsequent "depreparation," some wait too long in hopes that this latest alarm will also prove "false"; they begin their precautionary work too late if at all and consequently suffer, anyhow risk suffering, what sensible preparation would have spared them.

Sensible preparation, yes: neither on the one hand paranoically (and counterproductively) taking the most extreme defensive measures at the least alarm, nor on the other underprepping for the storm's most probable maximum intensity, time of arrival, and duration — that is the Reasonable Waterside Dweller's objective. Not surprisingly, RWDs of comparable experience and judgment may disagree on what constitutes the appropriate response to a given stage of a given storm's predicted approach. Indeed, such neighborly disagreements — serious but typically good-humored when the consequences of one's "judgment call" redound upon the caller only, not upon his or her neighbors — are a feature of life hereabouts in storm season: Not one of us but keeps a weather eye, so to speak, on our neighbors' preparations or nonpreparations as we go about our own.

In this respect, my situation is fortunate: I'm flanked on my upshore side by old "Better-Safe-Than-Sorry" Bowman, typically the first of us to double up his dock lines, board his windows, and the rest, and on my downshore side by young Ms. "Take-a-Chance" Tyler, typically the last. Both are seasoned, prudent hands — as am I, in my judgment. Neither neighbor, in my judgment, is either decidedly reckless or decidedly overcautious (although each teases the other with the appropriate adjective) — nor, in my judgment, am I. When therefore old Bowman sets about plywooding his glass or shifting his vintage fishing-skiff from dock to more sheltered mooring, I take due note but may or may not take similar action just yet with my little daysailer; should it happen that *Tyler* initiates such measures before I do, however, I lose no time in following suit. Contrariwise, the circumstance that Tyler hasn't yet stowed her lawn furniture or literally battened the hatches of her salty cruising sailboat doesn't mean that I won't stow and batten mine — but I can scarcely imagine doing so if even Bowman hasn't bothered. All in all, thus far the three of us have managed well enough.

Our current season's box score happens to be exemplary. Hurricane Abdullah (the Weather Service has gone multicultural in recent years, as well as both-sexual) suckered all of us, though not simultaneously, into full Stage Three, Red-Alert preparation, even unto the checklist's final item — shutting off our main power and gas lines, locking all doors, and retreating inland — and then unaccountably hung a hard right at our virtual threshold, roared out to sea, and scarcely raised the local breeze enough to dry our late-July sweat as we undid our mighty preparations. Tropical Storms Bonnie and Clyde, the tandem toughs of August, distributed their punishments complementarily: Predicted merely to brush by us, Bonnie took a surprise last-minute swing our way and made Tyler scramble in her bikini from Green Alert (Stage One, which we had all routinely mounted: the minimum Get-Readys for even a Severe Thunderstorm warning) up through Yellow (where I myself had seen fit to stop under the circumstances) to Red, while long-since-battened-down Bowman fished and chuckled from his dock — just long enough to make his point before lending her a hand, as did I when I finished my Stage Three catch-up. From Bonnie we all took hits, none major: an unstowed lawn chair through Tyler's porch screen; gelcoat scratches on my daysailer, which I ought to've hauled out before it scraped the dock-piles; a big sycamore limb down in Bowman's side yard ("Not a dead one, though," old Better-Safe was quick to point out, who in Tyler's view prunes his deadwood before it's rightly sick). No sooner had we re-de-prepped than on Bonnie's heels came Clyde, a clear Stage Two-er by my assessment, Stage Three again by B.S.T.S. Bowman's, Stage One once more by T.A.C. Tyler's. Clyde thundered erratically up the coast just far enough offshore to justify all three scenarios and then "did an Abdullah," leaving Bowman to prep down laboriously all day from Red Alert and me all morning from Yellow, while Tyler sunbathed triumphantly out on her dock, belly-down on a beach towel, headphones on and bikini-top off — just long enough to make her point before she pulled on a T-shirt and pitched in to return our earlier favor, first helping me Doppler-Shift from Yellow back through Green and then (with me) helping Bowman do likewise, who had already by that time Yellowed down from Full Red.

So here now at peak season, September's ides, comes dreadsome Dashika, straight over from West Africa and up from the Horse Latitudes, glaring her baleful, unblinking eye our way. She has spared the Caribbean (already battered by Abdullah) but has ravaged the eastmost Virgin Islands, flattened a Bahama or two, and then swung due north, avoiding Florida and the Gulf Coast (both still staggered from *last* year's hits) and tracking usward as if on rails, straight up the meridian of our longitude. As of this time yesterday, only the Carolina Capes stood between Dashika and ourselves.

"Poor bastards," commiserated Tyler as the first damage reports came in. Time to think Stage Two, she supposed, if not quite yet actually to set about it; Capes Fear and Hatteras, after all, are veteran storm-deflectors and shock absorbers that not infrequently, to their cost, de-energize hurricanes into tropical storms and veer them out to sea.

"Better them than us," for his part growled Bowman, as well as one can growl through a mouthful of nails, and hammered on from Yellow Alert up toward Red.

I myself was standing pat at Stage Two but more or less preparing to prepare for Three, as was Tyler vis-à-vis Two — meanwhile listening to the pair of them trade precedents and counterprecedents from seasons past, like knowledgeable sports fans. I had already disconnected my TV antenna, unplugged various electronics, readied flashlights and kerosene lamps, lowered flags, stowed boat gear, checked dock lines, snugged lawn chairs and other outdoor blowaways, and secured loose items on my water-facing porch: Green Alert. While Dashika chewed up the Outer Banks, I doubled those dock lines, filled jerry cans and laundry tubs with reserve water, loaded extra ice-blocks into the freezer against extended power outage, checked my food and cash reserves, and taped the larger windows against shattering: Yellow Alert, well into last night.

This morning scarcely dawned at all, only lightened to an ugly gray. The broad river out front is as hostile-looking as the sky. Damage and casualty reports from Hatteras to the Virginia Capes are sobering indeed, and while Dashika has lost some strength from landfall, she remains a Class Three hurricane vectored straight at us. Moreover, her forward velocity has slowed: We've a bit more grace to prepare (in Bowman's case to wait, as his prepping's done), but our time under fire will be similarly extended. Already the wind is rising; what's worse, it's southerly, our most exposed quarter and the longest wave-fetch on our particular estuary. In consequence, last night's high tide scarcely ebbed, and this morning's low tide wasn't. This afternoon's high bids to put our docks under and the front half of Tyler's lawn as well, right up to her pool deck (my ground's higher, Bowman's higher yet). If there's a real storm surge to boot, I'll have water in my basement and the river's edge almost to my porch; Tyler's pool — to which I have a generous standing invitation, although I prefer the natural element, and which she herself enjoys uninhibitedly at all hours, skinnying out of her bikini as soon as she hits the water — Tyler's pool will be submerged entirely, quite as Bowman the hydrophobe has direly long foretold, and her one-story "bachelor girl" cottage may well be flooded too.

A-prepping we've therefore gone, separately, she and I. While Better-Safe potters in his garden and angles from his dock with conspicuous nonchalance, savoring his evidently vindicated foresight and justifiably not coming to our aid until the eleventh hour, I've ratcheted up to Full Red: trailered and garaged my boat, shut off power and water to my dock, taped the rest of my windows (never yet having lost one, I'm not a boarder-upper; Tyler won't even tape), boxed my most valuable valuables, even packed a cut-and-run suitcase. Nothing left to do, really, except shift what's shiftable from first floor up to second (two schools of thought hereabouts on that last-ditch measure, as you might expect: Bowman's for it, although even he has never yet gone so far; Tyler's of the opinion that in a bona fide hurricane we're as likely to lose the roof and rain-soak the attic as to take in water downstairs) and get the hell out. Ms. Take-a-Chance is still hard at it: an orange blur, you might say, as she does her Yellow- and Red-Alert preps simultaneously. It's a treat to watch her, too, now that I myself am as Redded up as I want to be for the present and am catching my breath before I lend her a hand. Too proud to ask for help, is T.A.C.T. — as am I, come to that, especially vis-à-vis old Bowman — but not too proud to accept it gratefully when it's offered in extremis, and that particular sidelong "Owe you one" look that she flashes me at such times is a debt-absolver in itself. Under her loose sweatshirt and cut-off jeans is the trademark string bikini, you can bet; Tyler's been known to break for a dip in the teeth of a thirty-knot gale. And under the bikini — well, she doesn't exactly hide what that item doesn't much cover anyhow, especially when B.S.T.S.B. is off somewhere and it's just her in her pool and me doing my yard work or whatever. We're good neighbors of some years' standing, Tyler and I, no more than that, and loners both, basically, as for that matter is old Bowman: "Independent as three hogs on ice," is how T. describes us. Chez moi, at least, that hasn't always been the case — but never mind. And I don't mind saying (and just might get it said to *her* this time, when I sashay down there shortly to help shift *Slippery*, that nifty cutter of hers, out to its heavy-weather mooring before the seas get high) that should a certain trim and able neighbor-lady find the tidewater invading her ground-floor bedroom, there's a king-size second-floor one right next door, high and dry and never intended for one person.

No time for such hog-dreams now, though. It's getting *black* off to southward there, Dashikaward; if we don't soon slip Ms. Slippery out of her slip, there'll be no unslipping her. What I've been waiting for is a certain over-the-shoulder glance from my busy friend wrestling spring-lines down there on her dock, where her cutter's bucking like a wild young mare: a look that says "Don't think I *need* you, neighbor, but" — and there it is, and down I hustle, just as old Bowman looks set to amble *my* way after I glance himward, merely checking to see whether he's there and up to what. A bit of jogging gets me aboard milady's pitching vessel, as I'd hoped, before B's half across my lawn; by the time he has cocked his critical eye at my own preparations and made his way out onto Tyler's dock, she and I have got *Slippery*'s auxiliary diesel idling and her tender secured astern to ferry us back ashore when our job's done.

"Need another hand?" It's me he calls to, not Tyler —

let's say because I'm in *Slippery*'s bobbing, shoreward-facing bow, unhitching dock lines while T. stands by at the helm, and there's wind-noise in the cutter's rigging along with the diesel-chug — but his ate-the-canary tone includes us both. Bowman's of the age and category that wears work-shirt and long khakis in the hottest weather, plus cleat-soled leather shoes and black socks (I'm in T-shirt, frayed jeans, and sockless deck-mocs; Tyler's barefoot in those aforenoted tight cutoffs).

"Ask the skipper," I call back pointedly, and when I see B. wince at the way we're pitching already in the slip, I can't help adding, "Maybe she wants somebody up the mast."

He humphs and shuffles on out toward the cutter's cock-pit, shielding his face from the wind with one hand to let us know we should've done this business earlier (I agree) and getting his pantslegs wet with spray from the waves banging under *Slippery*'s transom.

"Just stow these lines, Fred, if you will," Tyler tells him pertly; "thanks a bunch." She has strolled forward as if to greet him; now she tosses him a midships spring-line and returns aft to do likewise with the stern line — just to be nice by making the old guy feel useful, in my opinion, because she *is* nice: tough and lively and nobody's fool, but essentially nice, unlike some I've done time with. So what if she's feeding B's wiser-than-thouhood; we're good neighbors all, each independent as a hog on ice but the three of us on the same ice, finally, when cometh push to shove.

Only two of us in the same boat, however. Tyler casts off her stern line and I the remaining bow line; she hops smartly to the helm, calls "Astern we go!" and backs *Slippery* down into full reverse. When Bowman warns me from the dock "Mind your bowsprit as she swings, or you're in trouble," I'm pleased to say back to him — loud enough for her to hear, I hope — "Some folks know how to swing without making trouble." Lost on him, no doubt, but maybe not on her.

Out we go then into the whitecaps to make the short run to her mooring, where *Slippery* can swing indeed: full circle to the wind, if necessary, instead of thrashing about in her slip and maybe chafing through her lines and smashing against dock piles. I go aft to confer on our approach-and-pickup procedure with Ms. Helmsperson, who's steering with her bare brown toes in the wheel's lower spokes while she tucks a loose sunbleached lock up under her headband. Raising her arms like that does nice things with Tyler's breasts, even under a sweatshirt; she looks as easy at the helm as if we're heading out for a sail on the bay instead of Red-Alerting for a killer storm. When she smiles and flashes the old "Owe you one," I find myself half wishing that we really were heading out together, my neighbor-lady and I, not for a daysail but for a real blue-water passage: hang a left at the lastmost lighthouse, say, and lay our course for the Caribbean, properties and storm-preparations be damned. Single-handing hath its pleasures, for sure, but they're not the only pleasures in the book.

Storm-time, however, is storm-time, a pickup's a pickup, and both of us know the routine. It's just a matter of confirming, once we've circled the mooring buoy and swung up to windward, that she'll leave it close on our starboard bow, following my hand-signals on final approach. T. swears she can do the job herself, and so she can in ordinary weathers, as I know from applauding her often enough from dock or porch when she comes in from a solo cruise, kills the cutter's headway at exactly the right moment, and scrambles forward just in time to flatten herself in the bow, reach down for the mast of the pickup float, and drop the eye of her mooring line over a bow cleat before *Slippery* slips away. In present conditions, it's another story; anyhow, once I'm positioned on the foredeck she has to follow my signals will-she nill-she, as I'll be blocking her view of the target. Make of that circumstance what you will; I myself mean to make of it what I can. Looks as if we're thinking in synch, too, T. and I, for now she says, "I'll bring us up dead slow; final approach is your call, okay?"

Aye aye, ma'am. That wind really pipes now in *Slippery*'s rigging as I make my way forward, handing myself from life-lines to shrouds and up to the bow pulpit while we bang into a two-foot chop and send the spray flying. My heart's whistling a bit, too. *Easy does it*, I remind myself: *Not too fast, not too slow; neither too much nor too little.* That pickup float has become a bobbing metaphor: *Don't blow it*, I warn me as we close the last ten yards, me kneeling on the foredeck as if in prayer and hand-signaling, *Just a touch portward, Skipper-Babe; now a touch starboard. Just a touch . . .* Then I'm prone on her slick wet foredeck, arm and shoulder out under bow rail, timing my grab to synchronize *Slippery*'s hobbyhorsing with the bob of the float and the waggle of its pickup mast — and by golly, I've got her!

Got *it*; I've by-golly got it, and I haul it up smartly before the next wave knocks us aside, and with my free hand I snatch the mooring eye and snug it over the bow cleat in the nick of time, just as six tons of leeway-making sailboat yank up the slack.

"Good show!" cheers Tyler, and in fact it was. From the helm she salutes me with her hands clasped over her head (that nice raised-arm effect again) and I both acknowledge and return the compliment with a fist in the air, for her boat-handling was flawless. By when I'm back in the cockpit, she's all business, fetching out chafe-gear to protect the mooring line where it leads through a chock to its cleat and asking would I mind going forward one last time to apply that gear while she secures things down below, and then we're out of here. But unless I'm hearing things in the wind, there's a warmth in her voice just a touch beyond the old "Owe you one."

No problem, neighbor. I do that little chore for her in the rain that sweeps off the bay now and up our wide river, whose farther shore has disappeared from sight. It takes some doing to fit a rubber collar over a heavy mooring line exactly where it lies in its chock on a pitching, rain-strafed foredeck without losing that line on the one hand or a couple of fingers on the other, so to speak; we're dealing with large forces here, pumped up larger yet by Ms. Dashika yonder. But I do it, all right, seizing moments of slack between waves and wind-gusts to make my moves, working with and around those forces more than against them. When I come aft again, I call down the cabin companionway that if she loses her investment, it won't be because her chafe-gear wasn't in place.

"Poor thing, you're soaked!" Tyler calls back up. "Come out of the wet till I'm done, and then we'll run for it."

When I look downriver at what's working its way our way, I think we ought to hightail it for shore right now. But I am indeed soaked, and chilling fast in the wind; what's more, my friend's on her knees down there on one of the settee berths, securing stuff on the shelf behind it and looking about as perky and fetching as I've ever seen her look, which is saying much. And despite the wind-shrieks and the rain-rattle and the pitching, or maybe because of them, *Slippery*'s no-frills cabin, once I'm down in it, is about as cozy a shelter as a fellow could wish for, with just the two of us at home. Concerned as I am that if we don't scram out of there pronto, there'll be no getting ashore for us (already the chop's too steep and the wind too strong to row the dinghy to windward; luckily, our docks are dead downwind, a dozen boatlengths astern), I'm pleased to come indoors. I stand half beside and half behind her, holding on to an overhead grab rail like a rush-hour subway commuter, and ask, What else can I do for you, Skip?

She cuts me her "Owe you one," does Ms. Take-a-Chance — maybe even "Owe you two or three" — and says, "Make yourself at home, neighbor; I'm just about ready."

Yes, well, say I to myself: Likewise, mate; like-wise. Seems to me that what she's busy with there on her knees isn't all that high-priority, but it sure makes for an admirable view. Instead of admiring it from the settee opposite, I take a seat beside her, well within arm's reach.

Arm's reach, however, isn't necessarily easy reach, at least not for some of us. When I think about Take-a-Chance Tyler or watch her at her work and play, as has lately become my habit, I remind myself that I wouldn't want anything Established and Regular, if you know what I mean. I've *had* Established, I've *had* Regular, and I still carry the scars to prove it. No more E & R for this taxpayer, thank you kindly. On the other hand, though I'm getting no younger, I'm no B.S.T.S. Bowman yet, getting my jollies from a veggie-garden and tucking up in bed with my weather radio. As the saying goes, if I'm not as good as once I was, I'm still as good once as I was — or so I was last time I had a chance to check. Life hereabouts doesn't shower such chances upon us loners, particularly if, like me, you're a tad shy of strangers and happen to like *liking* the lady you lay. There ought to be some middle ground, says I, between Established and Regular on the one hand and Zilch on the other: a middle road that stays middle *down* the road. Haven't found it yet myself, but now I'm thinking maybe here it perches on its bare brown knees right beside me, within arm's reach, fiddling with tide tables and nautical charts and for all I know just waiting for my arm to reach.

Look before you leap, proverbial wisdom recommends — while also warning that *he who hesitates is lost.* In Tyler's case, I'm a paid-up looker and hesitator both. *Nothing ventured, nothing gained*, I tell myself; *there is a tide in the affairs of men*, et cetera, and I plop my hand palm-down on her near bare calf.

"I know," frets Take-a-Chance, not even turning her pretty head: "Time to clear our butts out of here before we're blown away. Better safe than sorry, right?"

Dashika howls at that, and the rain downpours like loud applause. In one easy smiling motion then, Tyler's off the settee with my business hand in hers, leading me to go first up the companionway.

Which I do.

Well. So. I could've stood my ground, I guess — *sat* my ground, on that settee — and held on to that hand of hers and said, Let's ride 'er out right here, okay? Or, after that wild dinghy-trip back to shore, I could've put my arm around her as we ran through the rain toward shelter, the pair of us soaked right through, exhilarated by the crazy surf we'd ridden home on and breathing hard from hauling the tender out and up into the lee of her carport. I could've given her a good-luck *kiss* there in that shelter, to see whether it might lead to something more (nobody to see us, as Bowman appears to've cleared out already) instead of merely *saying* Well, so: Take care, friend, and good luck to both of us. At very least I could've asked Shall we watch old Dashika from your place or mine? or at very *very* least How about a beer for *Slippery*'s crew? But I guess I figured it was Tyler's turn: I'd made my move; the ball was in her court; if she wasn't having it, amen.

So take care now, is what I said. Good luck to all hands. I'll keep an eye out.

Whereat quoth T.A.C.T., "Thanks a bunch, nabe. Owe you one."

And that was that.

So an eye out I've kept since, and keep on keeping as Dashika roars in, although there's little to be seen through that wall of rain out there, and nothing to be heard over this freight-train wind. Power's out, phones are out, walls and windows are shaking like King Kong's cage; can't see whether *Slippery*'s still bucking and rearing on her tether or has bolted her mooring and sailed through Tyler's picture window. All three docks are under; the surge is partway up my lawn already and must be into Tyler's pool. Can't tell whether that lady herself has cut and run for high ground, but I know for a fact she hasn't run to this particular medium-high patch thereof.

I ought to cut and run myself, while I still can. Ms. T's her own woman; let her *be* her own woman, if she's even still over there. But hell with it. I moved a couple things upstairs and then said hell with that, too, and just opened me a cold one while there's still one cold to be opened and sat me down here all by my lonesome to watch Dashika do her stuff.

I'm as prepared as I want to be.

Hell with it.

Let her come.

" 'Yes, well,'

. . . as he likes to say."
. . . .

Presently: "Are you and I weathering what we can't avoid,
or vice versa?"

Both. Let's do it happily ever after. They. Them.

"There is no happily ever after. No ever after, period.
There's only the period."

Maybe suspension points? . . .

Activity, inactivity, meals, tears, love. Presently: "They *are*
as prepared as they want to be, no?"

No.

"As they'll *ever* be, then."

They'll never be.

"Same thing. So what are they waiting for?"

A god on wires, to save the situation.

"Don't hold their breath. There *is* no et cetera."

No wires, either, for better or worse. Only stories.

Presently: "Maybe they're out of stories."

Nope. But maybe *she*'s out of —

"Yup. Never mind her, though."

He'll never never-mind her.

"He's going to have to learn to never-mind her."

Meanwhile, he hastily interjects . . .

"Meanwhile?"

All the while there is. Which being the case . . .

5.

On with the Story

"In our collective headlong flight toward oblivion [Alice reads], *there are a few among us still, remarkably, who take time out from time to time to read a made-up story. Of that small number, dear present reader, you are one."*

The writer of these lines is another, and a third is the abovementioned Alice, chief character of this story-now-in-progress, whose attention has been caught by the passage that you and she together have just read. Leafing more or less distractedly through an in-flight magazine — Alice is, in fact, in flight, crossing the Mississippi River at cruising altitude aboard an aging DC-10 en route from Boston to Portland, Oregon — she has registered marginally its advertisements for attaché cases, notebook computers, highway radar detectors, collapsible luggage carriers "just like the ones your flight attendants use," and airport hotels. She has then fretfully scanned self-help articles on how to make more effective product presentations and (the same thing, really) a more forceful presence at job interviews. She's going to have to be doing that, for sure, now that her divorce-settlement negotiations — which both she and Howard vowed to keep amicable for young Sam and Jessica's sakes and their own — have, despite all, turned adversary and acrimonious.

With rather more interest, she has wistfully next perused

a photo-spread entitled "Island Paradises" — three of which, as it happens, she and Howard romantically "ran off" to, honeymooned in, and vacationed at, in turn, back in the palmy years before their children came along; before Howard's "mid-career course correction" failed to correct it; before her own work history mainly spun its wheels, and their marriage, to both parties' dismay, went belly-up. No Island Paradises in Alice's foreseeable future: For the past half-dozen years at least, her idea of a quality vacation has been a weekend's state-park camping with the kids (but they're in junior high and high school now, ever less interested in roughing it en famille, especially just with Mom) or a week at her parents' summer place on Cape Cod. It's from one of those latter that she's just now returning, leaving Jessica and Sam for an additional fortnight with their maternal grandparents. To Alice's embarrassment, all hands' airfares have had to be on the old folks' tab; she and Howard simply haven't the resources to finance cross-country family visits. They haven't even a savings fund for the kids' rapidly upcoming college expenses, for pity's sake, typically the middle-class American family's single largest capital outlay. After eighteen years of marriage, this decoupling couple's only real nest egg is a few thousand dollars gained not by programmatic saving but by refinancing the nest when home mortgage rates dropped a few years ago — and now Howard's insisting that that egg be split fifty-fifty. Likewise their equity in the house itself, which he wants sold; likewise further their children's custody, although his proposals for the logistical management of that last item strike Alice as risible if not disingenuous — possibly a ploy to reduce his child-support payments.

How in the world, she has wondered in mid–photo spread ("The *Other* British Virgins"), did her parents' generation — the generation that generated the postwar Baby Boom whereof she and Howard are dues-paying members — manage? Typically on one income, or one and a fraction, American middle-class couples like Alice's folks and Howard's contrived to send two, three, even four offspring through college — sometimes even through private colleges, not the local state diploma mills that Sam and Jessica will have to make do with — and in Alice's case to private high school before that, not to mention affording them piano lessons, dance and horseback-riding lessons, art lessons, a house to grow up in considerably more spacious than Sam's and Jessica's (in a better neighborhood, too), and in later years even a vacation home as well? Howard's father, moreover, managed all this while himself divorcing and remarrying at his son's present age; gave his first wife their commodious house free and clear for the children to finish their high-school years in, plus enough alimony to maintain her and them therein till they were off to college at his expense and she remarried — and on top of that paid all of her divorce-lawyer's fees as well as his own, with the result that Howard's mother (how Alice now envies her in this!) had had the luxury of protracting the negotiations at her leisure and at her estranged husband's cost. All this, mind, in a divorce action that, like Alice's and Howard's, was no-fault, by pained mutual consent — not one party dumping the other and therefore becoming willy-nilly the "buyer" of the divorce, the aggrieved other party the "seller." Alice's dad (still contentedly married to her mom) is a retired history professor of modest repute with a couple of royalty-producing textbooks as well as scholarly articles in his bibliography; her mother was for decades a part-time Special Ed teacher in the public schools. Howard's father and mother, a bit more affluent but scarcely rich, are or were respectively a research chemist with a few process-patents on the side and a classic 1950s "homemaker" who did volunteer charity work at her church and the county hospice. In those Kennedy/Johnson, *Leave It to Beaver* years, where on earth had the money come from?

Alice exhaled audibly, shook her head, and turned to the final page of "Island Paradises": Norman Island in the BVI, now about to be "developed" with resort hotels, but almost pristine fifteen years ago when Howard and she, already a few months pregnant with Sam, had anchored a chartered sailboat in its splendid Bight on the third Thanksgiving of their marriage.

"Beats Boston, right?" the fellow in the aisle-seat beside her commented at this point. He, too, she'd noticed, had been leafing through the airline's in-flight mag and, evidently, eyeing Alice's progress therethrough. Whether by coincidence or as a conversation-starting gambit on his part, they reached Norman Island separately together.

"Careful, there," Alice replied — cordially but coolly, in her judgment, as she was not much up for conversation: "You're talking to an old Bostonian."

"Am I, now?" To Alice (who wasn't looking closely) the man looked to be maybe twenty years older than herself, same general eth and class, standard navy blazer khaki slacks open sportshirt lanky build graying hair nice tan easy smile. "So are you, as it happens. But I don't object to an island paradise from time to time."

"Likewise, I'm sure."

His accent wasn't Boston — but then neither is Alice's, and "old Bostonian" scarcely describes her. Child of academic parents, she and her brothers were born in Bloomington, Indiana, spent their elementary-school years in Santa Barbara, California, and only their high-school years in suburban Boston, as their father moved from campus to campus up the professorial ladder. If Alice thinks of any place as her childhood home, it's that cottage on the Cape, where the family spent more summers together than school years anywhere.

Her tone and manner did the job, if there was any to be done. Both passengers returned to their magazines, wherein "Island Paradises" turns out to be followed — unusual for an in-flight publication — by a bit of fiction: a short story called "Freeze Frame," its author's name unfamiliar to our protagonist. Alice is not, these days at least, much of a reader, of fiction or anything else beyond the lease- and sale-contracts that come across her part-time office desk and the textbooks on real-estate law, of all things, that she's been cramming lately in half-hearted preparation for her Oregon licensing exam. As a girl (whose parents strictly rationed their children's diet of television) she consumed novels the way Sam and Jessica consume Nintendo and junk food — and not just kiddie-novels. In her first-rate private high school (she wished Sam's public one were half as good), Fitzgerald's *Great Gatsby* and Turgenev's *Fathers and Sons* joyously broke her heart and enlarged her spirit. At Reed College in Portland (where she'd met pre-law Howard), she'd been a sociology major with a serious minor in her favorite subject, literature; she read rapturously through the big Victorians and the early Modernists, and in her senior year considered with her dad and with Howard (by then her virtual fiancé) the merits of sundry graduate departments of literature as well as sociology, with an eye toward advanced degrees in one or the other and an academic career.

All that seems another world to her now. She and Howard "ran off" to Barbados on holiday after graduation and presently thereafter married. She followed him to law school in New York, where she did pickup copyediting to help pay the rent, and then — when he dropped out for reasons that they still argue over — to Chicago on an initially successful business venture with one of his father's chemical-patent partners (their Virgin Islands cruise and her happy first pregnancy date from this period). When the Chicago venture fizzled, she and young Sam and Jessica-in-the-works followed him back out to Portland and his present restless employ as a "product developer" for a pharmaceutical concern — while Alice herself, faute de mieux, "helps out" half-time these days in a suburban real-estate office. She has thus far resisted the mild advances of her more-or-less mentor there, although he's a civilized-seeming divorcé himself and she's lonesome for adult male company now that she and Howard have split; but she guesses unenthusiastically that she'll take his advice and go for her broker's license. In the interstices of her frazzled life: videos with the kids, when she can get them peaceably assembled; regular jogging, to keep her spirits up and her body in shape for whatever next episode in her life-story; telephonic set-tos with Howard about economic and parental matters; the aforementioned odd camping weekend; maybe half an hour's thumbing through some glossy magazine like *Elle* or *Vanity Fair*: snapshots from yet another world. She scarcely manages to read the daily *Oregonian* these days beyond its real-estate section, much less *literature*; indeed, she probably ought to be re-reviewing the R. E. Board–exam stuff right now, as she has spent most of her "vacation" week doing. But she's supersaturated in that line; also depressed by her parents' loving, unspoken, but obvious disappointment in their only daughter's life-trajectory thus far and even with her upbringing of their grandchildren ("*Mortal Kombat!*" her dad had groaned in disbelief when young Sam fished out that stupefying game from his backpack, like a junkie in need of a fix, the minute they arrived at the Cape Cod cottage).

Alice is, in fact, for perhaps the first time in her forty years, truly fearful of the future, whereof that real-estate-law manual is a token and wherefrom this in-flight magazine —

like the round-trip flight itself and the less than refreshing vacation that it has bracketed — is an all-too-brief reprieve.

Literature, hah: Those were the days!

Thus the odd opening of that "Freeze Frame" story catches her attention. As she reads on, moreover, she finds herself involved in (and she'll presently be stopped still by) one of those vertiginous coincidences that happen now and then to readers of stories, attenders of movies, even swappers of anecdotes with one's fellow passengers through life: a correspondence stranger than fiction (even when one of the corresponding items *is* fiction) between the situation one is reading or hearing about and one's own. "Freeze Frame" — its first half, anyhow — turns out to involve a forty-year-old White-Anglo-Saxon-(lapsed)-Protestant middle-class American woman (name not given) who, like Alice, acutely knows herself to have passed the classical *mezzo del cammin de nostra vita*, as the author puts it, quoting the opening lines of Dante's *Divine Comedy*: a little past the halfway point of the biblically allotted threescore-and-ten. Like Alice, "she" is a healthy human animal, though under sustained stress lately, and the daughter of still-living parents who themselves are in good health for their age. She knows therefore her expectable remaining life-span, barring accident, to be slightly longer than the span behind her — more trying, too, she expects, although her story thus far, while relatively privileged, has by no means been carefree. The story's narrator calls its lead character's malaise "the Boomer Syndrome": Just as her middle-class-American generation is, by and large, the first of the century not to surpass its forebears in physical height and general health, so with many exceptions are its members likewise falling short, or feel themselves to be, in material, perhaps even spiritual, well-being. "Her" father and mother respectively G.I.-Billed through state university and worked through secretarial school, the first in their families' history to "go past high school"; they flourished as a one-and-a-half-income family in the booming postwar U.S. economy and provided their children (four!) with a suburban upbringing at least as favored as Alice's and her brothers', substantially more favored than their own had been, and downright sybaritic compared to that of "her" grandparents. The parental generation managed the class-climb from small-shopkeeper to professional ("her" father was an estate-and-trust lawyer) and confidently supposed that their sons — maybe even their daughters — would likewise enter the professions on the strength of their excellent educations. But something — "Call it the countercultural Sixties," the author suggests in the story, "the oil-embargoed, 'stagflated' Seventies, the TV-narcotized beginning of the end of the American Century" — something had gone quietly but profoundly wrong.

And then less quietly. Of "her" two brothers, one has drifted from commune to hippie commune right up into the Reagan Eighties, his circuits blown on Sixties methedrine; in his late thirties he half-supports himself as a longhaired mower of suburban lawns who converses with spirits as he maneuvers his Kubota wide-blade rig through the greenswards of Newton, Massachusetts. The other, after dropping out of two colleges plus law school (shades of Alice's Howard), is doing modestly in rural Maryland as a remodeler of small-town kitchens and bathrooms; he likes to work with his hands. Of the two girls, one has broken her parents' officially liberal hearts by "coming out" as a lesbian and, after a creditable West African tour of duty in the Peace Corps, a halfhearted suicide-attempt, and a parentally subsidized stay in a Pittsburgh psychiatric hospital, settling down with her same-sex Significant Other to run a marginally successful New Age gift shop in San Diego. Not all that different a résumé, changes changed, from Alice's gay brother's in his Key West cappuccino bar, which her parents gamely visit every second or third winter, not to lose touch altogether.

As for Her herself, whom let's capitalize henceforth for clarity and convenience: After "Freeze Frame" 's opening address to the dear present reader, said reader finds Her gridlocked in downtown St. Louis traffic, not at morning or evening rush-time but, curiously, just a bit past noon — owing perhaps to a routine lunchtime-traffic congestion that She didn't know to allow for, perhaps to some out-of-view accident or other bottleneck. In any case, en route to the riverside expressway in her ailing, high-mileage Subaru wagon after an upsetting legal confrontation with her estranged husband — a confrontation between their respective divorce-lawyers, actually, through which the parties to the action sat in stony silence — and running late already for a job-interview appointment in University City (She'll be needing a better job than her current office-temping, all right, given the likely outcome of those settlement negotiations, but she's not at all sure that her indifferent work-history qualifies her for anything remotely approaching her vague expectations back when she took her M.A. in Art History fifteen years ago), She's stopped dead in this humongous traffic jam and verging on tears as her aged station wagon verges on overheating. How could "her" Bill have sat there so damned impassively — her longtime, once-so-loving spouse, father of their twins, her graduate-school lover and best of friends — in those hateful new wire-rimmed, double-bridged eyeglasses that She supposes are an aspect of this new, intransigently hostile William Alfred Barnes, and that she suspects are meant to please some other her than Her?

The cold-hearted bastard, Alice remarks to herself. The DC-10's captain announces at this point that owing to turbulent weather over Chicago, the plane's course has been diverted south; they are crossing the Mississippi just below Hannibal, Missouri — Mark Twain's birthplace.

She (I mean our distraught "Freeze Frame" protagonist) happens to be gridlocked in actual sight of that river: There's the symbolic catenary arch of the "Gateway to the West," and beyond it are the sightseeing boats along the parkfront and out among the freight-barge strings. As She tries to divert and calm herself by regarding the nearest of those tourist boats — an ornate replica of a Mark Twain–vintage sternwheeler, just leaving its pier to nose upstream — her attention is caught by an odd phenomenon that, come to think of it, has fascinated her since small-girlhood (happier days!) whenever she has happened to see it: The river is, as ever, flowing south, New Orleansward; the paddle-steamer is headed north, gaining slow upstream momentum (standard procedure for sightseeing boats, in order to abbreviate the anticlimactic return leg of their tour), and as it begins to make headway, a deckhand ambles aft in process of casting off the vessel's docklines, with the effect that he appears to be walking in place, with respect to the shore and Her angle of view, while the boat moves under him. It is the same disconcerting illusion, She guesses, as that sometimes experienced when two trains stand side by side in the station and a passenger on one thinks momentarily that the other has begun to move, when in fact the movement is his own — an illusion compoundable if the observer on Train A (this has happened to Her at least once) happens to be strolling down the car's aisle like that crewman on the sternwheeler's deck, at approximately equal speed in the opposite direction as the train pulls out. Dear-present-reader Alice suddenly remembers one such occasion, somewhere or other, when for a giddy moment it appeared to her that she herself, aisle-walking, was standing still, while Train A, Train B, and

Boston's South Street Station platform (it now comes back to her) all seemed in various motion.

As in fact they were, the "Freeze Frame" narrator declares in italics at this point, his end-of-paragraph language having echoed mine above, or vice versa — and here the narrative, after a space-break, takes a curious turn. Instead of proceeding with the story of Her several concentric plights — how She extricates or fails to extricate herself from the traffic jam; whether She misses the interview appointment or, making it despite all, nevertheless fails to get the university job; whether or not in either case She and the twins slip even farther down the middle-class scale (right now, alarmingly, if Bill really "cuts her off" as threatened, She's literally about two months away from the public-assistance rolls, unless her aging parents bail her out: she who once seriously considered Ph.D.hood and professorship); and whether in either of *those* cases anything really satisfying, not to say fulfilling, lies ahead for her in the second half of her life, comparable to the early joys of her marriage and motherhood — instead of going on with these nested stories, in which our Alice understandably takes a more than literary interest, the author here suspends the action and launches into an elaborate digression upon, of all things, the physics of relative motion in the universe as currently understood, together with the spatiotemporal nature of written narrative and — Ready? — Zeno's Seventh Paradox, which three phenomena he attempts to interconnect more or less as follows:

Seat-belted in her gridlocked and overheating Subaru, the protagonist of "Freeze Frame" is moving from St. Louis's Gateway Arch toward University City at a velocity, alas, of zero miles per hour. Likewise (although her nerves are twinging, her hazel eyes brimming, her pulse and respiration pulsing and respiring, and her thoughts returning already from tourist boats to the life-problems that have her by the throat) her movement from the recentest event in her troubled story to whatever next: zero narrative mph, so to speak, as the station wagon idles and the author digresses.

Even as the clock of Her life is running, however, so are time in general and the physical universe. The city of St. Louis and its temporarily stalled downtown traffic, together with our now-sobbing protagonist, the state of Missouri, and variously troubled America, all spin eastward on Earth's axis at roughly a thousand miles per hour. The rotating planet itself careens through its solar orbit at a dizzying 66,662 miles per hour (with the incidental effect that even "stationary" objects on its surface, like Her Subaru, for half of every daily rotation are "strolling aft" with respect to orbital direction, though at nothing approaching orbital velocity). Our entire whirling solar system, meanwhile, is rushing in its own orbit through our Milky Way Galaxy at the stupendous rate of nearly half a million miles per hour: lots of compounded South Street Station effects going on within that overall motion! What's more, although our galaxy appears to have no relative motion within its Local Group of celestial companions, that whole Local group — plus the great Virgo Cluster of which it's a member, plus other, neighboring multigalactic clusters — is apparently rushing en bloc at a staggering near-million miles per hour (950,724) toward some point in interclusteral space known as the Great Attractor. And moreover yet — but who's to say *finally*? — that Attractor and everything thereto so ardently attracted would seem to be speeding at an only slightly less staggering 805,319 mph toward another supercluster, as yet ill-mapped, called the Shapley Concentration, or, to put it mildly, the Even Greater Attractor. All these several motions-within-motions, mind, over and above the grand general expansion of the universe, wherein even as the present reader reads this present sentence, the galaxies all flee one another's company at speeds proportional to their respective distances (specifically, in scientific metrics, at the rate of fifty to eighty kilometers per second — let's say 150,000 miles per hour — per "megaparsec" from the observer, a megaparsec being one thousand parsecs and each parsec 3.26 light-years).

Don't think about this last too closely, advises the author of "Freeze Frame," but in fact our Alice — who has always had a head for figures, and who once upon a time maintained a lively curiosity about such impersonal matters as the constellations, at least, if not the overall structure of the universe — is at this point stopped quite as still by vertiginous reflection as is the unnamed Mrs. William Alfred Barnes by traffic down there in her gridlocked Subaru, and this for several reasons. Apart from the similarities between Her situation vis-à-vis "Bill" and Alice's vis-à-vis Howard — unsettling, but not extraordinary in a time and place where half of all marriages end in separation or divorce — is the coincidence of Alice's happening upon "Freeze Frame" during a caesura in her own life-story and reading through the narrative of Her nonplusment up to the author's digression-in-progress just as, lap-belted in a DC-10 at thirty-two thousand feet, she's crossing the Mississippi River in virtual sight of St. Louis not long past midday (Central Daylight Savings Time), flying westward at an airspeed of six hundred eight miles per hour (so the captain has announced), against a contrary prevailing jet stream of maybe a hundred mph, for a net speed-over-ground of let's say five hundred, while Earth and its atmosphere spin eastward under her, carrying the DC-10 backward (though not relatively) at maybe double its forward airspeed, while simultaneously the planet, the solar system, the galaxy, and so forth all tear along in their various directions at their various clips — and just now two flight attendants emerge from the forward galley and stroll aft down the parallel aisles like that deckhand on the tourist stern-wheeler, taking the passengers' drink orders before the meal service. Alice stares awhile, transfixed, almost literally dizzied, remembering from her happier schooldays (and from trying to explain relative motion to Sam and Jessica one evening as the family camped out under the stars) that any point or object in the universe can be considered to be at rest, the unmoving center of it all, while everything else is in complex motion with respect to it. The arrow, released, may be said to stand still while the earth rushes under, the target toward, the archer away from it, et cetera.

Her seatmate-on-the-aisle, fortunately, is too preoccupied with punching a pocket calculator and scribbling on a notepad (atop his in-flight mag atop his tray-table) to notice her looking up from her reading. Alice decides that she'll order white wine and club soda when her turn comes, and goes back to the suspended non-action of "Freeze Frame" lest he disturb her reflections with another attempt at conversation.

Back, rather, she goes, to that extended digression, wherein by one more coincidence (she having just imaged the arrow in "stationary" flight — but not impossibly she glanced ahead in "Freeze Frame" before those flight attendants caught her eye) the author now invokes two other arrows: the celebrated Arrow of Time, along whose irreversible trajectory the universe has expanded ever since the Big Bang, generating and carrying with it not only all those internal relative celestial motions but also the story of Mr. and Mrs. W. A. Barnes from wedlock through deadlock to gridlock (and of Alice and Howard likewise, up to her reading of these sentences); and the arrow in Zeno's Seventh Paradox, which Alice may long ago have heard of but can't recollect until the author now reminds her. If an arrow in flight can be said to traverse every point in its path from bow to target, Zeno teases, and if at any given moment it can be said to be at and only at some one of those points, then it must be at rest for the moment it's there (otherwise it's not "there"); therefore it's at rest at every moment of its flight, and its apparent motion is illusory. To the author's way of thinking, Zeno's Seventh Paradox oddly anticipates not only motion pictures (whose motion truly *is* illusory in a different sense, our brain's reconstruction of the serial "freeze-frames" on the film) but also Werner Heisenberg's celebrated Uncertainty Principle, which maintains in effect that the more we know about a particle's position, the less we know about its momentum, and vice versa — although how that principle relates to Mrs. Barnes's sore predicament, Alice herself is uncertain. In her own mind, the paradox recalls that arrow "at rest" in mid-flight aforeposited as the center of the exploding universe ... like Her herself down there at this moment of Her story; like Alice herself at this moment of hers, reading about Hers and from time to time pausing to reflect as she reads; like every one of us — fired from the bow of our mother's loins and arcing toward the target of our grave — at any and every moment of our interim life-stories.

"White wine, please," she hears her row-mate say affably in his non-Boston accent. "With a glass of ice and club soda on the side."

"The same," Alice says in hers. He has already fished out his wallet; for a moment Alice worries that he'll offer to pay for her drink, too, amiably obliging her to conversation. Peter, at work, is forever offering lunch that way, and sometimes, strapped for money and male social conversation, Alice agrees, but she inevitably feels thereby compromised, *transacted*, quid-pro-quo'd and unready to quo. This fellow does not, however, so offer; he goes back to his figuring while Alice scrabbles in her purse, pays, pours, sips (he does glance her way now, smiles slightly, and lifts his plastic tumbler in the merest of toasts to the wine-order coincidence, a toast that it would be gratuitously incordial of her not to respond to in kind), and then returns, glass in hand, to the freeze-framed "Freeze Frame," whose point she thinks she's beginning to see, out of practice though she is in reading "serious" fiction.

To the extent that anything is where it is [the author therein now declares], *it has no momentum. To the extent that it moves, it isn't "where it is." Likewise made-up characters in made-up stories; likewise ourselves in the more-or-less made-up stories of our lives. All freeze-frames* [he concludes (concludes this elaborate digression, that is, with another space-break, after which the text, perhaps even the story, resumes)] *are blurred at the edges.*

An arresting passage, Alice acknowledges to herself. Her reflective circuits stirred by the story-thus-far as they haven't been in too long, she smiles at the contradiction in that phrase. *An arresting passage*: Alice's First Paradox.

"Hmp," she hears herself say aloud, amused at that. Amused at *that*, she stifles a chuckle and helps herself to another dollop of wine.

"Fuff," the fellow on the aisle replies, anyhow says, as if to his notepad — and Alice remarks for the first time that he's been annotating not only that pad but the margins of the "Freeze Frame" story in his copy of the in-flight magazine: "Forgot continental drift."

"Excuse me?" She's still smiling, partly at her little witticism, partly at the pleasure, unfamiliar lately, of smiling spontaneously from pure innocent amusement rather than grimly, to keep her spirits up. Another brace of flight attendants — a brace of braces, actually, she supposes in her lingering amusement — is beginning the meal service in the DC-10's twin aisles. Bemused Alice decides to take time out from

"Freeze Frame" (whose author has been taking a prolonged time-out from telling the story) and give sociability a try through lunch.

"I'm rechecking the numbers in this crazy story," the fellow says wryly, "and it just occurred to me that continental drift wasn't factored in." He smiles: a friendly smile, confident but unassuming. "You're reading the thing, too, I see. Did you get to the numbers part yet?"

"That's where I am now, and the arrow business. Pretty dizzy-making." She sips her wine.

He taps the text with his ballpoint. "Shouldn't the Earth's rotational speed be corrected for the latitude of St. Louis, the way an LP record moves faster at its edge than halfway in toward its hole? And then there's the wobbling of the Earth's axis, right? — that causes the precession of the equinoxes. Plus or minus the couple of millimeters a year that the crustal plates grind along." He grins and shrugs his eyebrows. "Too late now. May I have another white wine, please, to go with lunch," he asks the steward who here hands them their meal trays.

"Another white wine. And you, ma'am?"

"I'm fine," Alice says, who isn't; who would quite enjoy a second drink, to enhance this recess from her troubles and lubricate the conversation a bit, but who feels she can't afford another four dollars. "Maybe just a refill on the club soda. How's it too late?" she asks the aisle-chap. "You mean too late for the author to throw in plate tectonics?" She's pleased with herself for remembering that term — Jee-sus, is she ever rusty in the areas of knowledge for its own sake and disinterested reflection! — and the guy responds to it with a clearly appreciative glance. She wonders whether he's some sort of academic like her dad, or, more admirably (what Howard used to be before he autodestructed, and she before the burdens of parenthood and downward mobility in a souring marriage numbed her mind to everything except economic and psychological survival), a *non*-academic who maintains a lively intellectual curiosity beyond his professional concerns.

"Right." He opens his second pony of California Chablis, pours some of it over the wine/ice/soda mix already in his glass, and with a gesture of his bottle-hand offers to top up Alice's as well. Caught off-balance, she shrugs acceptance and holds her glass himward. It is to prevent spillage that he rests the bottleneck on her glass-rim as he pours, but that light brief steady contact has a tiny voltage on it, as if their hands were touching.

"Much obliged, kind sir."

He lifts his glass to her again; Alice simply makes a pleasant smile and nods. He's not being pushy, she decides, sipping; just normally sociable.

"So what do you think of the story so far?" he asks her: a nondirective question if she ever heard one.

"Well . . ." Why not say it? With a smile, of course: "I happen to identify completely with the woman in the car, so it's not easy for me to be objective."

"Mm." His glance is sympathetic, but instead of inviting details, as she rather expected he would (there was no question mark after that "Mm"), he asks whether she happens to know what *Subaru* means in Japanese. Alice doesn't; he surprises her again by neither supplying that datum, nor acknowledging that *he* doesn't know either, nor explaining why he asked in the first place: what that question has to do with the story. He registers her amused negative headshake with a minimal nod and asks, "What about this gimmick of hitting the narrative Pause button and smarting off about relative motion and Zeno's paradoxes? Is that any way to tell a story?"

He has begun his lunch. Alice turns to hers: a grilled-chicken-breast salad, not bad at all and appropriate with the white wine, or vice versa. His question sounds to her more testing than testy (she likes that unspoken little wordplay: her second in five minutes, and maybe five years). "Well," she ventures, testing the idea herself: "The piece is called 'Freeze Frame,' right? The woman's stuck in traffic the way she's stuck in her life-story, and the author dollies back to give us the Big Picture. . . ."

"Nicely said."

Encouraged, Alice adds, "It's motions within motions, but it's also pauses within pauses. It's freeze-frames framing freeze-frames."

When was the last time she ever talked like this?

"Brava," her neighbor applauds: "The point being that all of those freeze-frames are in motion — spacewise, time-wise — just as we are, sitting here. So why is the time of day a bit past noon, instead of morning or evening rush hour?"

"Is this a quiz, or what?" For his tone, good-humored but serious, is clearly not that of puzzlement.

"More like a map-check, I guess," he allows between fork-fuls. "Or a reader-poll. I'm out of practice in the short-story way."

That makes two of them, Alice assures him. And she was so crazy about literature in college; couldn't get enough. But then, you know, the hassles of real life: scrabbling for a liv-ing, raising kids — plus television, and everybody's attention span getting shorter. God knows *hers* isn't what it used to be; it's only at times like this that she can settle in to really read: long plane-rides and such, and unfortunately her life these days doesn't include very many of those. Sometimes (she declares) she really thinks — well, he's older, halfway between her parents' generation and her own, she'd guess, so maybe he'll say this is just Baby-Boomer self-pity, but it really does seem to her sometimes that her whole American generation is . . . not *lost*, like Hemingway's Lost Generation, but there's been a real slippage: economic slippage, obviously, but *gumptional* slippage, too, if he knows what she means. Is that a word, gumptional?

He smiles. "It is now."

She's an attractive woman (I shift this story's narrative point of view to have our man-on-the-aisle affirm to himself); rather more so, actually, in her present agitation. Bright, articulate, well put together, well turned out in her light summer linens, and obviously as stressed for whatever reasons as is his nameless lady-in-the-Subaru. Not to play games or seem importunate, he was about to own up to her that the "Freeze Frame" story is his: a bit of a time out from his usual occupation. By temperament and profession he's a novelist, more accustomed to the narrative long haul than to the sprint. It has been decades since he last wrote short stories. Back in the Sixties, when his first and only collection of them was published, the woman beside him — laughing now at her sudden effusiveness and at the same time knuckling tears until he offers her a dry cocktail napkin to dab with — will have been a high-schooler. But as it happens he's between larger projects just now, and at his age and stage one never knows but what the pause-in-progress, so to speak, might be one's artistic menopause. That possibility, while certainly not cheering, doesn't greatly alarm him, any more than does the regrettable prospect of losing sexual desire and potency, say, somewhere down the road (in that order, he hopes). He has had a gratifying if less than epical career in both areas, and in others as well; he is in fact on tour just now to help promote his latest mid-list novel, and missing his wife, and feeling rather too far along for this sort of thing — while at the same time mildly enjoying the break in his unglamorous but still deeply satisfying daily routine of dreaming up people and situations, putting thoughts and feelings and actions into

English sentences, and in the process discovering what's on his imagination's mind, as it were: what his muse has up her sleeve; what she'll do for an encore this late in the day.

It was in this spirit, he's telling Alice now (Yeah, he 'fessed up. Why not? Strangers in transit, never see each other again, etc.), that he wrote the "Freeze Frame" story a few months back — all those motions-within-motions and pauses-within-pauses, as she accurately put it — and even urged his agent, half as a lark, half seriously, to try placing it in some in-flight mag, of all odd places, instead of in one of the few large-circulation American magazines that still publish "literary" fiction. But of course he hadn't anticipated the happy coincidence that he would first see it in print while flying virtually over the scene of its stalled action. Truth stranger than fiction, et cet.

"Not to mention the *un*happy coincidence that you'd get stuck with old capital-H Her," Alice says, "in the flesh." Her sniffles are okay now; not stopped, but under adequate control and anyhow okay.

She's impressed, mildly; has never met a writer in person before (she thinks now she remembers his name from some classroom anthology, light-years ago); is amused to hear him say "et cet" in his ordinary speech just the way it comes up in his story, almost a stylistic tic; recalls now that in fact he said he was *re*checking those numbers, not checking them. He doesn't seem boastful or otherwise pretentious or affected: a regular fellow, self-ironic but serious; *likable*, she decides, and okay-looking for his presumable age, but who cares about that? Who cares, for that matter, whether he's thinking Get this dip out of here! He seems all right, even nice: not pressing, not turning her off; letting her babble, but companionably running on a bit himself. She finds herself doing a self-surprising thing: actually catching his hand in hers for a moment — Thanks for the Kleenex — giving it a comradely squeeze (same small voltage as that wine-bottle/glass-rim contact), and declaring she can't spare a damn dime in her present pass but would certainly enjoy another glass of wine with him if he'll be kind enough to stand her one. She'll return the favor in some other life.

"There is no other life," he declares, pleasantly. "That's why some of us make up stories." As for the wine, no problem: He'll put it on his publisher's tab; she'll buy a copy of his current novel as soon as she can afford one, but no sooner, and if she enjoys it she'll tell her friends to do likewise. All debts squared.

"Done."

And so at six-zero-eight mph et cetera et cetera et cetera this pair relax as if suspended in space and time. Never mind the in-flight movie framing along now on the video screens: In the cozily darkened cabin, all its window-shades drawn for viewing purposes, they sip white wine and exchange information about their lives. Alice, forgivably, speaks mainly of her marital problems and her anxieties with regard to the future. He counsels courage, patience, and good will; he went through that wringer himself some decades back and can attest that, with luck, there's life after the mid-life crisis. He can't argue, however, with her envious observation that a man out in the world is better positioned to meet significant new others than is a full-time mother with a ratsy part-time job. How she wishes, now, that she'd taken her doctorate in whatever and made her own career moves instead of doing the Fifties-housewife trip like Howard's mother! Though she wishes even more that her husband's career had really flown, and that they'd aged and grown in synch, still loving each other and their life together. . . .

Out come the Kleenex: Excuse her.

With fair candor he responds to her questions, when she

thinks to ask them, about how it was with him Back Then. "I wrote a lot of short stories, for one thing," he reminds her. "Too scattered for anything longer."

She gestures toward the text of "Freeze Frame," tucked into the seat-back pocket before her, and raises her eyebrows at him. "Does this mean there's trouble again at home?"

He smiles at that, shakes his head, raps on the plastic tray-table in lieu of wood.

Does Alice really mock-sigh then and say, "Too bad for *our* story!" Or, perhaps, "In that case, how do we get me and Miz Whatsername out of gridlock?" Do they chuckle at her plainly experimental flirtsomeness and raise the intimacy-level of their dialogue a notch or two, so that by final approach their hands are touching freely? And when at the airport baggage-claim he offers her a lift downtown in his cab — even dinner at his hotel, if she's up for it (Portland's splendidly refurbished old Heathman), before his scheduled appearance that evening at Powell's Bookstore — does she say, in a spirit clearly ready for adventure, "I'll say I missed my connection," and then, as the circumstance dawns on her, snatch up his hand in both of hers and declare, "No, damn it: I don't have to say anything! *There's nobody home to say it to!*"?

More reasonably, their mid-flight tête-à-tête having run its transitory course along with that sufficiency of wine, do they presently unbuckle to visit the lavatories aft and then return separately to their seats: she to go on with the "Freeze Frame" story, more curious even than before to find out what its author has in store for Her; he to go back to his notepad, in which for all Alice knows he's now jotting notes for some story about *her* as they rush motionlessly together through the time of their lives, their life-stories meanwhile suspended . . . ?

Given the age and stage of the woman in the gridlocked car, that "just past noon" business in "Freeze Frame" strikes me as obvious to the point of heavyhandedness. I apologize on behalf of the author, who has also not gotten it said to our Alice that *Subaru* is Japanese for the Pleiades cluster (see the automaker's logo) in the constellation Taurus — much farther now from the dear present reader than it was even a sentence ago. On the other hand, *I* haven't yet managed to get it said (what the "Freeze Frame" story declares somewhere in that digressive pause before the space-break beyond which Alice is currently reading) that all stories are essentially constructs in time, and only incidentally in the linear space of written words. Written or spoken, however, these words are *like* points in space, through which the story-arrow travels in time. Just now it rests at *this* point, this word, this — yet of course never resting there, but ever en route through it to the next, the next, from Beginning through Middle et cetera. Even if and when we linger over an "arresting passage," we're only apparently at rest in the story's suspended but incessant motion; likewise in our manifold own.

There. Said.

"On with the story?"

"Maybe . . .

But it's suspensions within suspensions."

Et cetera ad infinitum, amen. I figure if we fractalize this pair enough, they're home free.

"You mean they'll never get there."

He'll settle for that.

"Dearest best friend, don't count on it. Achilles nails the tortoise. Stories end."

Don't count on *that*. As the fellow said, Delta rho times delta q equals or exceeds Planck's Constant.

"The fellow said that?"

Cross my heart.

Presently, in the dark: "Okay: She'll bite."

Herr Heisenberg, aforecited. The famous Principle.

"Explain. But she may drop off in mid-Principle; she's truly running on Empty."

Likewise.

"Poor thing. I need to hear your voice, though."

I'll sing her to sleep. *A cha-a-ange in momentum . . . times a cha-a-ange in position . . . equals or excee-e-e-eeds . . . Planck's Constant* (divided by two pi, divided by two).

Presently: "What's Planck's Constant?"

I thought she'd never ask. Planck's Constant is Physics for six point six two five times ten to the minus twenty-seventh power erg-secs. Approximately.

"Thanks lots. What's *that*?"

That's Math for the constant of proportionality relating the quantum of radiation-energy to the frequency of radiation. Nobody said Uncertainty was going to be easy.

"All Greek to her."

Ditto him: *Delta pee*, et cet.

"But he *knows* Greek. So explain, till she's asleep."

Explain, explain. He summons the fading ghosts of his college physics and his frat-house Greek and ventures that one's knowledge of a particle's speed is inversely related to one's knowledge of its position.

"Which is to say?"

That the only way to measure speed with any precision is to sacrifice precision in the measurement of position, and conversely. What you make in Boston, you lose in Chicago.

"Kiss."

Anon: "He can explain everything."

He wishes. Thought she was asleep.

"You wish. What can't you explain?"

Why she and he —

"Goes without saying. Unlike some folks we know, who say without going."

Let's do that! Forever after.

"Nope. But now that she's awake, maybe he can explain love to her."

Love?

"Love."

Hm. That'd take time. . . .

"Take. Till tomorrow."

Promise?
"Mm, she sleepily replies."
Mm's the word. Meanwhile . . .
"Mm."

6.

Love Explained

Mid-afternoon mid-life lovers, postcoitally lassitudinous and sweat-wet, skin to skin.

Presently: "Explain love to me."
    Mm?
    "Love: Explain."
    That'd take some doing.
    "So do."

Presently: The phenomenon in general? Or us-here-in-this-bed-on-a-weekday-afternoon-in-October?
    "Your pleasure. Just explain, please."
    Wuff. We may have to go back a bit. Perspective . . .
    "So go. I have a long attention span."
    You do.
    "Wait. . . ."

Presently: Well. In the beginning —
    "So far, so good."
    On with the story?
    "Please."
    The Big Bang, of course . . .
    "History."

Sensitive Dependence on Initial Conditions . . .

"Likewise later conditions."

If you'd gone to Macy's that day instead of to Bloomingdale's, or to Bloomingdale's but not through Housewares on your way to Bedding —

"As it were."

Or if you'd passed through Housewares a half-hour earlier or later — we wouldn't be lying here all these years afterward.

"Evaporating."

The great god Contingency. Scary to imagine.

"Yet he actually managed that time not to get his wires crossed."

But back to the *really* initial conditions for just a fraction of a second, from T-zero to the beginning of nucleosynthesis, let's say, one one-hundred-thousandth of a second later: the first hundred-thousandth of a second of Time. . . .

"To me it seemed like ages. I thought you'd never look up from those Krups coffeemakers."

I saw you. But after all that time I couldn't believe it was *you*. Anyhow, I wanted to look you over before I officially noticed you.

"I noticed."

The point is, even back at the virtual beginning there were already certain inhomogeneities —

"To put it mildly. Nice Hyphenated-American girl meets Hyphenated-American boy, equally nice but differently hyphenated. . . ."

Her a thirtysomething single parent? Him fortysomething and divorcing?

"If they hadn't known each other already, from before . . ."

Another set of sensitive conditions, thank goodness.

"They should thank the Institute's grant-funding policy,

which gives young post-docs and their mentors a chance to rub elbows."

Und so weiter.

"They could've got it on way back then!"

But he was too shy, and she too proper.

"Inhomogeneities."

Were it not for which, the atoms of matter that finally got their act together after Time's first three hundred thousand years would have scattered through space like buckshot instead of clumping together into sheets of galaxies with humongous voids between.

"Story of her life, till Bloomingdale's."

What concerns us here in this bed on this brilliant Thursday afternoon in October is that a zillion years after our story's beginning, we've got this still-expanding universe on our hands, with a scale of magnitudes ranging from superstrings of galactic clusters down to the electrons of the atoms of the molecules of DNA, for example. If we're going to explain love, we've got to adjust our focus.

"Like so?"

Oh my yes.

Presently: As one was saying, at a certain *very* critical point somewhere between those superclusters on the one hand and those subatomic particles on the other, one finds our friendly neighborhood galaxy and even our dear little solar system with its nine or so planets, of which the seventh from the edge happens to be this pretty blue-white-brown-and-green job, like the algae that got life going on it.

"I've been there! It comes complete these days with oceans, continents, and the Boston/Cambridge urban complex, as I remember, comprising not only streets and buildings and shopping plazas, but inhabitants too. . . ."

Including, though not limited to, rats and roaches, pigeons

and starlings, pet animals, and maybe a million *Homo sapiens*, teeming and swarming.

"Getting and spending. Dealing dope and composing music."

Hijacking cars and leveraging buyouts.

"Laundering laundry. Mugging and panhandling."

Learning long division. Staring at TV screens and computer monitors. Shooting baskets and one another.

"Mating in and out of wedlock with members of the same and differing sexes. Cooking up stir-fries and stories."

And even, in rare instances, contemplating the nature of the universe and the phenomenon of consciousness therein.

"But not explaining love, I notice."

Not quite yet. Among those last-remarked instances, however, is to be found here and there the oddball capable of formulating or at least of comprehending Einstein's relativity theories, Schrödinger's quantum-mechanical wave-function equations, and Heisenberg's Uncertainty Principle —

"*Along with other apparent esoterica which are in fact among the indispensable intellectual baggage of our narrative-historical moment*, right?"

As you may have heard.

"In spades, chez l'Institute. But play it again."

More than Freudian psychology, more than Marxist ideology, quantum mechanics has been the Great Attractor of the second half of this dying century — even though, speaking generally, almost none of us knows beans about it.

"The old songs are the best. That's love?"

We're getting warm.

"We *were* getting warm, back there with the mating and the stir-fry. Then we lost the picture."

So we fiddle with the clicker. The next-to-bottom line is that per Standard Theory, the position of any and every electron is a field of probabilities until we measure it; then and only then its "wave function" collapses and it truly *has* a position.

"Shall we cut to the chase?"

This *is* the chase. It follows that the universe aforementioned might be said to be as much an effect of our observation of it as we observers are an effect of its aforesummarized evolution, which happens to have happened within *extremely* critical parameters, like a cute re-meet.

"The Anthropic Principle! Kiss me quick."

It comes in three flavors —

"Don't we all: The Weak, the Strong, and the Participatory, if I remember correctly."

Whereof we democratic types have no time for any save the Participatory: "*The observer is as essential to the creation of the universe as the universe is to the creation of the observer.*" All hands on deck, and kiss me again.

"Nothing is but thinking makes it so."

Quod erat demonstrandum and voilà: The universe is a self-exciting circuit, like us.

"Not only *like* us, if I follow you, but *because of* us."

You're leading me. Don't stop.

"By turns and together we're *both* leading and following, no? At our best, I mean."

And at our best we're both both leading and following the observable universe as observed: So declareth the Participatory Anthropic Principle.

"Things are as we find them to be because we who are among both the causes and the effects of those observed conditions thus observe them. Kiss?"

No sooner said than.

Presently: "And no sooner done than said. Thus just as consciousness is both the impulse and the prerequisite for explaining consciousness, and so might be said to be equally subject and object, or question and answer . . ."

And just as Dante, led by Love to the final circle of Paradise, sees there that the big L is literally what "moves the Sun and the other stars," so you and I, about halfway through our expectable life-story just when our planet, mirabile dictu, happens to be about halfway through *its* —

"Time, time . . ."

See how it runs, and so we *make* it run.

"Love exists, like the world, you're telling me, as much because I asked my question as conversely."

You're telling me.

"Now that we've explained it, I knew it all along."

Presently: Much obliged, dear friend.

Presently: "Dear friend: my pleasure."

"You're putting words in her mouth."

Yes, well: my line of work.

"*Time, time* . . ."

Mere words in her mouth.

"Kiss them, then."

Later that same day, or maybe the next: "If only life were as simple as theoretical physics."

Mm?

"Love explained isn't love explained away."

Hallelujah. You looked simply terrific on the courts to-day, by the way.

"Spiffy to the end."

He fell in love with her all over again, as usual.

"Lust explained."

But not away.

In time: "Anyhow, thanks for trying. Really."

De nada.

"Exactly true, alas: The cupboard's bare."

Not so. Half full at least.

"Half empty, then. At least."

Not before he fetches from it, for her delectation and pos-sible diversion, this hefty item here. . . .

"Poor lucky dog, that gets thrown *that* bone. Let her have it."

They'll share it: a team effort on both ends.

"To the end of both?"

More words in her mouth. Shall I?

"To the end."

7.

"Waves," by Amien Richard

"Are we particles," Amy wants to know, "or waves?"

She's floating prone, trim, and naked on an inflated mat at the edge of our borrowed pool in the beachfront yard of our borrowed house in Freeport, Grand Bahama. Her cropped-blonde head rests on the heel of one hand; with the other she idly stirs the water-surface — at the same time reading, intermittently, a science magazine propped on the coping of the pool. Beyond our security-fenced and casuarina-screened lawn, the surf on our borrowed ocean, driven by a rising southerly, breaks first on the distant reef and then again, less roughly, on "our" shelved sandstone beach.

Reasonably, before he answers, Richard asks, "We human beings? Or *we* meaning you and me?" Likewise naked except for a canvas sailing hat, and as carefully sun-lotioned as is his mate, he's lounging in a towel-spread and palm-shaded poolside chair, dangling one foot in the water near his wife's hand and scribbling in a notebook. Utter luxury, the pair of us agree, after what we've lately been through, and in our shared and different ways we're soaking it up.

"Us, I guess. Yes. Waves or particles?"

Without looking up yet from his notebook, "Wherefore doth milady ask, her partner maketh bold to wonder," Richard likewises, "whilst he cobbleth up a reply?"

With wet fingertip Amy taps her borrowed *Scientific American*. "Says here that photons behave like particles sometimes and other times like waves. I'm wondering how it is with us."

"You and me."

"For starters."

Tucking his upper lip like President Bill Clinton in the Pensive Mode, her mate considers. "The same." And makes to make another notebook-note.

Amy, presently: "Hell with it, then, I guess."

"Her friend begs her pardon?"

"Her friend heard what his friend said."

"So he thought." Notebook closed. "Ame?"

"To hell," the woman of us now declares — to the surf mat, it would appear, face pressed into it, forehead resting on back of hand — "with everything."

"*Stressed out*, her husband, who loves her, helpfully suggests," the man of us etc.

Instead of responding "No response," Amy non-responds.

We talk this way, sometimes: occupational side-effect of our being professional articulators, so to speak; a couple of ironists married fourteen years exactly as of the date of this dialogue. Reader will have noticed, as has Richard, that Amy didn't ask for explanation — at least not directly, at least not yet — only for reply, and that her life-partner has supplied, so far, no more than she requested. Treading carefully, we'd bet.

"Partner *in* life, or partner *for*?" it might be inquired, and therefore by Amy now is. The woman reads and routinely questions our joint mind.

In most certainly, *for* presumably and we hope. That very presumption and mutual hope, it will turn out, happen to be what's at stake in this waves-or-particles story, now more or less launched and about to pause for a bit of cautious background exposition. Here's how it is with us Amy-and-Richards and what we're doing in a borrowed house on borrowed time in Freeport, Grand Bahama:

Well known in the free-lance trade and to readers of *National Geographic*, *Cruising World*, the *Smithsonian*, and other "nature" mags, also to followers of the *New York Times* nonfiction list and even to watchers of public-television nature-and-travel documentaries, "Amien Richard" (Incorporated) is the nom de plume of our long-standing and historically quite successful collaboration. To put it most baldly, Amy's the brains of this outfit, Richard the voice. Our original project-ideas are typically hers: "Let's pedal a tandem bicycle across the USA, sea to shining sea, switching positions at each time zone"; "Let's watch nature-watchers"; or maybe no more than (as in the present instance, after a two-year virtual hiatus) "What say we skip this winter altogether and sail down to the Caribbean?" She then takes that ball, if it appeals to her mate, and runs with it: thinks up the angles; negotiates commissions, sponsorships, contracts, tie-ins; does the lion's share of logistical planning, research, administration, even photography in cases where we don't need a camera crew. The woman resists *writing*, however, in the sense of composition, and so it's Richard who drafts our proposals and, most important, turns our homework into prose sentences like these: the finished product, which Amy will perspicaciously then edit and supervise the marketing of. Mainly, as instanced, we do nonfiction books and articles, including the odd television project; but "Amien Richard" (we give that surname a French twist — Ree-*shard* — to go with the Gallic-sounding "Amien") have one commercially successful novel to our credit, too, as you may remember: *The Watcher*, a fictionalized spin-off from our nature-watcher-watching documentary. Book-of-the-Month Club

Alternate Selection, film option twice renewed and looking reasonably positive: not bad for a first offense.

And that same pseudonymous entity may now be in process of gestating, of all labor-of-love enterprises, our maiden *short story* — to be entitled, possibly, "Waves," or, just as possibly, "Particles." Its Return on Investment ("Vive le ROI," practical Amy likes to say) won't approach that of a commissioned article in the *Times* Sunday magazine, for example; but we like to try different things. Anyhow, we're R&R'ing just now after our truly hairy Gulf Stream crossing, among other turbulences, and the R of us hasn't entirely suppressed his original youthful ambition to be a *writer*-writer: a capital-A Author. If this story gets written, he has promised the A of us, we'll change the couple's names to . . . oh, "Amy" and "Richard," maybe, to protect the presumably innocent.

What else? Well: Today's our Ivory Wedding Anniversary, as has been more or less mentioned, and info-rich Amy has come up with not only that bit of scrimshaw — the woman's a walking World Almanac, currently floating in place — but also this food for thought: that over the years of our corporate life most of the cells in our bodies have replaced themselves, not once but twice. More on this subject presently, we suspect. We're old enough to have undergone four or five previous such seven-year body replacements and one prior marriage apiece, of shorter duration now than our present and ongoing one. Each of those initiations issued offspring, and by gosh and by golly we've seen that blended duo through high school and into college: no mean accomplishment for a pair of peripatetics without institutional fringe benefits. For A. R. Inc.'s first near-dozen years, our own genes went uncombined; we regretted that, one of us maybe more than the other, but we couldn't see shelving our footloose rent-and-tuition-paying enterprises for the years it would take to raise another child to portability. . . .

We couldn't? Really, we couldn't; remember? We enjoyed our adventuresome life, much more than not. We valued and value still, to put it mildly, our vigorous marriage, which has weathered its share of storms (most recently and sorely . . . but never mind, yet). And we love each other.

Right?

Suffice it to say, then, that our current project — a leisurely cruise down the Intracoastal Waterway in *ARI*, our weathered but seaworthy secondhand ketch (same vintage as our marriage, and much of *it* renovated, too, over those dozen-plus years), from our home base in Annapolis down to Florida, across to the Bahamas, and on to the Caribbean and back, leaving a trail of magazine-pieces in our wake — was meant by the way to reconsolidate and reaffirm "Amien Richard," Inc., after a devastating, regrettably centrifugal season. In this, through September and the first half of October, it arguably succeeded, wouldn't we say? We would, on balance. Yes. Moseying down the ICW in the intimate quarters and simple rhythms of life afloat, following the end-of-summer weather south and putting daily more mileage between us and the venue of our unspecified late calamity, we went some way toward regaining, if not lost heart, at least reciprocal spontaneity and clarity of spirit.

Well said. Thanks. We lucked out on the regular season's hurricanes, as with crossed fingers we hope we shall on the late-season item now approaching: Hurricane Emile, of which the building seas out there on "our" reef are early stirrings. We even got an article out of Emile's immediate predecessor, Hurricane Dashika, a near miss who chewed up Beaufort, North Carolina, while we were snug in Beaufort, *South* Carolina ("The Battered Beauforts," *Sail* magazine, forthcoming). We did an eating-piece for USAir's in-flight mag on the splendid restaurants of Charleston's Historic District and an ecology-piece, not yet placed, on the savannas of Savannah. By pushing our timetable a bit and coordinating Amy's logistical prowess with Richard's navigational, we arranged to transit the Cape Canaveral area in time to witness, photograph, and project another nature-watcher-watching article, this one about a PBS television crew making a *Nature* documentary on wildlife reacting to a space-shuttle launch. In the Art Deco district of Miami Beach, while Amy's camera clicked away for a possible *Architectural Digest* commission down the road, we touched base with a Bahamian college-roommate of Richard's, now a successful speculator in that same real estate, who commiserated with our late loss and insisted that we make free with his Freeport beachfront spread after our maiden Gulf Stream crossing. He and his wife seldom find time these days to use the place themselves, he declared; they have others, elsewhere. He would notify their caretaker to expect us and to show us the workings of the house and grounds. We would find it more than comfortable, he was sure, and very likely we'd need a few days to rest and regroup before moving on to the Out Islands and down to the Caribbean.

Understatement of the season. But here comes that same caretaker now, cheerful ex-Haitian Georges; we hear him opening the automatic driveway gate on the house's far side to deliver our host's Jeep, which Georges has obligingly commissioned for us early this morning and will now put at our disposal for the duration (as yet undecided) of our visit. Time to end this water-testing exposition, wrap ourselves in beach towels, and return to our story's present action.

In which Georges, dressed as usual in clean khakis and white T-shirt, respectfully hails us from the nearest patio — "Mister Richard? Miz Amy?" — not presuming to approach more closely while we're undressed. A compact, dark brown, well-muscled, pleasant-faced, dignified, soft-spoken, near-hairless fellow in his forties, Georges has been in our absent hosts' loyal employ for a dozen years, ever since he "came ashore," as he quaintly puts it, from his troubled homeland and was taken up (and his irregular immigrant status regularized) by Richard's ex-roommate's Canadian wife, who functions as overseer of their several properties. To the various skills that Georges brought ashore with him, she has added reading, writing, and a spoken English more fluent than our French.

His beach towel knotted at the hip, Richard goes over and shakes the man's hand. From poolside, Amy waves and calls, "Bonjour, *M'sieur* Georges," teasing him for his declining to use our first names unadorned, as we use his.

Good-humoredly but resolutely, "Good morning, Miz Amy," Georges calls back, and returns her wave from the patio. Richard tends to shrug his shoulders at such cross-culturalities as this matter of address-forms, but liberal Amy takes them seriously, and Georges has therefore obligingly explained to her that one must "have respect" if one wants to get on in the world. Miz Evelyn, our absent hostess, evidently imparted that great truth to him along with English; Georges in turn hopes to have taught it to his children. Of those, we have learned from him, he has "about seven": four handsome sons "inside," who help him with his caretaking chores after school, and "about three daughters outside" — mainly in New York City, it seems. We (who have "about two" ourselves these days, so Amy has replied to Georges' polite inquiry) haven't yet sorted out the fellow's infobits and the sociology of Inside versus Outside children; we agree, however, that "having respect" cuts both ways, and that Georges is not to be pestered with our Yankee egalitarianism.

The two men stroll around to the driveway, Richard feeling fairly foolish in bare feet, beach towel, and large-brimmed hat. There Georges checks him out on the operation of the fat-tired, high-sprung, roll-barred, topless, fire-engine-red Wrangler, one of several vehicles garaged on the premises and the only one licensed for island-wide use beyond Freeport's posted "insurance district" — another info-bit not yet clear to us Amy-and-Richards. Georges has repeated with some pride our host's instructions to him that it is his "personal responsibility" to see to it that we have everything we need for a pleasant visit, the Jeep included; in discharge of that responsibility, he tries as earnestly to answer our questions about the island as we try not to overburden him therewith. It has become evident to us, however, that while he is an alert, industrious, guileless, and resilient fellow with a basketful of handyman's skills, the world of licensings and "insurance districts" is as beyond his compass as Miami real-estate speculation is beyond ours.

Having tried the 4WD's gearshift and reviewed the operation of the automatic gate (labeled *Warning: Attack Dog*, like most others in the neighborhood, but not, like many of them, correspondingly equipped, or topped with coils of razor-wire), Richard asks where on the island we might find good snorkeling from the beach, closer to shore than the half-mile or so between our doorstep and the wave-smashing reef out yonder. Georges' suggestions — he himself doesn't enjoy swimming, but several of his sons are ardent and knowledgeable spearfishers — are couched in detailed local references unfamiliar to Richard if perhaps not to Amy, who yesterday began hitting the guidebooks as is her wont and talking to restaurant servers and store clerks: a positive sign, R hopes, after her recent dark torpor.

"Gold Rock?" he asks her when Georges has gone to sweep leaves off the family tennis court against our possible later use of it. "Dead Man's Reef?"

"They're in the guides," Amy thinks she remembers, "or on the tourist map. Did you do the map with him?"

"Georges doesn't do maps," her husband replies. "But how's this for specificity? We cross the first main canal up yonder and follow the beach road along through Williamstown and up along farther till we come to the Haitian cemetery in the pine woods. We leave the Jeep at that cemetery and walk back along that beach to where those woods began and on along back to the first pine tree separate from those woods along that shore. Then we swim straight out from that lonesome pine tree to where the coral is, et voilà."

"Haitian cemetery?"

"It's where Georges came ashore," Richard reports, "whatever *that* means. He says we'll see, and maybe we should. Or is it to hell with everything?"

His wife cuts him a look. "Is it to hell with everything with you?"

"It is not. Let's go find that Haitian cemetery."

At this point in the text of our trial story, Richard himself inclines toward a space-break followed by a friendly-though-tentative conjugal sex scene, perhaps of a therapeutic character. Amy nixes that proposal and his unspoken proposition, however, and she's the editor-in-chief of this outfit. From the pool we've moved up to our bedroom, to dress and pack for our day's excursion; we have more or less decided to follow Georges' detailed directions and explore what our map shows to be the windward side of the island this morning (Williamstown village is indicated, likewise the adjacent beach, but no Haitian cemetery); then back to Port Lucaya, next door to Freeport, for lunch and a look at how repairs are proceeding to *ARI*'s rig, damaged in our Gulf Stream crossing. In the afternoon, we guess, if nature's weather and our own remain favorable, maybe we'll check out a reef or two off the leeward shore, where the water's less likely to be roiled by waves; then back to home base to see what we feel like doing this evening in the wedding-anniversary-celebration way.

If anything. We don't *want* this damned yearlong cloud hanging over us, you understand; we happen to like as well as love each other, and *neither of us blames the other for what happened* (at least no more than him/herself), and it's a drag to go about feeling bruised, licking our wounds, our spirit-gauges reading Empty. But you don't de-cloud just by saying "Get lost, cloud," any more than you make literal bruises disappear — and we're both carrying literal contusions, as it happens, from last week's mighty culminating knockdown that nearly took away our mizzen-mast — just by saying "Bye-bye, bruises." Having made our indirect way through our pretty remarkable borrowed house, avoiding the shortcut through its grand sunken living room for reasons presently to be explained, and having discarded our pool-towels and turned naked to the question whether to beach-bag our undies and wear swimsuits under our clothes or vice versa, Richard embraces his wife from behind as she's folding her towel on the king-size bed, cups a hand over each of her breasts, nuzzles her nape, and presses his nonerection against the cleft of her butt. In ordinary circumstances, that overture would likely suffice to precipitate the balming business that he warmly has in mind, especially given the added small titillation of a luxurious, unfamiliar bedroom (from its balcony/sundeck there's even a waterslide down to the pool) after the confined quarters of a cruising sailboat. Amy permits the embrace — our first such since Miami — and even puts her hands atop his; her body tension, however, says No, and so there goes our sex-therapy scene.

May Richard hope that what his friend's body tension really says is Not yet?

Of course Richard may; *Amy* sure as hell does. But who

knows how things will sort out with this troubled pair of particles? On with the story, and perhaps we'll see.

Amen, sigh Amien Richard, Inc. — and we put the space-break here instead:

After which, while we bounce down the potholed beach-road in our mighty Wrangler, Amy in the driver's seat fills her husband and the reader in on what she has learned about what we're seeing. Because the Bahamas, while politically in-dependent, remain still in the Commonwealth, we drive on the left, Brit-style, as we have done on such other once-British isles as Barbados and Jamaica. Nearly all of the island's cars, however, regardless of their country of manufacture, are shipped over from the States and, having been built for the American trade, sport left-side steering, with the interesting consequence that one passes other vehicles more or less blind to what lies ahead. No problem outside the "insurance zone" (we think we begin to understand the term), where there's little traffic on the straight, flat, often poorly surfaced roads; rather more ticklish in busy Freeport/Port Lucaya, especially at the roundabouts, but all hands seem to manage, by and large. Like its numerous smaller neighbors, Grand Bahama is topographically uninteresting: no mountains or rain forests, just a large flat cay of palmetto, casuarina, poison-wood, and Bahamian juniper, ringed by fine flat beaches, patches of mangrove, vast grassy conch-abounding shallows, coral reefs of varying health, and Caribbean-clear water. The Out Islands, everyone agrees, are more handsome; bustling Nassau, the archipelago's capital, is more colorful and lively. Freeport and environs, Grand Bahama's only conurbation, makes its living principally off cruise-ship and beach-resort tourism, although the resorts are more or less downscale as of this writing, and the port of call is less popular than oth-ers farther south. Two large casinos, Amy reports, one in

Freeport and the other in Port Lucaya, are the most conspicuous sources of hard-currency inflow; how much of it stays on the island is another matter. Perhaps owing to Grand Bahama's proximity to the States, its native culture seems less distinct to Amien Richard than the various cultures of the Caribbean.

What most forcefully takes our tourist/documentarist eye as we commence this A.M. Wrangler-tour is the scale and number of construction projects evidently stalled, shelved, or abandoned at various stages of completion. Much of the island's western half has been reticulated into a network of laboriously dredged and masonry-banked canals, fingering out from a series of main channels with outlets to the sea —the backbone of what was intended as a massive Florida-style real-estate development, every house with its private canal-front and dock. On the fingers of land between these fingers of water, scores, perhaps hundreds, of residential streets were laid out some years back, paved, named, and marked with signs; a handful of houses have been built, as many more begun, but on almost none of these latter do we see construction in progress. On the contrary, it is as if the entire vast enterprise has been abandoned: The building lots are overgrown with man-size scrub, which in places chokes the now-crumbling, cratered streets; the road signs rust and lean; unfinished houses, many with scaffolding still in place, are marked FOR SALE and overgrown with vines. Entire resorts-in-the-works, we will discover, have been similarly aborted in mid-gestation; others have changed hands downward from up-market franchises; one or two have been abandoned and reclaimed by nature, which in these latitudes moves in fast. Even the casinos have a slightly threadbare look: broken light fixtures unrepaired, decorative fountains algae-grown, worn carpeting on the entranceway steps.

What happened, our driver explains (according to the friendly and knowledgeable maitre d' of the restaurant where we dined last night in Port Lucaya, and with whom A made conversation while R was in the men's room), is that the island had looked in the early Eighties to be about to boom like the Caymans, under an Anglo administration friendly to outside investment and offshore banking (for which, to some extent, read "drug money laundering," we suppose). The massive canals were dug, the streets laid out, the resorts built or begun; real-estate speculators, mainly non-local, profitably bought and sold. But the Reagan/Bush administration's later "war on drugs," coincident with a new black Grand Bahamian administration's position that too much of that outside investment was bypassing native islanders, sharply chilled the action. Hence the García-Márquezlike disrepair and reversion to "nature" all about us: an abandoned "cinema village" out toward East End, meant for a nascent film industry that never took hold; the once-scenic "Garden of the Groves" now largely gone to weed, its pavilions plyboarded up; an enormous Loire Valley–style château almost the size of Chambord, its slate roofs and stone turrets wildly out of place in the tropics, perched empty and unfinished on a scrub-choked hill not far from Georges' modest village of tin-roofed cinderblock cottages painted in washes of aquamarine, coral, apricot, and umber — through which we roll now as Amy winds up her guidebook spiel. This arrested development, her maitre d' was confident, will prove temporary; despite the "Bahamas for the Bahamians" tone of the ruling party's billboards here and there about the island, the economic slump is so evident to all hands that the party will almost certainly have to come to terms with the development interests or lose the upcoming elections. In the maitre d's opinion, this present trough between waves of prosperity is exactly the time to buy into the distressed market.

Yes, well: Richard guesses not. Likewise Amy, although in another life she would enjoy being a wheeler-dealer like R's old roommate. We'll want to get *his* reading of this business eventually; meanwhile, the man of us is impressed for the umpteenth time at how much the woman of us found out in a single peesworth of time. Does she think there's an Amien Richard photo-essay in all this rather spectacular decay? "Grand Bahama Bides Its Time," say, for *National Geo*?

Without taking her suddenly tear-filled eyes from the pot-holed road — twin dirt-tracks now, leading bumpily through high weeds and wind-bent scrub along the empty beachside embankment between the village of Williamstown behind us and the stand of evergreen well ahead — Amy allows, "There might be, if our weather ever clears." She downshifts to ford a virtual pond in the road, hub-deep from last night's heavy rainshowers. "Just now this all reminds me too much of my other life" (in which she and her D.C.-lawyer husband came to realize — one daughter and a half-renovated Virginia horse-farm into their marriage — that they really weren't suited to each other *at all*, as they had romantically imagined themselves to be since undergraduate days, and their ambitious remodeling project sat idly depreciating for the two years it took them to work out a settlement and dispose of the property).

Let it not be a foreshadowing of ours, Richard says or prays, perhaps both, and gets no noticeable response in either case. Amy's maitre d's trough-between-waves image has chilled our man right through — and put him in mind, by the way, of his partner's story-opening question. Just now, he feels (likewise she, he might want to know), we two are decidedly in the Particle Mode: particles particles particles, minimally interacting but fundamentally discrete. If, as John Donne declared, no man is an island, that's because *every* man and woman is: "windowless monads," in Leibnitz's term, distinct as one Bahama from another (29 islands, 661 cays, and 2,387 rocks, Amy has informed us), bouncing waves off one another across the big and little gulfs separating them.

Speaking of which (waves), Q: Why does this particular pair of particles avoid their borrowed house's sunken living room, as has been demonstrated? A: Because upon our awed first inspection of the premises, over its massive coral-rock fireplace we were staggered to see a blown-up reproduction of Hokusai's famous woodblock print *The Breaking Waves Off Kanajawa* (a.k.a. *The Great Wave*, or simply *The Wave*), wherein a tsunami-size breaking sea towers over hapless fishing vessels dwarfed in the trough before it, and seems to tower likewise even over Mt. Fuji in the far distance.

"I myself have seen like those," Georges told us proudly as we stood stillstruck before the thing. "When I came ashore."

Replied grim Amy, "So have we, cher Georges. Nowhere *near* shore. May we never see another." Toward which end, we take the long way around great Hokusai in our comings and goings through the house.

Voilà? Okay, sure: voilà.

Et voilà now the promised woods, casuarinas for the most part, through which we bump per program after tentatively remarking the first free-standing shoreside specimen before it, our snorkeling landmark. And in those woods — strewn, alas, like much of the Grand Bahamian environ, with discarded plastic beverage bottles and other litter, but anyhow handsome, fragrant, and soughing in the rising wind — we find indeed a small rectangular plot of gravestones, trash-free and bordered neatly with conch shells. We pull off the main track into the scrub and de-Jeep for a closer look. An inscription on the central stone apprises us that on a stormy night in 1978, just outside the reef off from this spot, a boatload of Haitian refugees were put overboard (having been assured, we will later learn, that the scattered lights onshore were Florida) and told to swim to their promised land. In the nature of the case, neither the exact number of survivors nor that of nonsurvivors is known for certain, but the drowned bodies of twenty-one women, men, and children were found here and there alongshore over the next days and buried where we stand. Of the known survivors, most were returned to Port-au-Prince as illegal immigrants. A few — among them Georges, we now headshakingly infer — had better luck.

In a notorious passage in *De Rerum Natura*, Richard recalls, the Roman philosopher-poet Lucretius sings of the pleasure of standing safely on a storm-lashed headland to watch a vessel in distress offshore:

> *Not that we delight in other men's*
> *Afflictions, but because it's sweet to note*
> *That we ourselves (this time at least) are spared.*

Translation from the Latin by Amien Richard, who think we know what Lucretius means, all right, but who, having done time out there, feel in the presence of Hokusai's *Wave* and this Haitian refugee cemetery nothing whatever of that pleasure; not even the pained relief that Lucretius would have been better advised to specify. What we feel (and, feeling it, for the first time in a while we unself-consciously take each other's hand) is more akin to Aristotelian Pity and Terror: not yet cathartic, quite, but humbling, perspective-adjusting. Whether or not our partnership survives, our shipship did, and in it we two particles have managed to Come Ashore alive. Amien Richard's project-in-the-works (we mean both our interrupted voyage in progress and this story ditto) may come to be abandoned like so many projects round about us; but Amy and Richard, unlike some, are breathing air, holding hands, and feeling luckier after all than at least twenty-one other hapless human particles as we turn our attention now to mere amphibious pleasure.

What balm, to be *touring* and *doing* again instead of sitting around more or less in shock. The Jeep-ride; the cemetery-inspection, sobering as it was; now the sunny-breezy beach-walk back to that solitary casuarina, where we plop our towels, unbag our snorkel-gear and bag our outer clothing, lotion up, rub the insides of our masks with the juice of a beach-plant leaf to prevent fogging (a trick taught to Amien Richard on assignment years ago in Maui and here passed on gratis to the reader; it works better than spit), and wade into the tepid shallows to slip feet into swim-fins. Pleasurable as is this familiar routine, however, and new as we are to the art of short-story-writing, A. R. Inc. well understand that *action* is not to be confused with *plot*; that mere busyness — Wrangling down the road, citing Donne and Leibnitz and Lucretius, and swimming out now through the wave-stirred water in search of submarine diversion — so far from necessarily advancing our story, may in fact delay its progress. The classic curve of dramatic action is (excuse us) a Hokusai-like wave, rising conflicted from the trough of an initial ground-situation to a climactic crest and then crashing to its life-altering denouement. However diverting in itself, any particle of action that fails to increment that wave (e.g., perhaps, this paragraph) is indeed a diversion, quite beside the dramaturgical point.

So. Well. Through warm, sand-clouded water, over turtle-grass and sandstone and through isolated fingers of rust-brown coral, we swim out a few hundred yards, looking for the more substantial formations that attract marine fauna. Richard half-wishes we were back ashore holding hands again, en route somehow toward being *us* again; from the other side of some semicolon, Amy half-wishes likewise, but reminds Amien Richard that if wishes were horses, beggars would ride. Does any of that advance our plot? After deepening to maybe twenty feet, the lagoon reshallows like an inverse wave to eight or ten, and we begin to see brain corals, also some stag- and elkhorn, with such expectable denizens as squirrelfish, wrasses, sergeant majors, goat- and parrotfish, the occasional butterflyfish and French angel. Amy points out a medium-size stingray settling itself into a patch of white sand; Richard, who normally prefers to swim behind a bit and let Amy set our course and pace while he admires her body along with the other scenery, espies from the side of his eye a small shark. He turns for a better look — nurse shark, he decides, minding its own business down there among the brains and antlers — and then surfaces to call his wife's attention to the animal.

Doesn't immediately see her. Nothing extraordinary in that, losing track of a head and snorkel-pipe bobbing at surface-level among foot-high waves. He cons a full circle, confirming en passant our bearing on the now-distant pine and our relative proximity to the sea-crashed reef. No Amy. His nerves duly tingle a bit — but hey, we're veteran snorkelers, and these aren't dangerous conditions, merely too bestirred for good reconnoitering. She's probably diving to check something out. He ducks under, looks around, doesn't see her, resurfaces, doesn't see her, begins to think Oh my oh my but truly believes that the flat-out, tear-prostrated, what's-the-use-of-going-on part of our late loss and general moral devastation is behind us now. *It wasn't her fault.* He does another three-sixty, and sure enough there she is, thank Whomever, face down and snorkel up, finning unconcernedly midway between him and the reef, her hands clasped comfortably behind her back. Immensely relieved, he overtakes her; doesn't mention his alarm. We agree that conditions here to windward just now aren't worth it; let's go find lunch, check out the yard's progress on our boat, and look for calmer snorkeling waters to leeward. We commence the long but virtually effortless return to shore, thinking inevitably of how it must have been on that dreadful night for those wretched and terrified other swimmers. Not to mention . . .

Has any of this advanced the story? (It has, between the lines, Amy here opines in pained parentheses; but she isn't prepared to say how just yet. [What she did — unnoticed by Richard but not by the central joint narrative intelligence of this story — was give the slip to her mate's recently somewhat oppressive though understandable *monitoring* of her ((as she perceives it)) and dive down behind a pile of living coral to see whether she would carry through on her one-tenth-serious inclination to drown herself. As her held breath reached its limit, however, she happened to catch sight of the corkscrew inner spiral of a small, ground-down conch shell on the sea floor: a dainty, perfect, tapered blush-and-ivory auger, not uncommon in these waters but in this instance uncommonly fine in its coloration and its intactness-within-attrition. Instead of blowing out the last of her air therefore to find out whether she could actually inhale water as . . . others have done before her, she forced herself a fathom deeper, retrieved the token, and shot to the surface. No Richard ((he has ducked under in search of her)); then there he is, looking the other way, toward shore. She recovers her breath and inner balance; returns to snorkeling as if nonchalantly, although her heart still pounds; inspects through her mask the little treasure in her hand; tucks it for safekeeping into the crotch of her bikini, faute de mieux; then clasps her hands behind her back, the better to feign insouciance.])

* * *

On with the story, we suppose; anyhow with the narrative. Ashore, we towel, relotion and -dress, bid the drowned Haitians rest in peace. Amy considers leaving on their grave as tribute the little conch-stem (which, back on the beach, she has already surreptitiously uncrotched and pocketed) but then thinks *Ivory Anniversary* and decides to hold on to it for a while yet, in secret parentheses. We Jeep leftside in full strong sunshine back into Port Lucaya by the main highway, in places still as flooded in the absence of storm drains as if last night's rain had been a tidal wave. From the cab- and jitney-loads of elderly Americans splashing along with us toward the Lucaya Marketplace and casino, we infer that a cruise ship has docked in Freeport. We follow the crowd briefly in order to make dinner reservations for this evening at the best of its many restaurants, in case etc. Rather than buck the unexpected lunch crowd, however, we then retreat across Bell Channel — the Grand Canal of that aforedescribed network — toward the marina and repair yard. As we hoped and expected, along the way we see one of the island's many informal shellfish vendors, this one operating out of the back of a rusty Ford pickup under the hand-lettered notice CRACK CONCH STEAM CONCH SCORCH CONCH, and pause to share a standup paper-cupful of fresh-made conch ceviche with rum punch. We are the dreadlocked Rastafarian vendor's only current customers; to make conversation, Amy asks him brightly whether Hurricane Emile will pass us by. With cool but not incordial dignity (the fellow looks like dispossessed Ethiopian royalty), he halves the volume of Bob Marley reggae on his boom box and declares to her, "That be in *He* honds, mahm." Not meaning the late singer's.

I suppose so, Richard says to be agreeable, but he hopes for a more updated, less fatalistic opinion from the marina office. Thereto we Wrangle next — Richard at the wheel now, to get the feel of our borrowed vehicle and to relieve A, who has acknowledged feeling blah — and there in one of the service slips near the big travel-lift sits stout but battered *ARI*, our corporate ketch. Two native riggers, one in a bosun's seat at the mizzen masthead, are replacing the starboard shroud that let go in our Gulf Stream knockdown and would doubtless have cost us that mast if its sail hadn't happened to be furled at the time. As things turned out (since the boat's standing rigging is interconnected and more or less interdependent), when *ARI* finally self-righted and the storm passed, we were obliged to limp on to Freeport under cautious headsails and triple-reefed main, both to avoid overstraining the rig and because our mainsail's lower seams had blown out just seconds before the knockdown.

"We be done today," the elderly rigger on deck informs us. "You be good as new." He grins and calls up to his younger colleague, bandanna'd like an eighteenth-century pirate: "*Better* than new, Sahm, right?"

"You say," the fellow calls back. At risk of a patronizing stereotype, Amien Richard here report that our experiences thus far with Grand Bahamians of every station have been consistently agreeable. We have found them friendly, cheerful, and obliging without deferentiality (Georges excepted on that last score, but his case is special — and he, too, as aforereported, is rich in personal dignity and self-respect). The rigger-on-deck now shakes his head in good-humored awe at the power of the sea, what it has done to us. "But you should see some that come in here, mon! You lucky."

We suppose we are, all right, Richard agrees. The fellow is curious to know whether, when that rogue wave all but rolled us, the ketch's deep centerboard had been raised or lowered. He is of the opinion that, contrary to conventional wisdom, in breaking seas a boat so equipped should tuck up its board altogether, the way the islanders used to do in their fishing smacks in high seas. A sailboat can "trip on she keel," he declares, in such conditions; better to sacrifice a little normal stability, if necessary, and slip sidewise down the face of the seas instead of tripping and rolling. "Go *with the flow,* mon."

We are not inclined to argue that point. Amy's saying nothing, only smiling thinly; Richard, clutch-stomached at memory of that second-worst moment of our lives, merely nods. In all likelihood, *ARI*'s centerboard had indeed been fully lowered to dampen the vessel's roll in quartering seas; R's private opinion, however, is that given the weather's condition and his own at the time, the matter of centerboard-position is probably irrelevant. The British yard manager, to whose office we now repair, informs us that our ripped mainsail won't be quite so soon ready: next week earliest, as the sailmaker has a small backlog of similar transient orders and tends moreover to work on "island time." Just as well, don't we think? By next week, Hurricane Emile will be history, if indeed he's coming to visit: The latest reports have the Out Islands in for a passing blow but Grand Bahama in for no more than a spot of Force Seven winds and some heavy rain, probably toward morning and through tomorrow.

While delivering us these tidings, the fellow is half attending a Stateside baseball game on a countertop TV. "I say," he now says, indicating its diminutive screen: "Ever see one of *those* before?"

Looking more closely, we see that the fans at Oriole Park in Baltimore, of all familiar places, are engaged in that loosely coordinated fanly maneuver known as ... the Wave: Standing to stretch their legs between innings, they raise their arms en masse over their heads; those immediately behind the home team's dugout then bend leftward momentarily and restraighten, cueing their neighbors on that side to do like-

127

wise, et cetera, until, with no one leaving his/her particular place, the "wave" takes on a perceptible character and with apparent autonomy orbits the stadium twice or thrice before dissipating.

Says Amy, "Yup." "Ai yi," breathes Richard, and turns away.

The marina manager chuckles admiringly. "Enough to make a chap seasick, what?"

At this point in this trial draft of this trial story, Amien Richard declare another space-break in order to assess how things are going, plotwise, and for that matter *whether*, not to mention whither. Those accumulating *waves* coming at us and the reader from all directions are indeed enough to give this edgy brace of particles a touch of mal de mer. Amy considers editing at least a couple of them out, lest we be taxed with authorial heavyhandedness — the Hokusai, maybe, or the baseball fans — but *we* didn't put the damned things there: Coincidence did, for which, documentarists by temperament, we have a healthy respect. It is a fact, however, that whether owing to that particular "last straw" on the marina mini-telly or simply to our first reinspection of *ARI* since we checked that damaged vessel into the repair yard a few days back and moved our personal gear ashore, Richard finds himself, for the first time in his life, not afraid *at* sea, exactly (occasional scary moments are inevitable in sailboat-cruising, as in rock-climbing, horse-jumping, whitewater rafting, and any other sport that has in it an invigorating small element of danger), but, rather, afraid to *go* to sea; fearful of the prospect of returning to our ketch next week or whenever and reconfronting thereaboard both the elements and the limitations of our skills and strengths. This fear (which we don't doubt will subside in time if not pass altogether) both of us tacitly understand to be in the main a straightforward gut reaction to our literal knockdown; but in some measure, at least, it marks also our man's unassimilation of the figurative knockdown that preceded and perhaps even contributed to the literal. If A. R. Inc. have been withholding a lump of crucial exposition on that score, it's not out of archness or some minimalist program of seeing how much can go unsaid; it's out of mere fear of those abovementioned fears. Give us island-time, reader, if you can; give us till this day's Happy Hour, let's say, by when if we haven't paid that particular narrative bill we'll pack it in and to hell with it.

Meanwhile, we Jeep back through town (reminding ourselves aloud to go *clockwise* on Freeport's two roundabouts) and out toward West End, past small mountains of discarded conch shells from the native fishery; past a dispiriting though photogenic boat graveyard of wooden fishing-craft hauled ashore or into the mangrove shallows to decay; past fewer abandoned upscale construction projects but perhaps even more paper-and-plastic litter. At a particular spot confirmed earlier on our map by that senior rigger on *ARI*'s deck, we turn off the shoulderless main road onto a pothole-puddled, weed-grown track much like this morning's and bump along it, dodging bush-branches that smack our windshield, until at road's end we reach a stand of marsh grass and the handsome stretch of beach facing Dead Man's Reef — the largest of a row of exposed long coral rocks less than half a mile offshore.

"Whence the name?" Richard inquires of our database, who replies, "Don't ask." As we hoped, the water's calm here in the island's lee, and we have the splendid beach and Don't-Ask Reef to ourselves. Large clouds, however, are massing off to southeastward as we look for a suitable place to stash our gear; we agree we'd better get our snorkeling done before Nature's aquarium-lights go out.

"Anywhere'll do," Amy supposes. Like this morning's, this afternoon's high-tideline is lamentably strewn with washed-up plastic bags and containers, scraps of nylon fishnet and cork floats, empty bottles of Kalik, the local beer, and other detritus. Indeed, one little Bahamian juniper growing at the edge of that spartina-stand just behind the beach is so festooned with storm-driven litter as to remind Amien Richard of certain Buddhist prayer-trees we've seen while on assignment in Japan. A discarded auto-tire nearby becomes our gear repository, easily checkable from Out There with the prayer-tree landmark.

Says Amy, "You lead this time."

Yes, well. Reader will have noted that R has been silent since his reef-name query. Fact is, a wave (no other way to put it) of trepidation-cum-near-nausea has been building in him at the prospect before us — the literal flat seascape, we mean, in the first instance — and at the prospect of reimmersing ourselves therein. Has the man quite lost his nerve? Of course not; although his half-dizziness is real, he leaf-juices his mask, perches it up on his forehead, and wades out into a sandy aisle through the turtle-grass shallows, fins in hand, toward deeper water. Amy follows, registering her husband's still-trim body from behind in its tropicolored Speedo swim briefs.

Shit, she remarks to herself, her eyes re-tearing: *It wasn't his fault.* Nevertheless, shit shit shit.

Okay, reader: Amien Richard will go back to nature-watcher watching before we'll write a spill-our-guts sort of story. But while our protagonistic particles (waist deep now) fin out to Whatsitsname Reef, we'll take one final retrospective plunge, see how deep a dive our withheld breath permits and what, if anything, we see fit to fetch up from down there:

Our afore-invoked Lucretius accounts for the physical universe as we know it by imagining that as the aboriginal atomic particles, which have existed eternally, fall of their own weight separately together through infinite space like raindrops in a windless shower, from time to time they quite unaccountably *swerve* from their parallel paths, bump their neighbors, and thereby initiate the ongoing catenation of collisions, couplings, and decouplings that generate stars and planets, Richards and Amys, and the rest. This purely speculative premise of Lucretius's (wherewith he accounts for human free will and everything else of a nondeterministic character) has been said to anticipate the odd behavior of electrons and such according to modern quantum mechanics, but never mind that: What matters to our story is that one or the other or both of this bonded pair we're calling Amien Richard appear to have swerved just as unaccountably from their prevailingly scrupulous parental watchfulness. That the errant swervant(s) were expectably aghast, appalled, self-blaming and self-unforgiving, each earnestly exculpating any remissness on the other's part, but above all wiped out by grief at our immeasurable, irreplaceable loss — in a goddamn backyard *wading pool*, of all harmless places. That ARI's currently suspended winter-fleeing project was, as aforehinted, meant to put healing kilometrage between swerver(s) and site of swerve, and that it seemed to be doing that, on balance, from, say, the Great Dismal Swamp Canal down the Intracoastal to Miami. No condoling friends and supersympathetic relatives to keep the wound open with their good intentions, our separate off-to-college children included. No occasion to rehearse once more (except endlessly in our heads) the step-by-step that led each of us for the fell few moments to believe the other was on parental watch while he/she *a*) stepped indoors to fetch Lucretius from our library in order to check out an undergraduate memory of the poet's opinion that copulation hind-to was the surest route to impregnation, or *b*) to take a phone call from our New York agent about that latest movie-option on *The Watcher*. For the first time in a year-and-then-some, we came this fall to feeling almost like Amien Richard again, although to be sure . . .

It was our reunion with R's ex-roomie, alas, that unsettled our own reunition. The guy's a positively dashing, quite sophisticated and cosmopolitan fellow, apparently as cultured as he is evidently rich. If he strikes us as more Mediterranean than Caribbean (not to mention than Yankee), his wife, a stunner, seems to us more Continental than Canadian. They're forever off to here or there between deals or in pursuit thereof, separately or together, for extended periods, a sort of Amien Richard of real estate. As our Miami hosts, they were a model of polished and reciprocally affectionate couplehood; what was worse, they have, like us, grown children by earlier marriages and "their first grandchild": a darling late-born five-year-old son (our Michelle lived fourteen months) attended mainly by Cuban-American nannies (born into less affluence, Amien Richard's most beautiful collaboration was attended — lovingly, joyously, not to mention *meticulously* — by her parents). . . .

We can't talk about it. They condoled, of course, having heard the minimum necessary gist but no details, and of course they left us alone about the accident, merely offering us, tactfully, their Freeport place if we needed to "recoup a bit." But of course too the sight of that handsome "first grandchild" of theirs, so . . . alive, had the expectable effect. *Nobody's fault*, R tried to console weeping A, back aboard ARI. Stop *saying* that! It's both our faults! Okay: both, both; but it's time to quit blaming ourselves, no? Time maybe to blame each other, you mean? I didn't say that, for pity's sake. You as much as said it; you've as much as said it all along! Stressed out, Ame; stressed out. Damn straight I'm stressed out! Unlike *me*, I suppose you mean.

Et cetera. One sees how it went, alas, once it got going, as it happened to do in course of our backtracking a bit up the ICW from Miami toward Palm beach for the quickest shot across the Florida Straits to Grand Bahama. Truth to tell, if our accumulated and, so we'd thought, finally pretty well contained distress hadn't come untethered — a sore backtrack indeed, to the great dismal swamp of initial devastation, self-flagellations, and contritions — we would perhaps have exercised calmer judgment about the timing of that quick shot. From Delray Beach, our agreed-upon jumping-off place, across to Freeport is roughly eighty statute miles, about sixteen hours at the five-knot average we hoped to maintain under sail, power, or both: Leave the USA at five P.M., say, with enough daylight remaining for us to clear the coast; eat dinner in the cockpit under way; then trade four-hour watches through the night as we cross the shipping lanes, steering south of our target to compensate for the northward set of the current, and reach Bahamian waters with next morning's sun already high enough to illuminate their reefs and shallows and harbor-approach buoys. Piece of cake, it ought to be, absent foul weather, although we've never done the like before, and inasmuch as we've no pressing timetable (as we had, e.g., en route to our space-shuttle-launch rendezvous), we can stand by in Delray Beach till the forecast's clear.

As it reasonably was, Richard still maintains, at D-Day noon, when the earlier-predicted fifty-percent chance of nighttime showers, possibly thundershowers, had been reduced to thirty — which is to say, a seventy-percent chance of perfectly clear sailing. Why not sit tight, A wondered for us, until the Probability of Precipitation pops down to zero? Because, R pointed out on the weather map, those showers, when they *do* arrive, will be the leading edge of this big Norther here pushing down from Canada, which bids to blow hard against the up-running Gulf Stream for several days at least and whip up the steep seas for which that river-within-the-ocean is notorious. What's more, Tropical Storm Emile has chugged over from Africa to within a hundred miles of the British Virgins and is presently gaining strength as well as veering a bit north of west, toward Puerto Rico. Better to scoot across now and ride out those blows in snug Bahamian harbor, or ashore in the house so generously proffered us for recuperation. Point well taken, granted Amy; on the other hand, since we'll be snug-harboring it either way, why not stay put right where we are for an entire week, if necessary, until that weather map is menace-free? Because, replied her spouse, Delray Beach is no place to spend a week at anchor in a sailboat cabin or ashore in a cheapo motel, especially in the mood we seem to've lapsed into lately; and we're certainly not going to back-backtrack to Miami and then *back*-back-backtrack back here; and who gives a shit anyhow, come to that?

You're asking me? his wife countered, who could in fact have answered that rhetorical question (So could its asker have) but elected not to, it being plain to all hands which way our sore wind was blowing. Anchor aweigh, then, damn it, and Poseidon have mercy on A. R. Inc.

Alas, that deity didn't. We set out sullen, our demeanors muted but each of us considering the other by this time the reopener-in-chief of wounds we'd hoped were on the way to healing, our lapse having been a so clearly uncharacteristic swerve. Reaching east-southeastward on a fine mild southerly under all plain sail and autopilot, *ARI* dropped our home coast astern but not our bruised sensibilities — a pity, that, as it was a lovely evening's offshore sail, our first such. We both wanted to share the pleasure and excitement of it as we shared one glass of white wine and a delicious cold puttanesca that we'd made some days before; as we've shared so fortunately many pleasures and adventures large and small — but we could not, could not, and that inability (that impossibility, we felt) saddened and soured us one touch more. Dinner done, Amy in the cockpit then monitored our course and speed, Richard moped forward to watch twilit porpoises sporting in our bow wave, and a sudden cloud cover ended our daylight early. When presently R returned aft to stand the first evening watch, instead of keeping him company for a while as normally she would have, A excused herself and went below.

Our ship's log doesn't deal in causes and effects; it only reports the news. Through Richard's eight P.M.-to-midnight watch, the breeze freshened to twelve knots and swung southwesterly over our starboard quarter. R prudently decided to lower the small mizzensail, both to reduce *ARI's* rolling in the seaway and to decrease our sail area in case the trend continued. Thirty percent P.O.P., he several times reminded himself, means seventy percent P.O. *no* P. When he turned us temporarily around to windward in order to get that sail down, the flapping and hobbyhorsing brought A to the companionway hatch to offer help. "Don't need you," she was told.

Mm hm.

By watch-change time, the wind was dead astern at twelve to fifteen-plus, and the seas were building. The log indicates that we swung again to windward enough to tuck a first reef in the mainsail and shorten our big roller-furling headsail a bit, Amy at the helm, Richard tending sheets and halyards at the pitching mast. Seasoned hands, we executed this chore with a minimum of communication, suited up now in foul weather gear as well as life vests and safety harnesses. No moon, no stars, no running lights of vessels other than our own; black night, black wind, black ocean and spirits. Regretful of his earlier brusqueness, "I'll keep you company a bit," R offered.

"Don't need you."

Hmp. So he goes below, peels out of his foulies, and updates the log and our dead-reckoned position on the chart. Broad-reaching and running at an average six knots on the following breeze, we're ahead of our nominal schedule and, he notes with glum satisfaction, past the point of no return: With wind and seas astern and Grand Bahama now nearer than the coast of Florida, we must press on come what may. He stretches out and tries to sleep; is too agitated, rueful, depressed, excited. Must have dropped off anyhow, briefly, for he wakes with tears in his eyes from a ragged, wretched, fleeting dream (in which he was announcing to Amy's father, Mitchell, as once he had in happy fact, "We're naming her after you, old chap, sort of"). Three A.M., the boat's motion severe by our inland-waters standards but evidently under control and par for the course, he supposes, in offshore passagemaking. He suits up, swigs room-temperature cappuccino out of a bottle in lieu of hot coffee (which we're rolling too much for him even to consider making), and takes that bottle along for his wife's refreshment when he goes upstairs now to keep her company through the last hour of her watch, whether she goddamn needs him or not. Finds her steering by hand down the pretty scary following seas — too tricky for the autopilot to handle, she'll report — still barreling along on course at six knots plus under single-reefed main and a jib that she has somehow managed single-handedly to shorten further.

"You should've called me," he lets her know.

"Yeah, right." She waves off the proffered cappuccino; on irked impulse, Richard flings the half-full bottle overside. "Oh, terrific," Amy says: "Take *that*, ocean." She needs to stretch her legs and pee, she informs him, if Sir Galahad can contain his tantrum enough to mind the helm for a bit.

Ashamed of himself anyhow, Richard volunteers to begin his final watch now. Amy's tempted to say Piss on that; no half-ass martyrdom, s.v.p.; I'll call you when your time comes. But she's too pissed to give a piss: pissed at how we've pissed away what should've been a memorable adventure, not to mention whatever else we've pissed away or are in danger, perhaps even in process, of so pissing. So she shrugs and goes below to piss, maybe to stay unless the rolling makes her ill, pausing en route at the nav station to tune in the weather channel. The barely intelligible "nowcast" reports through much static that at one A.M. (i.e., two hours ago), the line of thunderstorms extending from Fort Lauderdale down to the Miami area had crossed the peninsula and was moving offshore southeastward at thirty-five miles per hour. The severe thunderstorm watch for that portion of Florida's Atlantic coast has been lifted. Amy restrains a sarcastic comment having to do with probabilities of precipitation. In our regrettably separate heads, we each perform the obvious calculation; diffused lightning-flashes astern verify our arithmetic.

What we ought to have done at this point, we both understand now and probably understood then as well, is heave to, drop and furl the mainsail while conditions still permitted that maneuver, and carry on under reefed headsail alone, shortening it further if necessary from the safety of the cockpit or furling it altogether and running before the wind "under bare poles" until the squall-line passed. But our own diffused lightning was flashing, too: Mad-sad Amy clunked the companionway drop-boards into place to keep spray and rain out of the cabin (Yup, it's raining now), perfunctorily bidding her husband to call her if he needs her; sad-mad Richard didn't even reply. Said each to him-/herself: *Let the damn boat sink.*

Enough, says the reasonable reader, who wants to get back to the present action, such as it is, of this "Waves" or "Particles" story. Enough, agree Amien Richard, still shaking our authorial head at how such prevailingly bone-deep unanimity can have come, if not unglued, at least more sorely strained than ever before in our connection. Whatever happened to magnanimity, to heartfelt gestures of reunion between essentially bonded particles? *Enough*, says Zeus the Thunderer, and lets fly, while Earth-Shaker Poseidon warms up in Davy Jones's bullpen. If we had been ourselves, we'll wonder later, could we have wrestled *ARI* head-to-wind enough, in that suddenly howling gale, that machine-gun rain, those black-towering seas rollercoasting us from astern, to wrestle the mainsail down etc.? But we were heart-hurt Amy hanging on for dear life down below to keep from being pitched right across the cabin (no chance of dropping foul-weather bottoms to use the head in these conditions) and hurt-heart Richard safety-harnessed to a cockpit strongpoint, clutching the wheel in both hands and schussing us blindly like a hot-dog skier down the black slopes of those watery alps. Overpowered by that single-reefed mainsail, the ketch wants to broach disastrously side-to; the seas rushing under us reduce our rudder control — and now the gods team up to throw their quick one-two punch. A particularly blasty blast from a slightly different quarter blows out our mainsail and pulls *ARI* maybe twenty degrees around just as a semi-rogue wave thunders up like a goddamn *cliff* from a slightly different angle — Who can see? — and one or the other or the two combined take us out. Despite hard corrective helming, the boat spins beam-on to the wave; whether or not *ARI* "trips on she keel" or is simply pushed over by the breaking sea, we're knocked flat on our beam-ends, masts and sails in the water and helmsman briefly *under* it, clutching the wheel with arms and legs, holding his breath, fumbling frantically for his harness-clip in case we truly turn turtle, and managing somehow to think *Oh god good-bye dear Amy I am so sorry* — while down in the tumultuous dark cabin, where such normally secured objects as books, audiocassette racks, settee cushions, and off-watch Amy are crashing perilously about, that last-mentioned projectile is thinking *Oh god good-bye dear Richard I am so sorry.*

It's all over pretty quickly. With no help from us, *ARI* staggers almost upright; is promptly knocked down again by the next wave but not quite so far; is re-resurrected by the hull's inherent stability and ample reserve buoyancy. By the next wave after that one, stunned Richard has managed to bring our bow just enough upwind to avoid another knock-down (the blown-out main, a blessing in disguise, reduces our windage; do we dare espy a metaphor in that?) and is hollering for his wife, who's hollering back for him. The gods wink at each other and turn to other amusements, elsewhere; by the time Amy gets those drop-boards out and struggles up into the cockpit, the squall has rolled by, the rain and wind are fast tapering. She secures her harness and takes the wheel; no words needed. Soaked through, her mate goes forward one careful tetherslength at a time and laboriously triple-reefs the flogging main; we bear off then in full control and relative comfort (although we're wet, cold, and traumatized) in the already-diminishing seas, which half an hour later have gentled to an easy swell that the autopilot —miraculously still functioning — can handle without difficulty.

The rest you've heard: How — bruised and spent in both body and spirit, surprised and on the whole grateful to be still alive, afloat, unwidowed or -widowered, and more or less intact — we jury-rigged our craft (with a spare rope halyard in place of that sprung starboard mizzen-shroud), likewise our conjugality (with heartfelt if not yet heart-healed embraces, reciprocal apologies, self-reproaches, absolutions, tears for the irretrievable, irrevocable, unreplayable, etc.), and together watched the sun come up over low-lying Grand Bahama.

What remains to tell, then, out here now at Dead Man's Reef? Storms pass, their damage lingers; repairs take time. As if tit-for-tatting from this morning, Richard disappears from Amy's sight while we're snorkeling the reef's handsome, fish-rich outboard wall; although she was supposed to be following *him* this time, her attention wandered off with a young sea turtle swimming by, and now she can't find the man either under or on the surface. Uh oh. But he has only, without realizing it, turned a coral corner at DMR's far end, a couple dozen yards off, having dived to inspect close up a moray eel warily inspecting him from its hole in the rock. He surfaces, sees where he is, paddles back into view, points landward. His wife nods agreement: Too cloudy now for optimally viewing these denizens of the not-so-deep. Side by side we swim toward shore until our downstrokes are brushing bottom, then shuck our fins and walk the last hundred-plus feet like the emergent amphibians we sort of are, hand in hand but saying little.

We don't know.

Back at our prayer-tree, while Amy slips into her shorts and shirt, Richard espies and plucks from the tide-wrack a hand-size lump of calcareous stone (tiny seashells, actually, by some natural process limed together) embedding on its upper face a single larger spiral shell — a small conch, most likely — whose exposed surface has been abraded by wave-action to reveal the delicate, self-replicating inner volutes. The effect is of an artfully mounted fossil. *Ecologically correct Ivory-Anniversary gift*, he notes to himself, and although it makes a mighty clumsy lump in his shorts side pocket, there he slips it for the Jeep-ride home.

In the course whereof . . .

But to hell with the course whereof. Back at la borrowed hacienda grande, Georges nowhere in sight, we strip at poolside, dive in to rinse the salt off us, wind up embracing in chest-deep fresh water. It's Amy, actually, who initiates *this* potential sex scene, embracing Richard from behind and snugging her womanly equipment against his back and backside. She feels him tense a bit, surprised; then he relaxes, takes her hands in his against his belly. "So what's that lump I saw in your pants a while back?" she murmurs between nuzzlings of his shoulder blades.

"A girl could check it out for herself," he suggests, and presently she goes and does, and Guess what?s, and invites him to a reciprocal frisking of *her* pants, dropped over yonder. That chuckly search successful, we exchange anniversary shells and kisses, lead each other indoors lest Georges or one of his Inside sons appear outside, and make consolatory love on the grand conversation-couch of that sunken living room, smack under Hokusai's dreadsome view of Mt. Fuji.

Happy ending? Not for the lost. As for us, too soon to say, say Amien Richard, Reincorporated; this is bona fide, true-to-life fiction we're floating here, not mass-paperback romance. We've recircled now to where our story started, Amy on mat and Richard in beach-toweled lounge chair, all hands feeling soundly loved and roundly laid despite whatever (or feeling Whatever despite being soundly-roundly etc.). Under a threatening sky we sip coconut rum with guava juice, munch munchies, raise eyebrows at the wind now whipping our casuarina screen and corrugating the pool surface, and return our postcoital attention to Amy's lead-off question.

"So," she still wants to know: "Are we particles or waves?"

Diplomatically, before he answers, Richard this time asks, "Which does it seem to you?"

Chin resting on fists: "When I think of . . . No: Never mind When I Think Of. I guess I think just waves."

"Mm hm."

"Not only *us*-us." The woman has never been more serious. "I mean everybody, every thing. Waves are all there is, is what *I'm* coming around to thinking. You?"

Her admiring husband agrees: "Waves, definitely. I even wonder now and then whether there *are* any particles, you know? I suppose there are, in a manner of speaking, but when you get right down to it, even particles are waves."

A. R. Inc. jointly second that particular motion, or proposition; wish we knew for sure how this maiden not-so-short-story of ours intends to end, but on reflection decide it's just as well we don't. Presently, no doubt, we'll do the Next Thing: dress for dinner and stroll or Wrangle the dozen-odd blocks into town for either our Ivory-commemorative or, if after all we haven't yet joint heart for that, something less affirmatory.

People can still prevailingly love each other, you know, and be nevertheless simply unable to go on with their story.

Contrariwise, you know, they can find to their vast regret that their love has gone the way of an inadvertently and momentarily unattended tot in a waveless wading pool and, despite *that*, decide for whatever reasons to keep their joint story going, if only faute de mieux.

Or not and not.

Or love and on with it, hoping that with time and large-spiritedness enough, the wave of their critical distress will sweep on without having sunk their ship altogether. While Amien Richard don't know for certain even whether this story of theirs will continue, much less how end, we're pretty sure now, as are its principal characters, that it won't be called "Particles." Waves everywhere, as Amy sort of said, in time or space or both. Our bodies are waves, for sure, as aforesuggested, their particular constituents ever in flux, their overall form evolving and then devolving, from infancy (with luck) through juvenescence to the full handsome maturity that we see naked here before us and on to the physical decline already begun but not yet conspicuously manifest in our joint case. Our minds? Likewise, as their contents and constructs, feelings and attitudes and even worldviews change, will-we nill-we, over time. And our selves, those posited centers of narrative gravity that we're in the habit of calling, e.g., Amy and Richard? Waves, definitely: mere ever-changing configurations of memories and characteristics embodied in those other waves, our minds and bodies. Okay, maybe not so "mere" — Look at splendid Amy there; look at excellent Richard there; look at . . . the inexpungeable dear image of the precious lost. All the same, our point is that the surfer is as much a wave as is the wave he surfs.

Does that not imply that A&R's marriage . . . that, indeed, all human relationships, are waves? Sure it does: the same wavish partners, by and large (although in each of the present cases, the "we" wasn't always us), but even in the stablest of instances the dynamic of their relation is ever in flux, continually disequilibrating and (Let's cross our fingers) continually returning toward equilibrium.

Our lives in general, then, it must go without saying . . .

Waves, absolutely, as are all our actions for good or ill, dissipating over distance and time. Ditto our stories, obviously; both our life-stories and (Shall we cross our fingers, dearest friend?) our made-up-and-maybe-even-publishable stories: waves waves waves, propagated from mind to mind and heart to heart through the medium of language via these particles called words.

But didn't Richard just say —

He did, and Amien Richard here corporately affirm: Even *those* particles are waves, coming into the language, often changing their spelling and sense, not infrequently dropping out of use. Waves all, all waves, from these riplets on our borrowed pool through yonder Hokusais chugging in from M'sieur Emile, right on out to the exploding universe. N'est-ce pas, amie?

"You say. Sure, I guess. Right."

Long may *we* wave, then. And concerning this evening ...?

"Let's cross our fingers."

"No comment."

None? His fingers were crossed.

"Hers, too. All the same . . ."

Sigh. Well, it was a long story.

"For one thing."

But it's *been* a long story.

"Not long enough."

Now you're talking.

"But it's finito. We just weren't lucky."

We were the luckiest.

"Not lucky enough. And this narrative striptease isn't working."

It's brought us this far. . . .

"No comment."

Presently: She's tired.

"Tired beyond tired."

All that tennis and beach volleyball.

"That was the relaxing part. That and our long long reef-swim."

In which neither swimmer lost sight of the other or played hide-and-seek like Amy and Richard.

"No comment."

Presently: "I guess I'm catching a sleep-wave."
   Ride it. *Love and on with it*, as the fellow said.
   "Yes, well."

Presently and very quietly, fingers crossed: Is she asleep?
   "No."
   Me neither.
   "It was a good wave, but I wiped out."
   Likewise.
   "Story of our lives?"
   No comment.

Next mid-day, perhaps; a rare spell of rainshowers, perhaps, ruling out tennis, beach volleyball, and other outdoor distractions. A cozy post-noon siesta, perhaps.
   Presently: He could read her a story about that.
   "About wiping out? She wrote the book."
   Not about wiping out.

8.

Stories of Our Lives

It has occurred to Ms. Mimi Adler, whom I like a lot, to wonder whether people reflexively think of their lives as stories because from birth to death they are exposed to so many narratives of every sort, or whether, contrariwise, our notion of what a *story* is, in every age and culture, reflects an innately dramatistic sense of life: a feature of the biological evolution of the human brain and of human consciousness, which appears to be essentially of a scenario-making character.

Ms. Adler's question may strike the reader of these lines as idle, academic, inconsequential — and it's certainly no grabber of an opening for a work of fiction, a bona fide short story. As I pen these words on my new friend's behalf, is not Bosnia bleeding, have not Rwandans been slaughtering one another wholesale, are not 154 pounds of deadly weapons-grade plutonium still missing from a Japanese nuclear reactor, and does not Haiti's immemorial misery more or less drag on, together with untold other large- and small-scale catastrophes right round the planet? In the face of so much wretchedness and gravity, what justification have Mimi and I for entertaining such chicken-or-egg questions as whether people's lives or their stories have, so to speak, ontological primacy?

That question, believe me, we take as seriously as we take the question that it questions. M's coming on to fifty, my wife's age, although you'd never guess so by looking at either of those trim, athletic, handsome, and energetic women. Like Mrs. Narrator, Mrs. Adler is a morally serious citizen as well as a dedicated teacher of young people. I myself am a dozen years older, Mimi's husband's a touch older yet, and you'd guess *that* at once if you saw us with our spouses, although both Robert and I are in good shape for our age — anyhow were, up to the time of this story. If less intense than our mates in the moral/political sphere, we too are unfrivolous professionals. Rob's a cognitive scientist, I've just decided, from whose acquaintance with current theories of consciousness Mimi will have picked up what she knows about the biological evolution of our brains and their propensity for spinning scenarios in order to sort out the data continuously flooding all our senses: in short, our experience of life. Rob cannot, however, speak to his wife's late perplexity on this which-causes-which question, as he's down in D.C. just now consulting for the National Institutes of Health. Yours truly, as aforenoted, makes up short stories — not for a living, as there's no living in it, but for the serious pleasures of dreaming up characters like Mimi and Rob and situations like the one I'm about to put them in, of working out plots and forms and themes and images and actions and voices (in a word, *stories*), and of finding the language wherewith to get those stories told. If that's not seriousness enough, I also teach part-time in a good American university, coaching graduate-student apprentices in my profit-poor but deeply gratifying trade.

In fact, that's how I came to know M.A. (so her initials just now suggest to me) — whose husband, I here decide, I already knew slightly as an extra-departmental colleague. Our university's M.A. storymaking program is age-blind, you

see, as well as gender-blind, eth-blind, prior-degree-blind —
blind to everything other than talent, accomplishment, and
promise. When we've sorted through the pile of applications
to select the dozen or so most likely-seeming, we're pleased
of course if they turn out to be a multiculturally mixed bag
of women and men, gays and straights, youngs and less
youngs, ets and ceteras; but as long as they're the most evidently talented, accomplished, and promising of the lot, we
don't finally care (so we tell ourselves) if our dazzling dozen
turn out to be uniformly middle-aged gay white (lapsed-)
Mormon doctors of philosophy from the province of
Saskatchewan. The group five years ago numbered only one
of those among the usual ethnic/sexual/actuarial/aesthetical
smorgasbord, which happened also to include this uncommonly attractive mid-fortyish Jewish-or-Italian-or-both-by-
the-look-of-her lady whose stories (as I knew from reviewing the application files) were poignant but playful
"postmodern" spin-offs from notable scientific or philo-
sophical propositions: Zeno's paradoxes, Schrödinger's
wave-function equations, whatever. They wanted revision
and polishing, to be sure, like everybody else's in the program, toward closing those crucial last millimeters between
gifted apprentice and truly professional work; otherwise their
authors would be applying to magazine editors instead of to
us. The woman's smile, however, needed no coaching at all:
a brilliant, knowing, persistent, disconcerting smile that said,
among other things, "We understand the tacit subtext here,
don't we?" and that would have been the more unsettling if
she hadn't directed it at just about everyone to whom she
spoke or listened.

My habit on opening day is to go around the seminar
room asking each new hand in turn to introduce her/him-
self: what name you go by, where you hail from, by what
waypoints you arrived among us, your past training and ex-

perience in the yarning trade, what you have in mind to do in your season here, whatever else it pleaseth you to mention of an identificatory nature. When Ms. Adler's turn came (she sat, as she would invariably through that academic year, at the opposite end of the long seminar table from me, dressed in the oversized university sweatshirt and black running tights in which she routinely jogged the five miles from campus to her house after class), she beamed that mighty smile the length of the room, declared matter-of-factly, "Mi chiamo Mimi," and then went on in her rich contralto speaking-voice to give us her résumé in an ad-lib paraphrase of that famous soprano aria from *La Bohème*. Most got the joke; some didn't. From that subtextual smile of hers, I could almost imagine that she had somehow guessed Puccini to have been, like tennis and sailing and the stories of Italo Calvino, among the touchstones of her new coach's courtship and marriage.

In a group whose average was better than average, the woman proved at least an average apprentice fictioneer, also a first-rate critic of her comrades' efforts (she really *did* see unspoken and sometimes significant "subtexts" lurking between their lines) and perhaps the most generally liked of that year's seminarians. Our cordial association continued, less closely, thereafter: the two couples at mixed-doubles tennis and certain university social events; Mimi and I at readings by visiting writers or *tout court* over occasional faculty-club lunches. As happens in more cases than not, her fiction, alas, for all its bright promise, got nowhere; she had reached the distressingly familiar stage of doing nothing correctably *wrong* in her art, really, but of doing nothing on the other hand so remarkably well as to distinguish her productions from the thousands of others that every magazine and book editor remains deluged with, even in the age of electronic visual media. Fortunately for her (now ex-) coach, if not for herself, the critic in her was too exquisitely aware of this state of affairs to make its articulation incumbent upon me; nothing to be done, we agreed, except cross fingers and soldier on until her muse smiles, if the bitch ever does. M's own smile, at that, told me she was already onto some tacit subtext between forkfuls of Caesar salad, but it was not one that I was privy to until early in the current semester, when over another such touch-base lunch she announced that her personal *Bohème* had reached Act Two's closing curtain: in this restaging, no echt-nineteenth-century tuberculosis for the soprano, but echt-late-twentieth AIDS for the tenor.

Rob? AIDS? No.

"Rob AIDS *yes*." Her splendid mahogany eyes filled right up. "HIV positive, anyhow, with AIDS to follow as doth the night . . . the day. . . ."

That *day* trailed into suspension-points and tears. When in time the tale got itself told (in the faculty-club parking lot, whereto we retreated for self-collection), it was of her steadfast, good-shape-for-his-age husband's feeling lately so under the weather that even as he completed his arrangements for early retirement (sixty-five is officially early in our institution), he underwent a physical exam more thorough than his routine annual checkups and thus learned the fatal news.

"So where'd it come from?" she spared me the discomfort of asking. No extracurricular sexual contacts, her husband swore, since back in the hyperpermissive Sixties, and his wife (who at his urging had had herself tested and been shown HIV-negative) saw no reason to question his fidelity. No needles except those in his doctor's medical lab and Rob's own cognitive-research facilities, where a certain amount of animal experimentation was carried on. Workers in such labs are not routinely tested for HIV; given the standard sterile precautions of any well-run laboratory, however, the chances of accidental virus-transmission in those venues must be near zero. Some while back, he'd had prostate surgery in the university hospital; Mimi, who regarded hospitals as dangerous anyhow, believed that place and occasion the likeliest suspect — although the patient had had no blood transfusions, for example, and our hospital is among the most prestigious in the land. Investigation was continuing. Through it all, my friend reported, her husband was being a brick, but Mimi herself and their two grown children were devastated: not only, in M's case, by the prospect of losing to that revolting malady her best friend and life-mate and the anticipated balance of their years together — as many as twenty, had luck been theirs, after which she had resolved to terminate promptly with Seconal her expectable widowhood — but for at least two other reasons as well, which may strike the reader as unseemly, although I confess that I myself found them not difficult to sympathize with:

• The dreadful turn of events had the incidental effect of relegating Mimi Adler to a supporting role, as she saw it, in her own life-story. More accurately (for I protested this idea at once, as had Robert, and as even more vehemently would my wife, when I recounted this tale to her), it forced a radical, lamentable revision of her lead role therein. Instead of Gifted Middle-School Teacher blossoming into Gifted Fiction-Writer (a scenario ever less tenable in any case), she had been recast as GMST obliged to become Heroic (or not so heroic) Nurse of Lovable and Competent but Otherwise Unremarkable Scientist.

These latter adjectives surprised me; I cannot dispute them, but had no idea that Mimi saw Rob so. Granted, she was distraught; all the same, I sensed a tacit subtext. Moreover,

• As aforementioned, she had become all but convinced that while she was not without literary talent, her gift was finally an amateur's flair, not a true vocation (I'm afraid I agree, but I'm not about to tell her so, and only time and perseverance can say for sure), and so she would not have that enviable life-preserver to help float her through her present pass and impending bereavement. She would be obliged to survive, if she chose to, on the strength of having been an okay mother, a quite good teacher, a truly loving and all but hundred-percent-faithful wife, a dedicated nurse of her husband's terminality, and a more or less stoical widow perhaps devoted to worthy causes, unless she decided to go the Hemlock Society route and to hell with it. She'd had more in mind, frankly, she told me (whose attention, for all my sympathy, was not undistracted by the subtext of that "all but hundred-percent-faithful"): How was she to come to terms with mere above-averagehood, especially in the face of this miserable new plot-twist, when all her life she had aspired to *excel*, to live *transcendently?*

It was these reflections and their accompanying guilt, she declared — turning on that singular smile now while making free with the pocket tissue-pack that I'd proffered en route to the parking lot — that had led her to thinking in this new way about people's lives as stories, etc., and thence to the question that *this* story opens with her pondering, quite as she might have opened one of her own. She supposed herself a monster even to think of such questions under the circumstances ("Maybe she is," my wife will allow); if so, so be it. She just thought her erstwhile coach might be amused.

I forgive you that *amused,* I told her then and re-tell her now — and I trust the reader to grant that M's introductory question wasn't entirely frivolous after all. It's going to have to wait for an answer, however, while the narrative camera cuts to a certain silver-alloy coin that fell out of my pants pocket onto the winter-dormant lawn of the faculty club as Mimi and I shortcut to the parking lot to avoid public display of her emotion and I fetched out on her behalf that little Kleenex-pack. A Canadian twenty-five-cent piece, that coin was, picked up casually in Toronto somewhere earlier when I happened to be author-touring up that way, and not yet recycled into some Baltimore parking meter (although to my eye all North American quarters are of identical dimension, soft-drink machines, unlike parking meters, know the difference): on one side, the head of ELIZABETH II D. G. REGINA in classic starboard profile; on the other, a bull-caribou portside ditto, haloed by CANADA 1984 and bearing in his mighty antler-rack the declared value 25 CENTS. On both faces, a circle of raised dots just inside the milled edge, to complicate counterfeiting. The I-character didn't notice his loss and never will, nor did my stressed-out lunch companion; the I-narrator of this stories-of-our-lives story, on the other hand, not only observed but *caused* the coin's fall from right trouser-pocket to campus grass, to the end of informing or reminding the reader, by association, of a certain schoolroom narrative exercise called "L'Histoire d'un sou" that used to be assigned in the French lycées. Imagine and recount the adventures of a common coin, that exercise demanded, as it circulates from hand to hand through one's society: perhaps from mint to bank and anon to some aristocratic lady's purse, thence serially to the pocket of that lady's pilfering chambermaid, to that chambermaid's middle-aged shopkeeping lover, to the young prostitute whose services that shopkeeper occasionally hires, to that prostitute's illegitimate but much-prized five-year-old son, Rodolfe (by the aristocratic lady's philandering husband, as it happens), to that lad's bullying seven-year-old alleymate, Victor, who snatches and runs off with it, to the gutter of the cobbled Montmartre street into which Victor darts and fearless little Rodolfe pursues him just in time to be struck by the aristocratic husband's carriage, and thence, tossed away by conscience-stricken Victor, down the storm-drain of that street into the sewers of Paris, where it goes unnoticed by Jean Valjean in flight from the detective Javert but not by that keen-eyed latter, who, though not an otherwise superstitious fellow, pauses for two seconds to pick it up lest toute la journée he have bad luck and thereby, ironiquement, affords Valjean the opportunity to elude him at least for another chapter. In analogous wise, this particular Canadian quarter in its ten-year tour of duty had passed through 240 hands, remaining in possession of each for a median fortnight over a range from ten seconds (given as change in what must have been the only gay bar in Saskatoon, Saskatchewan, in 1986, to a lapsed-Mormon Ph.D. candidate from Moose Jaw, and by him promptly passed to the friend with whom he was splitting the tab) to three years (in the miscellaneousforeign-coins ashtray of the Florida apartment of a Bahamian real-estate speculator whose travels took her to Canada occasionally but not often), before being given to me, again as change, in the delightful cafeteria/market/restaurant Mövenpick Marché in downtown Toronto, where that lady happened to have shopped and lunched on the same day that my wife and I happened to shop and dine there in mid-booktour. Now on a Maryland February afternoon it lies nearly vertical against blades of hybrid lawn-grass on a seldomcrossed sward of faculty-club turf, and there it could remain "forever," perhaps mashed into the soil come spring by the riding-mowers of campus groundskeepers and gradually thatched and sedimented over, the narrative camera locked uneventfully upon it ad infinitum like Andy Warhol's literal camera upon the Empire State Building in his 1964 film *Empire*, or perhaps accidentally excavated a year or a century hence by a crew relandscaping the area or digging footers for an extension of the building and examined by the nototherwise-superstitious finder for lucky numbers to use in playing the state lottery, thence on with its story.

In fact (so to speak), however, it gets noticed no more than an hour later by another colleague of mine, whom I've never met personally but know to be an art historian with a minor, as it were, in conchology, from which hobby he has acquired the half-conscious habit of keeping a beachcomber's eye out even in the city. An unorthodox fellow in several respects, Associate Professor Walter Ellison believes that paths should be laid where people walk, literally and figuratively, rather than constraining folks' walking to already-laid paths, and so he makes it his pedestrian practice, especially on campus, to take the most direct or otherwise convenient route to his destination, across lawns and even through flower-beds and shrubbery, as a sort of service to the university's landscape planners. Shortcutting like Mimi and me-the-character to the parking lot that she and I have already exited in our separate cars (M to go on with the grimly plot-turned story whereof she is the reluctant, ineluctable protagonist, I with the exfoliation of this, whereof I am teller-in-chief but wherein have only a walk-on, drive-off role), young Professor Ellison espies "my" coin in the grass and, recalling the folk-rhyme advisory, bends over as if to pick it up but in fact merely to inspect it before perversely *letting it lay* in order to defy, on principle, proverbial wisdom. Although Walt's only thirty-five and is in good physical condition from playing indoor tennis twice or thrice weekly at a suburban club, the muse of irony sees fit at this point cruelly to inflict upon him what will turn out to be a lifelong intermittent spinal-disc problem in consequence of that simple movement. Some fluke of leverage, one supposes; in any case, the pain is so sudden and shocking that between coin and car he hobbles in a sweat and at one moment nearly faints. It's all he can do to ease himself into his vintage bean-green Volvo wagon and drive home; by when he reaches his Mount Washington neighborhood, his lumbar area has so

seized up that he groans involuntarily at every major movement from driveway to lavatory (where he helps himself to
a tablet of Valium) to living-room rug, a second-hand Heríz
on whose central medallion he lies supine for the next two
hours, until Barbara comes home from her new job in the
reference department of the Enoch Pratt Free Library. She's
alarmed. He explains. She commiserates, and doses her recently anxious self with the Valium long ago prescribed for
Walter's wry neck by the same physician who, as it irrele-
vantly happens, diagnosed Rob Adler's AIDS (the drug, anyhow expired, will prove less effective in and for her case than
as a simple muscle relaxant in her husband's). The couple
then settle into a pained parody of their usual end-of-work-
day routine: As they're both Valium'd, in lieu of their customary glass of California Chardonnay they sip with their
trail-mix hors d'oeuvres a very weak solution of jug Chablis
and club soda, once Walt has gotten himself propped against
the couch-front. Even raising the wineglass in ironic toast to
the muse of irony — for they're scheduled to vacation next
week at the Club Méditerranée in Cancún, their first such
holiday, where they've been looking forward to tennis, snorkeling, beachcombing, and touring the nearby Mayan ru-
ins — makes him ouch.

"So what was your most interesting call today?" he asks
her as usual, though not usually in so clenched a voice.
Barbara works the Pratt's telephone information service
desk, "doing kids' homework for them," she complains, for
indeed they'll call to say "I'm writing this paper for eighth
grade? Can you tell me about Spain?"

"Nothing terrific. Some lady wanted Erwin Schrödinger's
equation for quantum-mechanical wave functions, and I
tracked it down easily enough but didn't know how to read
it to her. I mean, it's not like saying 'E equals mc squared,'
you know? The thing's humongous and full of hieroglyph-

ics. Then some guy needed the name and date of that Warhol flick where the camera stays fixed forever on the Empire State Building —"

"*Empire*. Sixty-eight or -nine? *Aiyi!*"

"Poor thing. Sixty-four." As to Cancún, they incline two days later to go on with the trip, although a statement from Walter's doctor would entitle them to a refund of their pre-payment. Thanks in part to a fresh prescription, the back pain has eased somewhat each day; they need the break — Barb especially, who finds life more stressful lately than does her inner-directed mate. They'll be able at least to read and sunbathe and eat and drink and perhaps visit the Tulum ru-ins down-coast from Cancún; maybe even snorkel the reefs, carefully, on calm days.

Do they go? Go they do, with unequally shared misgiv-ings. Walt, a workaholic by nature whose notion of holiday has historically been either wall-to-wall museum-touring or serious amateur conchology, merely hopes that their first real vacation-vacation won't be spoiled and that his pulled muscle or pinched nerve or slipped disc won't prove to be an ongoing or recurring disability (alas, it will). He has come to depend upon vigorous physical exercise, like sustained mental work, as a safety-valve in his life with Barbara, for one thing — a non-athlete and a bit of a complainer lately. She hopes the same, of course, for her sake as well as his; notwithstanding his inner and outer strengths, her husband's a real baby, in her opinion, on the rare occasions when any-thing's physically amiss with him, whereas she, at any given moment in her life-story, will likely be bearing up pretty sto-ically, without medication, under half a dozen assorted mi-nor ailments. Perhaps that is why, only three weeks into her job at the Pratt and just the week before this Yucatán vaca-tion, to her own considerable astonishment she permitted herself to go to bed with an attractive and rather famous senior departmental colleague of her husband's: an unmarried programmatic flirt who Walter himself suspects is either gay or asexual but who turned out — in the remarkable episode that followed one of the fellow's periodic consultancy-visits to the Pratt's fine arts collection, his coincidental path-crossing with Barbara as both were leaving the building at the end of her workday, his offering her a lift home in his bronze-gold Lexus to save her cab fare (Barb's little Honda was being serviced), and his all but daring her, en route, to stop in for a look at the rather grand condo he recently bought in a spiffy new high-rise overlooking the university — to be a decidedly more energetic and imaginative lover, on first and second go at least, than her husband of seven years. Now she is, if not quite guilt-stricken, at least guilt-nagged, the more because, with poor Walt hors de combat, on the day before their Club Med flight she took the initiative of telephoning Franco *from work*, ostensibly to tell him that she had really admired his new place and that, as between the two bedroom-drapery fabrics that he'd asked her opinion of, she definitely recommended the darker, "stronger" one with the seashell motif.

"I value your input, Barbara," he had replied in his only slightly accented but heavily testosteronic baritone. No mention, however, of *his* having enjoyed as had she their surprising roll in his high-rise hay; no insinuating suggestion that perhaps she would like to have a look at the seashell drapes when they were made and hung. Mortification, to have cheated on her husband with, of all people, the acting chair of his department, and to have been by him judged, perhaps, no good in bed! It makes her want to pile atop her ailing seat-mate now in contrite reaffirmation of their marriage-bond — but apart from the unseemliness of such behavior, the long charter flight has made Walt's back at least temporarily even sorer. As they circle in over the mangrove-and-chicle-thick expanse of Yucatán, her head begins to throb in a way that she can almost imagine signals migraine. She removes the prescription sunglasses that, for one reason or another, she has lately taken to wearing indoors as well as out, and massages the bridge of her nose. The ache neither disappears nor, thank heaven, comes on more strongly.

After they've checked in along with a festive busload of other new arrivals, been assigned their simple but comfortable quarters, and at Barbara's suggestion pushed the twin beds together to make one large one (she has to do most of the pushing), she asks, "Could we maybe sack out for a while before we explore the place?" Walt is disinclined at first — he didn't come to Yucatán to nap through this four-and-a-half-thousand-dollar vacation — but then he sees that it's not napping she has in mind, and although he'd rather go reconnoiter the resort's impressive spread and hit the beach, he tries to get into her sportive mood. "You'll have to get on top," he tells her.

She smiles behind her dark glasses. "That can be arranged." Moreover, when they're almost undressed she surprises him by suggesting that they remove each other's underpants with their teeth.

"Hot damn," her husband responds, assuming she's joking, and with his hands whisks off first his own briefs and then hers. In fact, however, she was quite serious: In her session with Franco, he had not only insisted that Barbara bestride him with her sunglasses in place ("So *barbaric*," he had teased) but had proposed, as they subsequently redressed, that next time they undress each other with their teeth. It was her amused excitement at that prospect that had prompted her follow-up phone call: a disappointment, but surely for the best.

"Take those damn *glasses* off," Walt now mock-scolds her when she mounts him — just as she was about to reach back and down to do with her forefingertip a certain little thing to him that Franco . . .

"Isn't it sexier like this?"

Smiling, he reaches up and removes the offending item. "I like to see who it is I'm making love with, okay?" He folds the sidepieces and sets the sunglasses on a nightstand. Feeling her headache rethreaten, Barbara declares, "It's just the same old wife as always," and hobbyhorses him straight to ejaculation so that she can dismount, dose herself with aspirin, and get those glasses back on. "Rain check," she tells him when he makes to reciprocate.

But as she unfolds the eyeglasses (before even washing up), one hinge-screw works loose and drops out, and the earpiece comes off in her hand.

"Oh god. We've got to find it!"

Naked on all fours she goes, searching the rugless quarry-tile floor in vain for the tiny screw.

"What am I going to *do*?" She's borderline-frantic. "They're my only glasses!"

Her startled husband reasonably supposes that all eyeglass-hinge screws are alike, unless some are metric and some not; they can buy the cheapest pair of overpriced nonprescription shades in the Club's boutique and use one of its screws to replace hers.

"It'll never work!" She sits Turk-fashion on the bare tiles, head in hands. "What am I going to do with my life?"

Surprised at her near-hysteria, Walt does his best to calm her — "Jesus, Barb!" — although experience has taught him that his efforts in this line are as liable to aggravate as to soothe.

The headache comes on: in fact, her first full-fledged migraine. To bed she retreats, not for sport this time. Seeing their vacation-week on the verge of going down the drain, Walt half-ruefully, half-resentfully goes to check out the boutique as proposed, acquiescing however to his wife's insistence that he buy nothing until she inspects and approves. In her judgment, he's reckless with their money. He finds, of course, sunglasses a-plenty for sale there — muchos pesos per pair, but so what compared to the cost of this trip? If the parts prove incompatible, perhaps he can use a screw from his own eyeglasses to repair his wife's and then jury-rig his with a wire paper-clip scrounged from the establishment's business office. He strolls the hibiscus- and bougainvillea-rich grounds, noting bitterly that their luckier plane-and-bus-mates are already enjoying the magnificent beach and the splendid Mexican Caribbean out there — its reefs abounding, no doubt, in jim-dandy shells.

Back at their room he finds a note on the dresser: *Sorry to've come unhinged (!) Gone to infirmary. Don't follow; will be okay. Will look for you on beach. Love you.*

His resentment melts, leaving only pity and affection; he knows *he*'s not the easiest person in the world to live with, either, and he doesn't for a moment doubt the bond between them. He changes into a swimsuit, loads their beach-bag with towels, sun-lotions, his snorkel mask, a plastic shell-identification card, and a book on Mayan artifacts, and advises his wife, on the back of her note to him, to look for him and/or the bag on the narrow stretch of beach just in front of their unit.

Properly to reach that stretch, one is meant to follow a paved and landscaped walk for several hundred yards toward the Club's central buildings, to the pool area and main beach access, and then backtrack along the strand itself, separated from the landscaped grounds by a low fence atop a five-foot embankment. Walt, however, takes the direct route, picking up a white plastic lounge chair as he crosses the lawn. That chair's one-piece molded curves — designed for nested stacking and for reclining in average though nonadjustable comfort — remind him of the recumbent stone figures of the Mayan god Chacmool, ubiquitous in the region: There are full-size replicas at the resort's entrance and miniatures for sale in the boutique. Careful of his back, he hefts the chair over the fence and slides it down the bank, then climbs over and down after it with their beach-bag. He has the strip to himself. "Chacmool" he positions where Barbara is most likely to notice it from their second-floor balcony, and he seats the bag in plain view on its belly, so to speak — just as, if he remembers correctly, sacrificial victims were once positioned on the original. Then he wets his mask-lens with saliva against fogging and enters the welcoming sea at last.

The water is warm, clear, and beautiful, with a moderate current from upshore, where the main beach is. Without swim-fins (he means to borrow a pair from the snorkel shack after Barb settles down) it takes a bit of effort to hover in place; easier to ride downstream on the current and walk back. He does that for a hundred yards or so, admiring the clean sand bottom, the mostly healthy-cooking coral, the flamboyant fish, and the occasional top shell or other mollusk, which he inspects and identifies but refrains on principle from collecting. No Barbara in sight when he returns to Chacmool. Deciding that the beach-bag is reasonably safe, he walks farther this time in the other direction — perhaps a quarter-mile, to the edge of the main bathing area, in order to snorkel the current home.

His wife's surprising question — "What am I going to do with my life?" — haunts him as he floats. He knows himself to be an antidramatic, even a plodding soul, at least by contrast to her higher-strung sensibility; he cannot imagine putting that question to himself, for example, in the absence of objective crisis, such as disablement so crippling that he couldn't work, or the loss of his wife to accident or disease (divorce doesn't occur to him; over the course of their marriage he has been tempted no more to infidelity than to illegal drugs, nor has he ever thought to wonder whether Barb has been). He sometimes regrets, even keenly, their not having children, especially when he's with his young nieces and nephews, but he finally shrugs at his infertility, as at his not being wealthy or movie-star handsome, and gets on with it. What is he going to do with his life? He's going to snorkel this stretch of sea-floor, then read up on the Mayans or beachcomb or both, go to dinner this evening, perhaps try tennis mañana if his back permits (the swimming seems to help it), then tour the Tulum ruins, where he particularly looks forward to viewing the astronomically calibrated temples of Marriage and Birth. . . .

A non-marine something on the bottom catches his eye, rolling lazily with the current over a sandy patch between coral rocks ten feet under: a pair of sunglasses, of all things, in design rather like Barbara's, though with hot pink frames rather than black. Amused (and careful of his back), he dives and retrieves them, noting as he surfaces that the hinge hardware seems uncorroded and moves freely. If the lenses were prescription-ground, he would turn the glasses in at the Hostess desk; as they're not — just an ordinary pair of ladies' shades, perhaps knocked off some bikini'd young miss upbeach an hour ago as she frolicked with her boyfriend in the gentle surf — he'll cannibalize them on Barb's behalf, then reassemble and return them if the experiment fails. Truly, while he can understand his mate's despairing question in a hypothetical way, on the gut level he finds it virtually incomprehensible.

There she is, he sees now in the downshore distance: a fetchingly bikini'd and sun-visored miss herself, stretched out on Señor Chacmool with the bag beside her and reading a book. That last he takes for a hopeful sign, as is her apparently making shift with her one-stemmed sunglasses instead of throwing up her hands. He tucks his treasure into the crotch of his swimsuit and happily strokes herward.

Shading her eyes with one hand, Barbara watches him wade ashore, his mask perched up on his forehead (her own forehead, though less ax-edged than before, feels still like a seismic fault about to let go). He reaches down into the front of his swimsuit as if about to expose himself.

"Hubby to the rescue!"

"Where'd you get those?"

"Frutas de mar, and more where these came from." Pattering on, he rummages through the beach-bag. "Want to check for yourself? How's your head these days, by the way?"

"A wreck. But it'll pass."

"*All passes*," he intones, fishing out the Swiss Army knife that he carries with him everywhere; "*art alone endures*. John Ruskin? Omar Khayyám? Art Garfunkel?" He has expected to have to use the point of the knife's smaller cutting blade to unscrew the hinge, but finds to his gratified surprise that while the main screwdriver/cap-lifter blade is, as he anticipated, too broad and thick to fit the tiny slot, on the can-opener blade there's a finer, narrower screwdrive tip that he'd never particularly noticed, evidently designed for just such employment. "Ah, those Swiss," he natters happily: "I hope our army never has to cross knives with their army. Voilà!" He displays the minuscule part in the palm of his hand. "We lose this one, we've still got a spare. The patient, please."

"The side-piece is up in our room. . . ."

No matter, he replies; he can anyhow test the threads. Better yet, they'll start a new fashion. In less than a minute he has installed a hot pink leftside earpiece in place of the absent black one. "If the screw fits, wear it," he proposes. Or he can restore the original next time they're in their room;

or she can go pink both port and starboard; or they can mix-and-match each time she takes her shades off to bestride him. "Whenever you need a little you-know-what," he concludes, presenting her with the odd-looking but perfectly serviceable specs. "On with the story?"

To his dismay, he sees she's weeping and shaking her head. For a moment he fears he's done something amiss — but now she takes in both her hands not the sunglasses but *his* hand, and covers it with tears and kisses, sobbing the most soul-wrenched, soul-wrenching sobs that he has ever in his innocent life heard the human animal give forth, although in truth it is capable of much greater.

The loser of those serendipitously found sunglasses, Mme Jacqueline Masson of Lyons, France, is, as it happens, neither young or currently bikini'd nor a miss; nor was she frolicking with a boyfriend in the surf at time of loss, although she has been and done all the above in years gone by. A veteran member of Club Méditerranée, at age fifty she has vacationed in some two dozen of that organization's resorts over as many winters. This is, however, her first visit to Cancún; she and her husband inclined to the literally Mediterranean clubs or, of the Caribbean ones, those in departments of France, such as Martinique and Guadeloupe. Moreover, it is her first vacation-trip as a widow, in the company of women friends from Lyons instead of her dear Bertrand, a physician in that city who succumbed to leukemia just about this time last year. Three days into this experiment, she supposes it's going neither well nor badly. Her two friends, somewhat younger (one recently divorced, the other "on holiday" from spouse and children), have been consistently animated, even festive — in part no doubt to keep her own spirits up. They have flirted harmlessly with the handsome young Gentils Organisateurs who manage the sports and other activities; they've tisked together at the rowdy

American teenagers and the resort's cuisine, which is generally inferior to that of the clubs they're used to and is directed, they're convinced, at less discriminating Yankee and Canadian appetites. They've done aerobics and yoga and archery and tennis and have even tried windsurfing. In amused defiance of Mexican law (nobody seems really to care), they have declared a certain stretch of beach at the far end of the resort Topless, and have been gratified to see half a dozen other women guests of various ages and nationalities follow their bare-breasted lead. Solange, the divorcée, today even proposed escalation to total nudity; proud of her still-sleek derrière, she wears bikini bottoms with only the tiniest of triangles in front and a mere string up the cleft behind, but even that, she has reminded them, is more than they would be cumbering themselves with at Guadeloupe's Caravelle or Martinique's Buccaneer Creek.

"Vive la France," Edith agreed, and although her body at forty-six is holding up less well than Jacqueline's at fifty, not to mention Solange's at forty, she took the lead in going bottomless on the spot — which happened to be hip-deep in the gentle surf.

"Pour la patrie!" Solange cheered, and was soon brandishing her famous thong-bottom over her head like a banner.

"Liberté, egalité, sororité," Jacqueline affirmed, and bent to follow suit just as a somewhat larger wave pushed her off-balance. Hobbled at the ankles by her dropped bikini, she tumbled with a little whoop and was unable simultaneously to slip her feet out of the garment and to hold her sunglasses in place. By when she regained her footing, the swimsuit-bottom was in hand, the glasses were gone, and all three women were laughing merrily.

"Là, là!" Solange pointed at a hot pink flash on the sand-stirred bottom, and redoubtable Edith dived for it, but the undertow of the approaching next wave swept the glasses out of sight. Their loser shrugged: Tant pis. She would be stopping at the boutique anyhow before dinner, for post-cards, and would buy another pair. A trifle.

But in fact the little loss provokes an inward sigh: She bought those particular sunglasses in Agadir, Morocco, five or six years back, when at Bertrand's urging they spent a few days at the old original Club Med there, and they sub-sequently became her unofficial beach-holiday specs. Her marriage, she supposes, was not extraordinarily satisfying, but it was at least ordinarily so; she misses it and her always-too-busy husband terribly (his terminal illness was their most time together since their honeymoon). Her grown son, the image of his father, rather bores her, and his wife she can scarcely abide. As for her women-friends, bless them, they were altogether more enjoyable as supplementary compan-ions than they are as the principal ones that, faute de mieux, they have become for her; Solange is quite naturally more involved with her current lover back home, Edith with both her husband *and* her current lover back home, than either is with her. The naked trio now wades ashore, animatedly dis-agreeing en route to their towel-spread lounge chairs whether the several American and two Italian members of their un-acknowledged topless sorority will presently join them in bottomlessness or whether the not-unhandsome Mexican se-curity guard at the resort's perimeter (who has plainly ob-served but so far chosen to ignore their rule-flouting) will feel moved to nip this escalation in the bud, so to speak.

Jacqueline Masson supposes that she'll become accus-tomed to the horrid emptiness of her present life and grad-ually fill it with other interests. Just now, however, she is so bored with its pointlessly ongoing story that she wishes she could simply close and toss it like a tiresome book — the way that sexy American girl, at the moment the women pass, tosses her paperback onto the sand beside the molded plastic beach chair in which she has been lolling like Venus on the halfshell, pulls her Oakland A's baseball cap down over her face, and rests her head on her upraised arms, lifting her perfect breasts as if to make them declare, "Here we are, guys; resist us if you can."

That *as if* is not Mme Masson's: She takes only the most perfunctory woman-to-woman notice of that brace of maraschino-topped vanilla sundae specials and then, with her companions, exits this narrative to deal with her unenviable own (while, just offshore, the moderate undercurrent tumbles like a vagrant subtext a certain pair of hot-pink sunglasses along the sandy sea-floor, leisurely under the moored Mistral sailboards and Laser sailboats, among the feet of bathers at the central swimming area marked with floats to warn off water-skiers and windsurfers, thence down-beach toward where another rule-flouter has dragged a lounge chair over the low-fenced bank from the landscaped lawn of the guest-compounds down that way). No: Those salivary tropes are courtesy of William Allen Wentworth III, American teenager for the four months remaining till his twentieth birthday, for whom the spectacle of three middle-aged French or French-Canadian (anyhow French-speaking) women wading merrily naked from the gentle surf merely makes more delectable the *Playboy*-centerfoldworthy blonde in orange bikini pants and Oakland A's cap, off whom he has scarcely been able to take his eyes for the past three-quarters of an hour. Praise God for sunglasses, which permit one shamelessly to ogle those Häagen-Dazs double scoops from thirty feet away while pretending to draft a letter to one's parents, back in Cincinnati, Ohio, explaining why, after a prolonged soul-search, one has decided to drop out of the University of Virginia in one's sophomore year in order — after a bit of R&R south of the border on the last of one's "college" inheritance from Grandpa Bill — to pursue what one is all but certain now is one's true calling: the management not of Wentworth Office Systems, Inc., the half-century-old family firm, but of sound-and-light effects for heavy-metal rock concerts. Although he shares the lanky build and troubled facial complexion of those rowdy Yank youngsters tut-tutted by Mme Masson, likewise their unseasoned mien and their currently de rigeur uniform of clunky black basketball shoes (unlaced), long baggy shorts, oversize T-shirt, and backwards ball-cap, Bill Three is a polite and rather shy boy, actually, indifferently successful with girls, more at ease with the unambiguous signal lamps, switches, and meters of an electronic console than with the complexly voltaged interactions of his peers. He has had his eye increasingly on Miss February (so he can't help thinking of the awesome blonde in the Oakland A's cap) since her arrival yesterday — Bill himself is three days into his unauthorized vacation — and has spent most of today virtually stalking her, so taken is he with her physical beauty and, more and more, with the way she handles herself. Among his impressions:

• "American" as she looks (to William the Third, this adjective still reflexively connotes white Anglo derivation, although he certainly knows better and gets along quite agreeably with his peers of other ethnicity), her name has an exotic, sort of Middle Eastern sound in his ears, at least as it's pronounced by the Chef du Village and other G.O.s with whom he has seen her speaking animatedly from time to time, both in English and in French: Jedee, Zhedí, something like that.

• Like himself, she's unaccompanied; she has doubtless been assigned a roommate, as has he (Bill scarcely sees his from one day to the next), but she prefers to move about on her own. More gregarious and athletic than himself, she has been observed by him playing power volleyball on the beach (she sets up a mean spike), dancing energetically at the disco, and laughing and chatting with the G.O.s and her fellow G.M.s (Gentils Membres) in the buffet-style main restaurant. Nevertheless, she appears to be essentially content with her own company: While most of their coevals lounge sociably about at poolside between activities, Bill takes it as a mark of their shared independent-spiritedness that Zhedí, like him, prefers the uncrowded far end of the beach. Enchanting as is her meticulous sun-lotioning of that perfect body, as yet untanned, in his opinion she is not displaying herself to encourage approach; she's simply taking the sun, reading and communing with herself between sessions of physical and social activity. He admires that, as also the unaffected friendliness of her conversation a while ago with the similarly topless and not at all bad-looking Italian or Latino woman nearby, whose handsome brown-nippled jugs the young man classifies as more coffee-almond-fudge than vanilla; Ms. Feb evidently doesn't regard other attractive females ipso facto as rivals. Bill's sense of her, moreover — but he'll readily grant that here his imagination is running free — is that she herself goes topless not out of exhibitionism (like that older French trio) but simply for the pleasures of nonrestraint and, perhaps, unaggressive nonconformity.

• She has, withal, has Ms. Zhedí/Jedee/Whatever, an air of unassuming self-possession and general maturity for her age that young B Three (as his Virginia musician-friends call him) finds almost as impressive as her lovely face and magnificent near-nude body: a refreshing absence of affectation that both encourages and intimidates him. He guesses she's a year or two older than himself, and feels that differential as acutely as he used to back in high-school days. Could she possibly find him interesting? Just possibly, he decides: In a freshman-year computer-science class at U Va, he was befriended by a girl less striking than Miss February but quite good-looking all the same who actually asked *him* out before he could ask her; they had "related" with an ease and reciprocal interest unprecedented in his experience, and might well have gotten it on as a couple if he hadn't still been honorably carrying a torch for Karen Baker, his high-school girlfriend (who turned out to be already involved with another guy, at her own university, in Vermont).

At exactly this juncture in our narrative, Chance presents William Allen Wentworth III with a chance indeed to test this possibility. As the three topless — and now bottom-less! — French-speaking ladies emerged laughing from the surf some moments ago and strolled past Zhedí en route to their beach chairs, she casually dropped her paperback onto the sand beside her, lay back in her own chair, pulled her ball-cap down over her face, and tucked her hands behind her head, with the aforenoted salivary effect on the observer. A breeze now ruffles the leaves of that book and blows a loose page free of it, almost directly toward our Bill; he tosses aside his clipboard with the half-drafted letter of explanation to his parents, piles out of his lounge chair, and makes a diving interception before the precious leaf can flutter past him down the beach and maybe into the water.

Gotcha! he exults to himself. He brushes sand from his shorts, restraightens his cap (Cincinnati Reds, a different league altogether from Oakland's; they might discuss that), carefully uncrumples the shortstopped paper, and considers how best to head for first base. Neither Miss F. nor the Italian/Latino woman nor the Frenchies appear to have noticed his flurry of action. His impulse is straightforwardly to return the book-page — "Excuse me, ma'am; this is yours, I think" — and, depending on her reaction, take it from there. That's how his buddy Fred Sims in Charlottesville would do it, drummer and backup singer with the Cold Fusion and cocksman extraordinaire: "If she doesn't cover her tits when you say hello," Fred would advise him, "you're home free, man." On the other hand, it might make better sense to wait until she puts her top back on before approaching her: "Didn't want to bother you while you were catching the rays," etc. (wink wink). He bets she'd appreciate his thoughtfulness.

To gather his nerve and consider his options, he returns to his chair, smooths the page out on his clipboard, and scans it; some idea of what she's reading might give him a good opener. Although B Three himself reads next to nothing as a rule except from video display terminals, and did poorly in his college literature courses (which anyhow had more to do with ethnic and gender politics than with art), and although he takes for granted that what isn't electronic isn't relevant except maybe historically, he has from time to time enjoyed specimens of science fiction and "cyberpunk"; maybe he and she can discuss that. From his monitoring of Jedí/Jaydee, he can't hazard a guess at her taste in books — but then, neither his life-experience nor his imagination affords him much sense of the range of possibilities, either in literature or in the reading proclivities of young women.

Out of context, at least, neither side of pp. 179/180 (so the leaf is numbered, bottom center) makes much sense to its present reader. A more knowledgeable and perceptive eye than B Three's might register that since the leaf's *recto* (179) happens to conclude one chapter of or selection from the overall text, and the *verso* (180) therefore to begin another, the title of the book itself — which would normally appear as a running head on the left-hand, even-numbered page — is missing; further, that inasmuch as no author's name appears under the (unnumbered) title of the item commencing on 180, the unnamed book must consist of articles, stories, or whatever by a single (unnamed) hand rather than by various authors. Neither a novel-page on the one hand, then (if it's fiction at all), nor an anthology-page on the other. What Bill registers is simply that the lines constituting page 179 (under the running sub-head STORIES OF OUR LIVES) read less like fiction than like . . . Bill can't say what. The page comprises a clutch of rhetorical fragments, concluding with *Rwanda, Haiti, Bosnia, Kurdistan. The doomed Marsh Arabs. The web of the world.*

Over *his* head.

Page 180, perhaps because it opens a missing text rather than closing one, is rather more intelligible, though scarcely less baffling. *I'm holding,* it begins (under the quotation-marked title *"Hold on, there"*), and a sort of dialogue ensues:

> *"That fellows's Page Whatever ended with* The web of the world?"
> *So the story goes.*
> *"And the next page says* 'Hold on, there'?"
> *Et cetera. The web of the world.*
> *"What's going on here?"*

Damned if Bill knows, but he's disposed to be impressed by anything associated with Ms. Zhedí-Feb over yonder, who has risen yet a notch higher in his estimation for presumably understanding and maybe even enjoying such stuff. Brains, too!

"Bonjour, Zhayr*dee*!" he hears called now in rich baritone — he hadn't noticed the *r* sound in her name before, actually overriding the *d* — and there's stocky, sun-browned, black-curled Marcel, the much-muscled and high-spirited Chef du Village, in his round-lensed, wire-rimmed specs, his shell necklace, and the bikini swim-briefs that he and all the other non-American G.O.s prefer to boxer trunks, not to mention knee-length "jams."

"Bonjour, Marcel," Miss Feb replies smoothly, once she

has lifted her cap to see who's saluting her. Just as smoothly, as Mar-*sayl* hunkers beside her chair to exchange pleasantries (he patrols the beach twice daily, Bill has observed, socializing with the G.M.s), she fetches from behind her back the orange bra of her swimsuit and unhurriedly dons it. Bye-bye, sweet Häagen-Dazzlers.

"You weel be on zuh red *team* in tomorrow's games, okay?" Marcel amiably proposes, and displays a handful of the colored yarn wristbands used to distinguish the competing teams in the Club's weekly "olympics."

"S'il vous plaît," Zhayrdee replies in pert and perfectly accented French, so it sounds to B Three at least. Then she adds, in her pure network American, "Wherever I'm needed."

"Red *team*," Marcel affirms. "We meet at zuh volley*ball* at ten o'clock, okay?"

"Entendu." She obligingly extends her right wrist for banding, and with her left hand adjusts her hair while the Chef du Village ties on the red yarn. The pair then chat awhile further in French, less jocularly (she even shows him what she's reading, and Marcel makes Gallic exclamations), before bidding each other cordial au revoir.

The heart of William Allen Wentworth III is stirred by an emotion complex and potentially dangerous to his self-esteem. He understands not a word of the pair's conversation, nor would he have if it had been in any other language than his own. For perhaps the first time, it occurs to him that it would be desirable — that it would be, in very truth, more *cool* — if such were not the case; if he could converse easily, animatedly, and seriously with people of other backgrounds than his. It is not finally difficult for him to acknowledge that a fellow like himself doesn't stand a snowball's chance in hell with Miss February, not simply because she's almost movie-star gorgeous but because she is (evidently) knowledgeable, sophisticated, and serious as well as "fun-loving" — all to a degree superior to anyone he has ever dated or been at all close to, the Virginia computer-science girl included. It is quite another matter, however, for him to see in another light, as now he dimly begins to, how "a fellow like himself" must appear to the likes of Zhayrdee and Marcel. When and if that light becomes clearer, he may chasteningly understand that real "cool" consists in impressive competencies together with firm principles and a degree of worldliness — that is to say, in character, capability, and polish — rather than in any particular costume and attitude; that to the excellent likes of Jerdí, nothing could be less cool than to be "cool" by his and Fred Sims's standards; that, in fact, he probably appears to her ridiculous: a clown, a creep.

"Red *team*?" Marcel is cheerfully asking him now, having resumed his tour of the beach.

"Nah, I guess not."

"You don't want to play? Is just for fun, okay?"

What a dork he thinks I am, thinks wretched Bill, and lamely smiles and says again, "Guess not, thanks."

"So," the Chef du Village says with a shrug, already scanning down the line. "May*be* you change your mind later, okay?" To the Italian or Latino girl he now calls "Red *team*?" She flashes teasingly at him her blue wrist-yarn and calls something back in what sounds to Bill like Italian but might as well be Greek. Marcel replies animatedly in the same tongue and goes to hunker beside *her* lounge chair; the girl doesn't even bother to cover her chocolate-kiss breasts.

Jerdí, Bill glumly observes, has gone back to her book.

For reasons that he is barely equipped to analyze, W.A.W. III will not much enjoy the remainder of his truant holiday. He'll mail to Cincinnati a version of his drop-out letter, return to Charlottesville just in time to join Cold Fusion for an extended gig in Chapel Hill and another in Durham before the band disbands over a feud between drummer and bassist on the one hand and lead guitarist and female vocalist/tambourinist on the other. Thereafter he'll make his way across the United States of America and back with Fred Sims, picking up random work here and there for a couple of years and eventually mending fences with his indulgent parents. In his mid-twenties he'll enter the family business after all, marry and sire children upon some clone of Karen Baker, and devote the decent balance of his life to his family and to Wentworth Office Systems, Inc. — which enterprise, however, will not prosper under his uninspired stewardship. In years to come he'll remember his abortive road-tour with Cold Fusion as being, in its way, the most satisfying episode in his entire listless life-story. Although his recollection of it decades hence will include his bolting the university and his Cancún escapade, he will not recall his uncharacteristic stalking and ogling of young Ms. Geraldine "Gerri" Fraser of Palo Alto, California — with whom, really, he has next to nothing in common beyond WASP ethnicity and U.S. citizenship. He slumps back into his beach chair, crumples into a ball the sibylline page that was to have been their link, side-arms it onto the sand, pulls his Cincinnati Reds cap over his face, and for a considerable while stares wide-eyed and soul-troubled at its convergent seams and evenly spaced ventilation-grommets.

Ms. Fraser — B.S. Stanford summa cum laude and currently a second-year student at the Johns Hopkins Medical Institutions — may happen to have the face and figure of *Playboy*'s centerfold-of-the-month, but from kindergarten to the present she has undeviatingly aspired to follow in the professional footsteps of her mother and father, an endocrinologist and obstetrician/gynecologist respectively. An accomplished all-round athlete and a serious amateur cellist, she has yet to choose her medical specialty; at age twelve it was pediatrics, at fifteen cardiology. Her love of scientific research inclines her toward a Ph.D. in medicine rather than a straight M.D.; on the other hand, her strong social conscience urges her toward clinical practice. The book to which she has returned is *Médecins sans frontières*, about the international volunteer physicians' organization thus named, devoted to heroic relief work in Somalia and similarly catastrophized venues; Gerri hopes to serve in that capacity for a year or two after her residency and before embarking on a career of medical research, private practice, or some combination of the two. Although she has lost her bookmark (a page that her current Baltimore boyfriend, a graduate-student apprentice poet at the university's Homewood campus, obligingly ripped from some Postmodernist story-collection that he happened to be perusing when Gerri casually asked him, as the pair were reading in bed, for something with which to mark her place while they make love), she knows quite well where she is, in the *Médecins* book and generally.

Has she even noticed the oddly dressed young fellow with the semi-punk haircut who's been following her about ever since she checked into the resort at her parents' urging for a bit of respite from her workaholism? She has, marginally: He reminds her, a little, of her kid brother back at Stanford, a preppie at heart who however feels compelled to ruffle the parental feathers by flirting with the punk subculture. They all know that Derek will outgrow such affectations; meanwhile, he takes their teasing good-humoredly.

That Mexican security guard, the lineaments of whose impassive face are directly descended from those that inspired the Mayan sculptors of dread Chacmool . . .

That topless young Bolognesa, a stewardess for Alitalia who aspires to be a travel agent in Rome, or perhaps in Milan . . .

The embryo, its existence unknown to both of its parents, busily and quietly multiplying its cells in Barbara Ellison's uterus . . .

Gerri Fraser's ex-lover back in Palo Alto, whose ball-cap she keeps as a souvenir of that pleasant life-episode, although she has switched allegiance to the Orioles and to her new poet-friend, and prefers soccer to baseball anyhow . . .

Franco the senior art historian, just now masturbating pensively before the draperied window of his condominium overlooking the university's lacrosse field, where the women's varsity squad is working out. Mimi Adler's sub-textual smile and narrative-ontological question. That Canadian quarter, still unretrieved from the campus grass. That balled-up book-page on the Club Med beach, slowly unballing itself now by the force of its own resiliency like a time-lapse movie of a sprouting mushroom, until another breeze catches and rolls it lightly seaward.

Rwanda, Haiti, Bosnia, Kurdistan. The doomed Marsh Arabs.

The web of the world.

"Hold on, there."

I'm holding.

"That fellow's Page Whatever ended with *The web of the world*?"

So the story goes.

"And the next page says '*Hold on, there*'?"

Et cetera. The web of the world.

"What's going on here?"

Life-stories. Life-or-death stories. Stories-within-stories stories, tails in their own mouths like the snake Ouroboros. Bent back on themselves like time warps.

"Time-tricks, you mean. Temporizings."

Name of the game. You've a better idea?

"Yes."

Forget I asked that question. *He didn't ask that question.*

"Hold on tighter."

He's holding. Everything's on Hold.

Presently: "We've got to just do it."

They. Why?

"*Us*. No more dodges. No more stalling. No more tricks."

More of everything. More more more.

"No. I'll do what I have to; you do what you have to."

What I have to do is talk you out of doing what you have to do. You don't *have* to do what you have to do, you know.

"Who says?"

He says.

"Speak for yourself. She's out of here."

Not yet.

"No? Explain."

He thought she'd never ask. They can't go before they close up shop.

"One more stall."

Name of the game.

Presently: "You win another round. Explain."

His pleasure:

9.

Closing Out the Visit

Good visit, we agree — fine visit, actually, weatherwise and otherwise, everything considered — but as with all visits agreeable and disagreeable its course has run. Time now to get our things together, draw down our stock of consumables, tidy up our borrowed lodgings, savor one last time the pleasures of the place, say good-bye to acquaintances we've made, and move along.

"The *light*," you want to know: "Have we ever seen such light?"

We have not, we agree — none better, anyhow, especially in these dew-bedazzled early mornings and the tawny late afternoons, when sidelit trees and beachfront virtually incandesce, and the view from our rented balcony qualifies for a travel poster. That light is a photon orgy; that light fires the prospect before us as if from inside out. Mediterranean, that light is, in its blue-white brilliance, Caribbean in its raw tenderness, yet paradoxically desert-crisp, so sharp-focusing the whole surround that we blink against our will. That light thrills — and puts us poignantly in mind of others who in time past have savored the likes of it and are no more: the late John Cheever, say, in whose stories light is almost a character, or the nineteenth-century Luminist painters, or for that matter the sun-drunk Euripides of *Alcestis*: "O shining clear day, and white clouds wheeling in the clear of heaven!"

"Such light."

Major-league light. This over breakfast bagels and coffee on the balcony — the end of these Wunderbägeln, freckled with sesame- and poppyseed, as good as any we've tasted anywhere, fresh-baked by the little deli that we discovered early in our visit, in the village not far from "our" beach. So let's polish off this last one, to use up the last of our cream cheese and the final dablet of rough-cut marmalade lifted from the breakfast place downstairs along with just enough packets of sugar to go with the ration of House Blend coffee that we bought from that same jim-dandy deli on Day One, when we were stocking up for our stay. Can't take 'em with us.

"Have we measured out our life in coffee spoons?"

We have, and canny guesstimators we turn out to have been. No more than a spoonful left over, two at most, which we'll leave for the cleanup crew along with any surplus rum, wine, mineral water, fruit juices, hors d'oeuvres, what have we, and I'll bet that the lot won't total a tipsworth by this afternoon's end, checkout time, when we've had our last go-round. Adiós, first-rate bagels and cream cheese and marmalade, fresh-squeezed juice and fresh-ground coffee, as we've adiósed already our fine firm king-size bed: Here's to sweet seaside sleep, with ample knee- and elbow-room for separateness sans separation! Here's to the dialogue of skin on sufficient square footage of perfect comfort so that the conversation begins and ends at our pleasure, not at some accidental bump in the night. Hasta la vista, maybe, in this instance, as it has become almost our habit here, after an afternoon's outdoorsing, to relish a roll in the air-conditioned hay between hot-tub time and Happy Hour.

*   *   *

Our last post-breakfast swim! No pool right under our balcony where we'll be this time tomorrow (no balcony, for that matter), nor world-class beach a mere shellsthrow from that pool, nor world-girdling ocean just a wave-lap from that beach, aquarium-clear and aquarium-rich in calendar-quality marine life for our leisurely inspection and inexhaustible delight; no scuba gear needed, just a snorkel mask fog-proofed with a rub of jade- or sea-grape leaf from the handsome natural beachscape round about us.

Now, then: Our pool-laps lapped, which is to be our first next pleasure on this last A.M. of our visit (not forgetting the routine and parenthetical but no less genuine satisfactions of post-breakfast defecation and stretching exercises on the bedroom wall-to-wall: Let's hear it for strainless Regularity and the ever-fleeting joy of able-bodiedness!)? A quick reconnaissance, perhaps, of "our" reef, while we're still wet? Bit of a beachwalk, maybe, upshore or down? Following which, since this visit has been by no means pure vacation, we'll either "beach out" for the balance of the morning with some serious reading and note-taking or else put in a session at our make-do "desks" (balcony table for you, with local whelk- and top-shells as paperweights; dinette table for me, entirely adequate for the work we brought along) before we turn to whatever next wrap-up chore or recreation — not forgetting, en passant, to salute the all but unspeakable good fortune of a life whose pleasures we're still energetic enough to work at and whose work, wage-earning and otherwise, happens to be among our chiefest pleasures.

Tennis, you say? Tennis it is, then, and work be damned for a change; we've earned that indulgence. You're on for a set, on those brand-new courts at our virtual doorstep, with a surface that sends our soles to heaven, pardon the pun, and so far from pooping our leg-muscles for the morning, has seemed rather to inspire them for the scenic backcountry bike ride up into the village for provisions, in the days when we were still in the provisioning mode. Extraordinary, that such tournament-quality courts appear to've gone virtually unused except by us — like those many-geared mountain bicycles free for the borrowing and for that matter the pool and spa and, we might as well say, our beach and its ocean, or ocean and its beach. Where *is* everybody? we asked ourselves early in the visit: Does the rest of the world know something that we don't?

"Vice versa," you proposed and we jointly affirmed, and soon enough we counted it one more blessing of this many-blessinged place that our fellow visitors were so few, as who but the programmatically gregarious would not: those couples who for one cause or another require for their diversion (from each other, we can't help suspecting) a supply of new faces, life-histories, audiences for their household anecdotes. Well for such that the world abounds in busy places; well for us who binge on each other's company to've found not only that company but a place as unabundant in our fellows as it is rich in amenities: just enough other visitors, and they evidently like-minded, for visual variety on the beach, for exchange of tips on snorkel-spots and eateries, for the odd set of doubles on those leg-restoring courts, and for the sense of being, after all, not alone in the restaurants and on the dance floor, at the poolside bar and out along the so-convenient reef, in this extraordinary place in general, in our world.

Auf Wiedersehen now, tennis courts! Arrivedérci, bikes and bike-trails, charming little village of excellent provisions agreeably vended by clerks neither rude nor deferential, but — like the restaurant servers, reception-desk people, jitney drivers, even groundskeepers and maintenance staff of this jim-dandy place — cheerful, knowledgeable, unaffectedly "real."

*   *   *

Lunchtime! You incline to the annex restaurant, up on the ice-plant-planted headland overlooking "our" lagoon, a sweet climb through bougainvillea, hibiscus, and oleander to the awninged deck where frigate-birds hang in the updraft from tradewinds against the cliff and bold little bananaquits nibble sugar from diners' hands. I incline to a quicker, homelier "last lunch," so to speak: fresh conch ceviche, say, from our pal the beachfront vendor down by the snorkel shack (who knows precisely how much lime juice is just enough lime juice), washed down with his home-squeezed guava nectar or a pint of the really quite creditable local lager. But who can say no to the stuffed baby squid and crisp white wine up at our dear annex, with its ambiance of seabirds and fumaroles, its low-volume alternation of the sensuous local music with that of the after-all-no-less-sensuous High Baroque, and its long view through coconut palms out over the endless sea?

"Endless *ocean*," you correct me as we clink goblets of the palest, driest Chablis this side of la belle France and toast with a sip, eyes level and smiling, our joint House Style, which would prohibit our saying *endless sea* even if we hadn't already said *seabirds* just a few lines earlier. *Sea* is a no-no (one of many such) in our house, except in such casual expressions as *at sea* or *on land and sea* or *moderate sea conditions*, and of course such compounds as *seaside*, *seascape*, *seaworthy*, and *seasick*, not to mention the aforementioned *seabirds*. One does not say, in our house, "What a fine view of the sea!" or "Don't you just love the smell of the sea?" or "Let's take a dip in the sea," all which strike our housely ears as affected, "literary," fraught with metaphysical pathos. Thus do longtime partners of like sensibility entertain themselves and refine their bond with endless such small concurrences and divergences of taste, or virtually endless such. But here's an end to our self-imposed ration of one wine each with lunch, especially in the tropics and only on such high occasions as this extended work/play visit; and there's an end to our unostentatious, so-delightful annex dinery, as pleasing in its fare and service as in its situation. Au revoir, admirable annex! — or adieu, as the case will doubtless prove.

Next next next? A whole afternoon, almost, before us, whether of sweet doing or of just-as-sweet doing nothing, since we have foresightedly made our departure arrangements early: scheduled the jitney, packed all packables except our last-day gear, settled our accounts, put appropriate tips in labeled envelopes for appropriate distribution, penned final hail-and-farewell cards to our far-flung loved ones, and posted on the minifridge door a checklist of last-minute Don't Forgets that less organized or more shrug-shouldered travelers might smile at, but that over a long and privileged connection has evolved to suit our way of going and effectively to prevent, at least to minimize, appalled brow-clapping at things inadvertently left undone or behind and too late remembered.

This air: such air, such air. Let's not forget not simply to breathe but to be breathed by this orchid-rich, this sun-fired, spume-fraught air! Off with our beach tops, now that we're lunched; off with our swimsuits, while we're at it, either at the shaded, next-to-vacant nudie-beach around the upshore bend — where we innocently admire lower-mileage bodies than our own (though no fitter for their age) of each's same and complementary sex; likewise each other's, trim still and pleasure-giving; likewise each's more than serviceable own, by no means untouched by time, mischance, and vigorous use, but still and all, still and all . . . — or else at our idyllic, thus far absolutely private pocket-beach in the cove two promontories farther on.

Pocket-beach it is. We lotion each other with high numbers, lingering duly at the several Lingerplatzen; we let the sweet tradewinds heavy-breathe us and then the omnisexual ocean have at us, salt-tonguing our every orifice, crease, and cranny as we slide through it with leisurely abandon: hasteless sybarites in no greater hurry to reach "our" reef for a last long snorkel than we would and will be to reach, in time's fullness and the ad lib order of our program, our last orgasm of the visit.

Good wishes, local fishes, more various, abundant, and transfixing than the local flowers, even. Tutti saluti, dreamscape coral, almost more resplendent than these fish. Weightless as angels, we float an aimless celestial hoursworth through spectacular submarinity, not forgetting to bid particular bye-bye to the shellfish and those calcareous miracles their shells, their shells, those astonishments of form and color, first among equals in this sun-shimmerish panoply, and virtual totems in our house. Faretheewells to our fair seashells, no more ours in the last analysis than are our bodies and our hours — borrowed all, but borrowed well, on borrowed time.

"Time," you sigh now, for the last time side-by-siding in our post-Jacuzzi, pre-Happy Hour, king-size last siesta; no air conditioning this time, but every sliding door and window wide to let the ceaseless easterlies evaporate the expected sweat of love. "Time time time."

Time *times* time, I try to console you, and myself. World enough and time.

"Never enough."

There's all there is. Everlasting Now, et cet.

"Neverlasting now."

Yes, well: The best-planned lays, as the poet says, gang aft a-gley.

"Not what I meant."

Appreciated. Notwithstanding which, however . . .

We beached out, you see, post-snorkelly, first in the altogether of that perfect pocket-beach on our oversize tripleterry beach towels, thick as soft carpeting, fresh from the poolside towel dispensary; then on palm- and palapa-shaded lounge chairs on the beach before the pool beneath our balcony, books in hand but ourselves not quite, the pair of us too mesmerized and tempus-fugity to read. Fingers laced across the beach-bag between our paralleled chaises longues, we mused beyond the breakers on the reef, horizonward, whither all too soon et cetera, and our joint spirits lowered after all with the glorifying late-day sun, so that when time came to say sayonara to that scape, to stroll the palmshadowed stretch to our last hot soak and thence, pores aglow, to take the final lift to passion's king-size square, we found (we find) that we can't (*I* can't) quite rise to the occasion.

"Me neither."

We do therefore not *have sex* — that locution another house-style no-no for a yes-yes in our house — but rather make last love in love's last mode: by drifting off in each other's arms, skin to skin in the longing light, no less joyful for our being truly blue, likewise vice versa or is it conversely, the balmy air barely balming us.

I pass over what, in this drowsy pass, we dream.

Have we neglected in our close-out prep to anticipate a snooze sufficiently snoozish, though alas not postcoital, to carry us right through cocktails to miss-the-jitney time? We have not. No mañana hereabouts for thee and me: On the dot sounds our pre-set, just-in-case Snoozalarm (which in our half-dreams we have half been waiting for); half a dozen dots later comes our backup front-desk wake-up call —

Thanks anyhow, Unaffectedly "Real" and pretty punctual paging-person — and we've time time time for the last of the rum or le fin du vin or both, with the end of the Brie on the ultimate cracotte, while we slip into our travel togs and triple-check our passage papers, button buttons snap snaps zip zippers lock locks. One last look, I propose, but you haven't heart for it nor do I sans you, hell therefore with it we're off to see the blizzard heck or high water. Adieu sweet place adieu, hell with it adieu adieu.

Time to go.

"That says it. Time to go."

Time goes without saying.

"So should we. Pack it in. Get it done with."

Time takes care of all that. In no time.

Presently: "*Time time time*, she sighs again. Boyoboy."

Time *times* time, he gently et ceteras.

"So let's say they've done all that close-out stuff. Now what?"

He'll think of something. Give him time.

Presently: "Three two one zero."

Right. Good-bye time.

"Sounds almost as if you really mean it this time."

Presently: "*Do* you really mean it?"

I do, as they said to each other once upon a time. E.g.:

10.

Good-bye to the Fruits

He agreed to die — stipulating only that he first be permitted to re-behold and bid good-bye to those of Earth's fruits that he had particularly enjoyed in his fortunate though not-extraordinary lifetime.

What he had in mind, in the first instance, were such literal items as apples and oranges. Of the former, the variety called Golden Delicious had long been his favorite, especially those with a blush of rose on their fetchingly speckled yellow-green cheeks. Of the latter — but then, there's no comparing apples to oranges, is there, nor either of those to black plums: truly incomparable, in his opinion, on the rare occasions when one found them neither under- nor overripe. Good-bye to all three, alas; likewise to bananas, whether sliced transversely atop unsweetened breakfast cereal, split longitudinally under scoops of frozen yogurt, barbecued in foil with chutney, or blended with lime juice, rum, and Cointreau into frozen daiquiris on a Chesapeake August late afternoon.

Lime juice, yes: Farewell, dear zesty limes, squeezed into gins-and-tonics before stirring and over bluefish fillets before grilling; adieu too to your citric cousins the lemons, particularly those with the thinnest of skins, always the most juiceful, without whose piquance one could scarcely imagine fresh seafood, and whose literal zest was such a challenge for kitchen-copilots like himself to scrape a half-tablespoons-worth of without getting the bitter white underpeel as well. Adieu to black seedless grapes for eating with ripe cheeses and to all the nobler stocks for vinting, except maybe Chardonnay. He happened not to share the American Yuppie thirst for Chardonnay; too over-flavored for his palate. Give him a plain light dry Chablis any time instead of Char-donnay, if you can find so simple a thing on our restaurant wine-lists these days. And whatever happened to soft dry reds that don't cost an arm and a leg on the one hand, so to speak, or, on the other, taste of iron and acid?

But this was no time for such cavils: Good-bye, blessed fruit of the vineyard, a dinner without which is like a day without et cetera. Good-bye to the fruits of those other vines, in particular the strawberry, if berries are properly to be called fruits, the tomato, and the only melon he would really miss, our local cantaloupe. Good-bye to that most sexual of fruits, the guava; to peaches, plantains (fried), pomegranates, and papayas; to the fruits of pineapple field and coconut tree, if nuts are fruits and coconuts nuts, and of whatever it is that kiwis grow on. As for pears, he had always thought them better canned than fresh, as Hemingway's Nick Adams says of apricots in the story "Big Two-Hearted River" — but he couldn't see kissing a can good-bye, so he supposed that just about did the fruits (he himself preferred his apricots sun-dried rather than *either* fresh or canned).

The *literal* fruits, he meant, of course. But surely it wouldn't overstretch either the term or anyone's patience to include in these terminal bye-byes such other edibles of the vegetable kingdom as parboiled fresh asparagus served cold with sesame oil and soy sauce, sorely to be missed in the afterlife if there were one and if food-consumption were a feature of it; likewise tossed salads of most sorts except fruit salads, which for some reason never appealed to him and to whose principal ingredients he had severally made his good-byes already, Q.E.D. Also pasta, if pasta's a vegetable; he had long been a fan of pasta in all its protean varieties, in particular the spiriferous and conchiform but including also the linear and even the non-Italian, such as Japanese "cello-phane" noodles (which he presumed to be some sort of pasta despite their transparency) and German Spätzle. Moreover, if he remained untouched by the popularity of Chardonnay among his countrymen, he was a charter member of the Yankee pesto-lovers association. Addio, then, pasta con pesto! Faithful to his homely origins, however, he insisted on equal farewell-time for the simple potato, whether boiled, baked, mashed, or French-fried with unhealthy but delicious salt and vinegar — no ketchup, please — and the inelegant Fordhook lima bean, which, out of some childhood impulse to diversify his mother's simple cookery, he used to stir into his creamed chipped beef or mix with his mashed white pota-toes and pan-gravy on the plate beside his southern-fried chicken: culinary items to which he had bidden good-bye decades ago and so needn't clutter his present agenda with. Friendly and nutritious veggies, vale! Although he never quite achieved vegetarianism and to this ultimate or all-but-ultimate hour continued to regard you essentially as the gar-nish to his dinner entrée, you are a garnish that he would miss almost as much as table wine if missing things were posthumously possible. Good-bye, garnís.

Moving nearer the center of life's plate, as it were, with only a bit more stretching of the parameters (if parameters can be said to be stretched at all by centripetal motion), might one not add — *must* one not add — to one's hail-and-farewell list the fruits of the sea, succulent in all languages but to his ear especially so in those of the Romance family: fruits de mer, frutti di mare, frutas de mar, and however it goes in sensuous Portuguese. He could, reluctantly, get by without red meat (grilled lamb chops, especially, it pained him to contemplate giving up, seasoned with salt, pepper, crushed garlic, and ground cumin), and only a tad less reluctantly without the flesh of light-fleshed fowl, in particular the breast-meat of barbecued Cornish hens. But finfish and shellfish of all varieties had for so long been at the center of his diet, it was scarcely an exaggeration to say that his flesh, by the time I tell of, was largely composed of theirs. If one had been permitted to slip in a request among one's farewell waves and kisses, his would have been that his remains be somehow returned uncombusted to his home waters, there to be recycled to the fauna whereupon he had so thrived and thence on out into the general marine food-chain. Rockfish, bluefish, sea-trout, shad; blue crabs, oysters, scallops, mussels, clams; billfish, tuna, and other steakfish; octopus and squid, in particular the stuffed baby Spanish variety called *chiperones*; sushi and sashimi of every sort; and, last because first among equals, that king of crustaceans, the New England lobster, *Homarus americanus*, whose spiny Caribbean cousin was in his estimation but an overrated poor relative, though undeniably handsome. Adieu to you, noble Down East lobster, all-too-rare-because-so-damned-expensive treat, that shouldst be steamed not a minute longer than *half* the time recommended by James Beard and most other seafood-cookbook authors. Ten minutes tops for a less-than-two-pounder, mark these parting words, or the animal has suffered and died in vain. "A quick death, God help us all," declares the character Belacqua in Samuel Beckett's story "Dante and the Lobster" — to which the story's narrator replies, in propria persona, *It is not*. (There is, by the way, a little-known technique for apparently hypnotizing and perhaps even anesthetizing lobsters on Death Row by standing the luckless creatures on their heads in a certain way, like arthropodous yogis, on one's kitchen-countertop. Had he time, had he world enough and time . . .)

But as the true soul-food is beauty, who could leave this vale of delights without farewelling at least a few representative examples of those flora and fauna that one eats only with one's eyes, and in some instances one's ears and nose? He meant, e.g., the very nearly overgorgeous fish and shellfish of saltwater aquarium and coral reef, whether viewed firsthand or on public-television nature shows and *National Geographic* photo-spreads; the astonishing birds of tropical latitudes and the butterflies of even our temperate zone, particularly the Monarchs hanging in migratory clusters from California eucalypts between November and March; the unabashed sexuality of flowers and the patient dignity of trees, large trees especially; certain landscapes, seascapes, skyscapes, cityscapes, desert- and marshscapes — in particular, he supposed, for himself, if he had been obliged as perhaps he was to choose only one of the above to pay final respects to, the vast tide marshes of his natal county: marshes which, while considerably less vast than they had been even in his childhood, remained still reasonably vast as of this valediction — always assuming that one was permitted to valedict. Nursery of the Chesapeake and, by semicoincidence, of their present valedictorian ("semi" in that it might be presumed to have been unpredestined that he be born and raised in or near the marshlands of Maryland's lower Eastern Shore, but it was no coincidence that, he having been therein B & R'd, those home marshes loomed so large in his imagination, if a marsh can properly be said to loom. For the sake of variety and euphony, he had been going to say "home bogs" just then instead of "home marshes," but it suddenly occurred to him for the first time, surprisingly enough at his age and stage, what the difference is between bog and marsh, particularly tide marsh. As between *marsh* and *swamp*, he confesses, the geological distinction eludes him still, although their connotations surely differ) . . .

Marshes, he was saying; saying good-bye, good-bye, good-bye to. Good-bye, still-considerable and fecund wetlands, at once fragile and resilient, neither land nor sea, symbolic equally of death and of regeneration, your boundaries ever changing, undefined, negotiable, your horizontality as ubiquitous as your horizon is horizontal, etc., etc. — and withal so eloquently sung, in your East Anglican manifestation, by the novelist Graham Swift in his novel *Waterlands* (not to mention by the novelist Charles Dickens in such of his novels as *Bleak House*, *David Copperfield*, and *Great Expectations*) that one would scarcely have presumed to do more than refer the attender of these farewells to those novelists' novels, were it not that as between East Anglia and the Eastern Shore of Maryland, the differences are at least as noteworthy, even unto their fenlands, as are any similarities. To "his" dear spooky, mudflat-fragrant marshes, then, a cross-fingered fare thee well.

But he could not leave the subject of marshes (hard enough to leave the marshes themselves) without a word of concern for the Marsh Arabs: the Madan people, he meant, whose fortune it had been for four thousand years to inhabit the marshes at the confluence of the Tigris and Euphrates rivers, in southern Iraq, and whose current misfortune it was to have been, for the past few hundred of those four thousand years, at least nominally Shiite Muslims who — self-reliant and wary of outsiders, like most marsh-dwellers — resisted the despotic Baathist regime of Saddam Hussein and were therefore, as one prepared to make these rhetorical farewells, being systematically exterminated by that regime via the dreadful expedient of *drying up their marshes* by diverting the inflow of those primordial, civilization-cradling rivers: an ecological atrocity on a par with the Iraqis' firing of the Kuwaiti oil fields. Good-bye indeed, one feared and fears, to the oldest continuous culture on the planet, numerous of whose communities have lived generation after generation on floating islands of spartina, continually replenishing them with fresh layers of reed on top as the bottom layers decompose and recycle; good-bye, poor hapless Marsh Arabs about to be destroyed in an eyeblink of time while still believing, after four millennia of harmlessly habitating your marshes, that somewhere in their labyrinthine fastness lies the *Arabian Nights*-like island of Hufaidh, complete with enchanted palaces of gold and crystal, Edenic gardens, and the Sindbaddish aspect of transforming into babbling lunatics any marshfarers who stumble upon it. May all destroyers of marshes serendipitously so stumble! Nothing quite like Hufaidh, one supposes, in the solitudinous wetlands of one's home county (only the odd goose blind, muskrat house, and, within living memory, moonshiner's still), though there is an uncanniness about even *their* low-lying, uninhabited islands — to which he truly now bade good-bye and better luck than the Madans'.

No marsh, however, one might say (paraphrasing John Donne), is an island. Indeed, in Nature's seamless web, if one might be permitted to mix metaphors so late in the day, no *island* is an island: When we lose the enchanted isle of Hufaidh by losing the marshes that sustained the culture whose imagination sustained that realm, we lose an item from the general cultural store and thus, figuratively at least, lose a part of ourselves — just as, literally, when we lose Poplar Island, say, in the upper Chesapeake, to the less malign forces of natural erosion (as happened to be happening apace even as he bade these good-byes), we increase the exposure of Tilghman Island, just behind Poplar, to those same forces, et cetera if not ad infinitum anyhow to the end of the chapter, as Cervantes's Sancho Panza puts it from time to time in *Don Quixote*: the geological chapter of Chesapeake Bay As We've Known It Since the Last Ice Age, continuously being reconfigured not only over millennia but over the span of a single lifetime (Where now was Sharp's Island, e.g., which he well remembered at the mouth of the Great Choptank River in his boyhood?), whereto — he meant equally that island, that river, that bay, and that lifetime — he now bade good-bye.

In the calm urgency of farewell, he hereabouts noticed, he had inadvertently changed the thrust of this valediction by conflating, in the passage above, the callous despoliation of the natural environment by Saddam Hussein's Baathists (and, Stateside, by the likes of real-estate developers, clear-cutting timberfolk, and toxic dumpers, in which last category our military-industrial complex stood out as a particularly egregious offender) — conflating these, I say, with such "natural" rearrangers of that environ as hurricanes, tornadoes, earthquakes, volcanic eruptions, tsunamis, and suchlike forces, ranging from Earth-destroying asteroidal impact on the scale's high end to the gentle, continuous attrition, on its low, of the mildest rain shower, gentlest wave, softest breeze, mere cellular decay — the inexorable rub of time.

Time, yes, there was the rub: Barely mortal time enough to kiss Earth's fruits hello before we're kissing them good-bye, and here he had so lost himself in the marshes, as it were, hoping perhaps to stumble upon his personal Hufaidh (if he has not stumbled itupon already: See how he babbles!), that he'd not even gotten around yet to Earth's salt, so to speak — nor, for that matter, even to animals other than human, except en passant in their aspect as table-meat. Fellow humans! He did not mean, yet, the nearest and dearest of those; they went without saying, although most assuredly not without saying good-bye to, if that unimaginable prospect could be imagined. No: He meant, in the first instance (which is to say the last, in order of importance), those anonymous others just enough of whom kept a restaurant, say, or a street or town or planet, from being unbearably lonely. Good-bye, insignificant others, if he might so put it without offense, understanding that he helped play that background role in your life-narrative as did you in his; would that your numbers were not so burgeoning — by runaway population-growth in some places, demographic shifts in others — as to threaten the biosphere in general and countless particular environs, not excluding his beloved Chesapeake estuarine system.

Farewell next to such only slightly less anonymous but considerably more significant others as ... oh, trash collectors, for example: Never, at any of a lifetimesworth of urban, suburban, and rural addresses, had he had reason to complain of the efficiency of the collection of his trash, both recyclable and non- — no small tribute from one whose profession was the written word. Same went, except for the odd and usually inconsequential glitch, for the several mail carriers and deliverers of daily and Sunday newspapers to his serial places of residence over the decades. What a quiet, civilized pleasure, to step outdoors of a morning in any season, sometimes before first light, and to find one's refuse collected for disposal, one's morning newspaper snugly folded in that way that newspapers are folded for tossing into driveways or tucking into newspaper-boxes, and moreover bagged in (recyclable) plastic if the weather even looked to be inclement — and then, somewhat or much later in the day, depending on where one's address happened to fall on one's postperson's route, to find one's outgoing mail duly picked up and incoming mail delivered. He shall miss that, chaps and ladies so approximately faithful to the motto of your service — or, rather, *should* miss it, if etc. Good-bye and thanks, and may neither rain nor snow nor sleet nor gloom of night et cetera. How fortunate it is, Aldous Huxley some-where remarks, that the world includes people pleased to de-vote their mortal span to the manufacture and sale of *sausages*, for example, so that those with no interest in that pursuit may nevertheless have their cake and eat it too, if you follow my meaning and possess wherewithal to purchase what, after all, those folk don't give away free.

People, people, people: builders of roadways, tunnels, and bridges, and of reasonably reliable vehicles to drive there-upon, therethrough, thereover; designers and fabricators too of such spirit-lifting artifacts as great art, to be sure, but also for example of jet aircraft in flight — particularly, to this valedictor's eye, those now-classic sweptwinged, rear-engined jetliners viewed passing overhead — likewise of most but not all sailing vessels under sail, of Krups coffeemakers, of Swiss Army knives in the middle range of complexity, of steel-shafted hammers with cushioned grips — in short, of all well-made things both functional and handsome, as agree-able to regard and to handle as to use.

Supreme in this category of human constructions to be farewelled — so much so, to this fareweller, as to be virtu-ally a category in itself — was that most supple, versatile, and ubiquitous of humanisms, language: that tool that de-constructs and reconstructs its own constructions; that uses and builds its users and builders as they use, build, and build with it. Ta-ta, language, la la language, the very diction of veridiction in this valley valedictory. Adieu, addio, adiós, et cetera und so weiter; he could no more bear to say *good-bye* to you than so to say to those nearest dearest, in particular the nearest-dearest, so to say, themof: He meant the with-out-whom-nothing for him to bid farewell to whom must strain the sine qua non of language even unto sinequanon-sense. Impossible to do, unthinkable to leave undone, and yet the mere prospect did undo him. Back to the apples! Back to the oranges! He'd say good-bye sooner to himself (he said), and soon enough would, than say it to —

But it went without saying that he had been assuming not that he might say without going, so to say, but say *before* going: say good-bye to the fruits, et cetera. Permission granted, surely?

"No."

"*I'll say yes to that.*"

Much obliged indeed.

"Yes to that No, she means, I'm afraid."

Ah, Permission *not* granted, then?

"As the fellow said, 'It is not.' Sorry."

Likewise.

Presently: "I *am* afraid."

Likewise.

"It's getting light out."

So he noticed. Maybe they could sleep a bit now?

"She's so tired she could sleep forever after, if she could sleep."

But she'll settle for a nice nap, yes? Though there's no timetable . . .

"We'll see. Good night, love."

Likewise.

Presently and quietly, fingers crossed: Is she asleep?

II.

Ever After

✒ 1

About human happiness in general and happy marriage in particular, not nearly enough has been written, in Frank Pollard's opinion, of a celebratory character. If *he* were a writer — of novels or of stories, say, such as this one — he would address that deficit, beginning perhaps with a dramatized rebuttal of Tolstoy's famous remark that all happy families are alike. Our Frank, however, is only a retired prep-school American History teacher (whose wife, a successful painter, would hotly contest that self-deprecating *only*): a happy consumer of art and ideas and, for four gratifying decades, their ardent transmitter to the boys of Highland Academy, but never, alas, among their producers.

Frank's experience is that happy *couples*, anyhow, like him and Joan, are alike in few respects beyond their taking much more pleasurable satisfaction than dissatisfaction in themselves, each other, their jobs and projects, their children, if any, their friends and colleagues, their life together — in short, beyond their being happy. Otherwise, they may be as different as apples and aardvarks: gregarious or asocial, profligate or frugal, educated or ignorant, high-energy or low-, Democrat or Republican. His mind is on this subject just now because, among other reasons, he and Joan are stretched out in side-by-side lounge chairs on the night-dark deck of their rented summer cottage at Fenwick Island, Delaware, sipping wine and stargazing, and Frank, for one, has just been vouchsafed an almost overwhelming soul-flood of peace, of grace — of something, anyhow, in that spiritual category.

The time here is deep August, an hour or so before midnight. The seashore air is muggy; dew stands in drops and pudlets on everything outdoors; the Pollards have spread beach towels on their chairs and removed all clothing except underpants, to let their skin breathe. A small white citronella candle in net-covered glass flickers off Frank's lean chest and Joan's ampler, well-bosomed torso. Together with a spray repellent, it's doing a reasonable job of misleading the mosquitoes so abundant after dark on the bay side of this coastal barrier island, especially in calm air. To westward, out over that shallow bay, hangs a first-quarter moon, on which Joan is trying to focus the family binoculars before training them on brilliant Vega, overhead. The day has been hazy-steamy, subtropical, but earlier this evening a thundershower rolled over Delmarva and out to sea; now the sky's clear enough for them to look forward to an annual ritual: toasting with champagne the first meteor of the Perseid Shower (and the end, virtually, of one more pleasant summer's work and play) before turning in for a good-night embrace under their bedroom paddle fan and a peaceful sleep. In years past, they stayed up on these occasions till the small hours, when in ideal conditions the meteor-count might exceed one per minute, all apparently radiating from the constellation Perseus over in the northeast; nowadays they're content with a single sighting, provided it be shared.

Meanwhile, as is also their end-of-evening custom, they're asking each other what was the highlight of each's day. It happens to be Frank who this time puts the question; Joan, as she often does, counters by asking "So far?" — for she maintains, sincerely, that her favorite part of any day is the ending of it in her husband's arms, before they roll apart into sleep.

"So far."

She has to choose between saying "Now" — that is, their waiting to retire to that sleepy embrace — or "Waking up this morning and holding each other till we got out of bed." She gives those alternative responses roughly equal time, at least as a preliminary reply before proceeding to some particular feature of the day. The woman quite means what she says, too — and this couple, mind, have been together for thirty years, since Joan was twenty-seven and Frank thirty-five.

"After that," she adds (having opted in the first instance for "Now"), "my favorite thing so far was getting that damned *lavender* right this morning" — in a watercolor she's doing of puddled dew in the forenoon shade of that same deck: one of a summer series that she calls variously her Puddlepaints, her Waterworks, her H_2O-Squareds — watercolors of *water* in sundry forms, moods, lights. If her track record holds, the dozen-odd items will fetch between five hundred and twelve hundred each at her fall show in Philadelphia; she would have painted the same number, however, of the same subject, with the same concentration, if she knew in advance that not one would ever be exhibited, let alone sold. Getting right that wash of lavender light was her A.M. project, and by dint of talent, training, luck, repeated trial, and much experience, she got it to her satisfaction: a small triumph that none besides the artist (and now her mate) will likely recognize.

"Yours?" she asks in turn, still twisting the eyepieces of those binoculars and flexing their angular separation — and Frank Pollard, who as always takes the question seriously, realizes that he can't choose a favorite moment or event, for the reason that this entire day has been ideal, not in its extraordinariness but, on the contrary, in its serenely perfect typicality, enhanced by contrast to the day before. The couple woke at first light this morning, as usual, to the sound of crows and mockingbirds in the black pines round about and crickets in the dew-soaked grass. Naked and sheetless under the slow-moving overhead fan (the Pollards share a distaste for air conditioning, among a thousand other shared likes and dislikes), they made lazy love, to both parties' satisfaction, and then breakfasted on the deck: fresh-squeezed orange juice, cinnamon-pecan buns from an Ocean City bakery, coffee from Hawaii's Kona Coast. Frank then read poetry on the toilet, as is his habit — in this instance, Yeats's *Sailing to Byzantium*, an old favorite, which duly moved his mind and heart while nature moved his bowels. After stretching exercises à deux and a wake-up dip in the tranquil, mist-mantled ocean, he read the morning newspaper down on their barbecue patio, out of Joan's way, while she turned to her easel and its challenge-du-jour. Before the air stoked up, he took a ten-mile bike ride along the flat ocean road up into the state park dunes and back; then he read a handsomely illustrated essay on logarithmic spirals, a pet subject of his, in the magazine *Sciences*, to which the Pollards subscribe as much for its art as for its articles. After that, he composed on their laptop computer a witty, perfectly routine end-of-summer newsletter to Joan's grown son by her short-lived first marriage and to his grown daughter by his rather longer-lived ditto: a pair whom F & J can't help wishing were married to each other (no consanguinity, after all) instead of to their actual spouses, hers an arrogant, womanizing lawyer, his a good-for-nothing layabout, in their parents' opinion. In that letter he declared, in passing, his intention to devote his next life to the history of science rather than to that of Colonial America. Of yesterday's pathology report — rather, of Frank's doctor's report of that report, together with his projections and recommendations therefrom — the letter made no mention, although some soon-to-follow one must. Too fine a day, too late in the season, to becloud with the likes of that; he wished his Paula in Minneapolis and Joan's Harold in Atlanta a day as fine, a season, a life. Lunch, presently, in a still-shaded corner of the deck: Joan's cold zucchini soup with Frank's garlic croutons and iced coffee, over which they sorted out the day's mail, compared notes on their respective mornings, and planned their afternoon. To the beach then, the pair of them, for some hours of swimming in the breakers, walking the strand, and reading in umbrella-shaded sand chairs, after which, back at the cottage, Frank did a bit of bookkeeping and Joan some preliminary packing for their return to the city two days hence. By car down to the market for their final light provisioning, then frozen fresh-peach daiquiris with crudités and hummus back on deck at Happy Hour. The evening headlines on TV; barbecued lamb patties with acorn squash and jug rosé for dinner as the sun set behind the pines; then a short bike ride together around the twilit neighborhood. A shower bath while nature considerately thundershowered Fenwick Island and cleared the air; a cheery phone call from the daughter just written to (it never fails), in which again Frank spoke only of such agreeable matters as the grandchildren's camp adventures, the anticipated Perseids, and their usual mixed feelings about exchanging the summer rhythms that they so enjoy for the busier urban-autumn routine that, historically at least, they have also much enjoyed. And now back on their excellent deck to sip Codorníu blanc de blancs brut, watch for meteors, and review their day, in order — vainly, for Frank Pollard — to choose a favorite moment from it.

"Grocery shopping with you," he declares, as he not infrequently does when stuck. It is a fact that in their younger years, especially back when they began keeping house together but were not yet married, he found it erotically rousing to stroll supermarket aisles with his new lover, then his bride, then his wife, selecting with her the foods they would prepare and enjoy together, as well as such homely necessities as lightbulbs and laundry detergent; returning home with their purchases in those days, they would sometimes pause to make love on couch or carpet between fridging the perishables and stashing the rest. He still finds it more pleasure than chore to steer the cart and check off items from their list while Joan plans and improvises menus down the line; today, e.g., as she stretched for a top-shelf jar of sun-dried tomatoes in oil, he could not resist a surreptitious pat on her pleasant behind. *There*, he now provisionally supposes, was his single favorite moment of the day — so far.

It is upon that recognition (while Joan rescrews those binocular eyepieces and declares, "I can't do lenses. Lenses hate me") that Frank Pollard experiences the aforementioned soulflood — of quiet joy, whatever. Come what may, they've had thirty blessed years together, by no means hassle-free but profoundly loving, profoundly satisfying; in a word, *happy*. That adjective gives him focus-troubles of his own: Happy tears blur bright Vega, the setting moon, the citronella candle on the low table between the lounge chairs, with its sweating icebucket of champagne and tray of acrylic flutes. Indifferent to this and every other emotion, in his pancreas meanwhile the robust tumor cells proceed with their inexorable division, redivision, and unhurried metastases: settlers, colonizers, unstoppable possessors and dispossessors of their new world.

2

Thirty feet southwest of and ten below the Pollards' chairs, on a leaf of ground ivy under one of the black pines near the deck of their rented beach cottage, a solitary dog tick, *Dermacentor variabilis*, unaware of doing so, bides its time, unwittingly carrying in its body great numbers of the microorganism *Rickettsia rickettsii*, the virus or bacterium (Rickettsias have characteristics of both) responsible for Spotted Fever in humans and some other mammals. As uncognizant of their patient host as are Frank Pollard's pancreatic-cancer cells of theirs, the microorganisms placidly metabolize, in effect "standing by" like the tick itself, to whom the Rickettsia colony was passed via its mother's eggs, independent of mammalian hosts. To the moon, the stars and planets, Earth's impending convergence with cometary debris, the Pollards' Fenwick Island deck and its occupants, not to mention their concerns, the *D. variabilis* is oblivious, though not quite to the sandy soil, the dew, the muggy air, the leaf on which it rests, the black-pine needles round about, and the dark-denimed leg now inching through those needles, now kneeling on the ground-ivy patch. The tick moves unhurriedly onto that dew-wet, serendipitous trouserleg and, presently, toward the warm animal tissue sensed thereunder and the blood-meal that is its program's goal. Its thousands of unknowing passenger-Rickettsias sense not even this, nor will they even when their vessel moors upon human skin, runs out its figurative gangway through the epithelium, and, in course of onloading its blood-cargo, unwittingly discharges them from one world to another, their unwittingly promised land.

❧ 3

"Microscopes and telescopes," Joan Pollard believes that it was Goethe who remarked, "distort the natural focus of our eyes." In fifth-grade science class it was invariably she who had the most trouble resolving paramecia under the school's old chrome-and-bakelite monocular microscope. Now she sees twin lunar quarters magnified up yonder, neither of them clearly, and can't locate Vega at all. Moreover, when she lowers the binoculars in order to see where to re-aim them, a midge or eyelash falls into her left eye, and the firmament swims.

"I give up," she declares, and, taking advantage of the fortuitous cover, lets flow a discreet measure of the tears never recently far away. A child of acrimonious divorce and herself early divorced, an overpermissive B-minus mother by her own assessment, more committed finally to her painting than to parenting, she neither expected nor particularly hankered for remarriage, and never seriously imagined that hers would be the extraordinary fortune (three decades later, she still inwardly shakes her head at it) of loving a man *profoundly*, despite his inevitable shortcomings; of being by him loved reciprocally despite hers, and of feeling their bond grow and deepen over the by-no-means-carefree years instead of abrading into resentment or callusing into indifference. Thirty years! The equivalent of twice that in most couples' lives, actually, thanks to the nature of his profession and hers; even before Frank's retirement from Highland Academy, in a typical week they spent more hours in each other's proximity than any "normal" working couple spends in a fortnight. And except during their never-frequent and ever-rarer quarrels, she has gone to bed nightly feeling blessed in their connection, and has morningly woken ditto. As has he.

"Something in her eye?" her husband asks now, accepting from her the failed binoculars; they often playfully address each other in third-person pronouns.

"Yep." Joan clears her throat and knuckles her eyeball. "Freaking *time*."

Frank focuses, with more success. "She's got time in her eye?"

"Also up her nose and in her face generally, but not out her kazoo. Where'd it all go, hon?"

Steering away from that question, "The thing is," Frank declares, "Goethe *liked* microscopes and telescopes. His remark's not a complaint; it's a reminder."

"Well, mine's a complaint," Joan decides. "And while I'm at it, T. S. Eliot's got his head in his pocket: It's *great* to measure out your life in coffee spoons. What sucks is running out of coffee."

Levelly but sympathetically, her husband observes, "She's distressed. Ah, so," he says then to Vega: "*There* you are, old girl."

"She is," his wife acknowledges. She pours herself and him another splash of champagne. "Let's spot us a meteor and pack it in. No: Let's stay out here forever."

"Easy on that eye, okay?" For she's knuckling it again. "Think of all those happy families of mites that colonize human eyelash follicles. You're making Apocalypse Now in there. The end of the world."

"Hell with 'em," says Joan. "What'd they ever do for me?" Soft-focused by her tears, the plastic glass of Catalonian champagne refracts the candlelight in a way that interests her painter's (right) eye. "Anyhow, Goethe was right. And it *is* the end of the world."

"Joanie?"

"Sorry sorry sorry." Bare forearms on bare thigh-tops, she slumps sidesaddle on her lounge chair, turning her wine-flute in the light. "I'm not going to be good at this, Frank. I'm going to fail you."

"So fail me." He pats her knee. "After all these years, you're entitled."

She looks away, skyward. "Was that a meteor?"

Frank considers. "Lightning bug."

4

In 1992, when Comet Swift-Tuttle last transited the inner solar system, the Pollards happened to be touring Spain. They watched for "their" Perseid Shower from the old city walls of Ciudad Rodrigo, in the province of Salamanca, where they were stopping at the Parador Nacional. Although they found the old city delightful — as much for its informal community park along the Rio Agueda, where the whole town seemed to gather at the hot afternoons' end to stroll and swim and socialize under the trees, as for its medieval walls and buildings — and although the night was satisfactorily dark out over the plain and the dry air brilliantly clear, they were disappointed at the apparent fizzle of the promised once-in-a-lifetime supershower. There hung the clustered constellations of the myth — Perseus, Andromeda, Cepheus, Cassiopeia — but by midnight they'd seen only one meteor together and one each separately. Since they planned an early start in the morning for their drive up into the Gredos Mountains, where they hoped to hike in the high forests, they bade the Gorgon-slayer buenas noches and turned in. It is from this happy Spanish driving-tour that Frank dates the intermittent onset of what he took to be a mild but increasingly persistent gastroenteritic discomfort: something in the food or water, he presumed, although both were excellent, and Joan felt nothing similar, and neither of the Pollards has been prone, historically, to more than the occasional transitory episode of nausea, diarrhea, or fever in their frequent travels and ardent culinary adventures. For as long as possible thereafter, he ignored the symptom.

In 1862, Swift-Tuttle's next-previous transit, Johann Wolfgang von Goethe was already thirty years in his grave alongside that of his friend Schiller in the ducal crypt at

Weimar, and no person currently alive on Earth had yet been born. In 1737, the transit believed to have been next prior to that, neither Goethe nor Schiller had yet been born; by Swift-Tuttle's next predicted transit, 2126, all persons alive on Earth in August 1994, the time of both the action and the writing of this story, will be dead. Mark Twain declared in 1910, correctly, that he had come in with Halley's Comet and would go out with it; among Earth's animate creatures, however, only trees might span such intervals as Comet Swift-Tuttle's orbital period — including, in special instances, *Pinus thunbergii*, the Japanese Black Pine, among still-young specimens of which hunkers the dark-clad interloper in the Pollards' yard, unconscious of the dog tick engorging on his right ankle, just above the black sock-top.

⇜ 5

Five days into his annual vacation-week at Ocean City, Maryland, his cash reserves a touch low and his mood a touch resentful of the fair but too-cool weather, Samuel Buffett, the Duct-Tape Rapist — so called by the media for his modus operandi in suburban Wilmington and Newark, Delaware, the venue of his serial assaults — is scouting Operation Nine, as he thinks of it, despite the possibility that its atypical location will narrow slightly the police search for him. How many hundred other Wilmingtonians, after all, are spending mid-August at the nearby Delaware and Maryland beach resorts? And everyone knows of the "copycat" phenomenon associated with unusual crimes. Thirty-two and single, the dependable and knowledgeable if sometimes short-fused assistant manager of a Radio Shack retail outlet in a shopping mall outside the state's major city, Sam has over the past two years taken up rape-robbery as an exciting and dangerous hobby. In the sexual attacks themselves

he takes considerable though secondary pleasure: They are
the bonus payoff for what he really enjoys — reconnoitering,
planning, and stalking; penetration of the premises; subdu-
ing and binding the frightened victim altogether into his
power. The associated robbery is almost perfunctory, a third-
order reward for his audacity, meant as much to deflect suspicion from a well-employed middle-class white man with
thinning brown hair and double-bridged eyeglasses as to aug-
ment his finances. He takes only cash, and has invested the
$1,953 gross from his operations thus far ($1,320 of it from
a single windfall, his seventh) in a one-year certificate of deposit at the bank branch in "his" mall. At that certificate's
first expiry-date, reminded of his falsetto commands to his
"targets," with an inward smile he "rolled it over."

Ordinarily, Sam Buffett selects as those targets attractive
young women who either live alone or have been observed
by him to be alone in their domiciles at the appropriate strike-
time. It was the extra challenge and quirky variety, as Sam
sees it, of the middle-aged couple in Operation Seven — the
only one that he remembers with less than entire pleasure —
that prompted him to "go for it," and although he had at
one point to inflict more pain than is his rule to pacify the
tape-trussed, freckle-pated husband while he sodomized the
tape-trussed, freckle-butted wife on all fours in the couple's
club basement, the unexpectedly large take helped compensate for his annoyance and the increased risk. By contrast,
Operation Eight — on a girl he knows cordially as a teller
in his bank and once came close to asking for a "date" —
went so easily, enjoyably, and perfectly per plan that he
stretched it out for nearly four hours, permitting frightened
but courageous Ms. Claudia Tully to natter earnestly on, between spells of tears and his assorted violations of her, about
the psychology of rape (on which subject she seemed knowledgeable indeed) and various resources that he might "ac-

cess" confidentially for help with his "problem." Thirty-seven dollars and twenty-nine cents, that operation yielded, which sum he looks forward to depositing with Claudia herself as soon as he can disguise it by combination with whatever the take from Operation Nine.

To that end, he brought along with him to Ocean City his kit: a loaded .22-caliber target pistol, its bore too small and its size too large for this purpose, really, but a relatively innocent-seeming piece to own, and meant only to intimidate, not to kill; the requisite ski mask, an itchy nuisance in hot weather; a small sheath knife; latex gloves and condoms (Sam fears AIDS); and the trademark roll of two-inch duct tape with which he blindfolds, binds at wrists and ankles, and intermittently gags his victims — all of these items (except the belted sheath knife) tucked into a black Land's End fanny pack in order to leave his hands free. It would not have surprised Sam Buffett to return to Wilmington and his job never having taken the kit out of his suitcase; nor does it surprise him to find himself daily more "up" for using it. The only child of a choleric father severely disabled in the Korean War and dead of a heart attack before the boy's thirteenth birthday and a scattered, indulgent mother who in her widowhood gave herself over to alcohol and chocolate, Sam grew up tidy, timid, taciturn, a touch irascible and officious: a fussy, asexual bachelor, so his neighbors and workmates indifferently suppose, who still lives in his now-obese mother's house and responsibly maintains her and it, his only known hobbies ham radio and, more recently, networking on his personal computer.

The man's methodicalness extends to his covert "operations," in which he has come to take an almost professional pride. Although the first three or four of them were "learning experiences" in which he developed his procedures and techniques, he has never botched one or even made a seri-

ous blunder. On the couple of occasions when something un-
foreseeable jeopardized the operation (Number Three's
young apartment-neighbors' rapping on her door and
singsonging merrily, "Come *on*, Do-reen; we-know-you're-
in . . . there!"), his resourcefulness has proved equal to the
challenge (gun barrel at her nape and tape-gag removed, at
his whispered instruction Doreen singsang back, "No-I'm-
not, guys; try-me-tomorrow-*mor*-ning!"). Except in the regrettable instance of Number Seven's hysterical husband,
whom it still distresses Sam to remember swatting angrily
with the .22, he has in his own opinion never "hurt" his victims — beyond the trauma of seizure, mortal threat, and
bondage followed by forced fellatio, rape both vaginal and
anal when he can manage it, and incidental robbery.
Particularly since attending Claudia Tully's spiel during
Operation Eight, he has read with interest articles in
Psychology Today about sexual predators "like himself,"
nodding Yes or No to sundry items of the profile and ultimately shrugging his shoulders. On infrequent past occasions
he has experienced unforced sex; agreeable enough, but by
his lights there's no comparing it with the excitement of the
forced variety. To the feminist assertion that rape has to do
with power, not with sex, Sam Buffett replies, "Bullshit"; to
the psychologists' assertion, however, that it has to do *at
least as much* with power as with sex, he readily nods assent.

Does Sam hate or anyhow resent women? He doesn't
think so, but grants the possibility. If he had been sexually
more successful in the normal way, would he feel impelled
to rape? Probably not, but who knows, and anyhow he
wasn't, so so what? He doesn't feel *impelled*, by the way, he
would object; merely inclined, and inclined to pursue that
occasional inclination. Is he a sadist? Well: No question but
he enjoys the forcing and threatening — except in the case

of old Seven's husband, and so he supposes he *does* have it in for women, sort of; so sue him! On the other hand, he would take no pleasure at all in carrying out his intimidative threats to shoot, knife, or mutilate his victims or in subjecting them to sexual violations beyond those aforespecified. In fact, he's not certain what he'll do if and when one vigorously resists him; perhaps retreat, perhaps shoot, knife, or mutilate. Except when "out hunting," he regards himself as an ordinary, peaceable fellow, politically conservative but environmentally concerned, with no taste for pornography or the violence so ubiquitous in American movies and network television.

Does Sam think about sooner or later getting caught, convicted, and jailed, or does he imagine raping an infinite series of women with impunity? Neither: He takes considerable pleasure in the recollection of his past operations but is not given to long-term projections. He has never regarded any next operation as his last; he takes them, so to speak, one at a time, as circumstances warrant. If asked whether he has ever reflected that it's only a matter of time until he's *doing* time, he would shrug, annoyed. He understands, more or less, that the risk factor in his serial operations has a cumulative aspect; his woozy mother is fond of declaring, apropos of nothing in particular, "The pitcher that goes always to the well eventually gets broken," but he does not imagine himself as going *always* to the well, only for some indefinite number of times yet.

It is Sam Buffett's practice to maintain a casual lookout for appropriate operational targets even when he's not in the actively hunting mode; indeed, it is the casual observation of a likely target that typically prompts the hunt, not vice versa. Standing at Claudia Tully's bank-window to deposit his take from Operation Seven, he happened to overhear her remark to the teller beside her that she'd be house-sitting through the month of March in her parents' place on Shawbridge Road and that she looked forward to rattling around all by herself in that big old house while they toured Greece and Italy. Mm hm, thought the Duct-Tape Rapist, and did a bit of subsequent reconnoitering, and bided his time till the appointed month. Strolling the Fenwick Island beach at afternoon's end yesterday (the first real beach-day of the week), he casually followed an attractive young mother and her two small children across the ocean highway and back to their cottage and observed that she seemed to be its only adult occupant; an after-dark reconnaissance and more extensive surveillance today confirmed that observation, suggested an operational plan, and piqued his interest: He has never "done" a woman with sleeping children, and imagines that there'd be no problem keeping her quiet and compliant. But that same unobtrusive scouting turned up the late-middle-aged couple next door to her — an easier mark approachwise (the ground slopes up to one rear corner of their raised sundeck) and very likely more cash-productive, but problematical as to management and what the hell, there's an ATM up the road in Bethany Beach if he runs short, so why risk it?

Why? Because that unpleasantness in Operation Seven still rankles him; for a moment there he was clear out of control, almost panicky, might actually have shot the guy. If he were running that operation again . . .

So: Supermom (thus he's come to think of the woman on the beach, admiring the tough-gentle way she manages the kids, roughhousing with them in the surf one minute, soothing their distresses or adjudicating their differences the next, and always talking to them *straight*, not in a put-on Mommy-voice) is unquestionably his target of choice: a succulent number, and there'd be no present indecision on his part if her sundeck had a ground-level corner like her neighbors', for easy access. Prepping for Operation Nine after a dinner of not-bad fajitas in an Ocean City Mex place, he pretty much decided to go for it once the sun was well down and Supermom's children were presumably asleep; it is only that bad aftertaste from Seven that has led him, while he's giving the kids time to crank up the old Z's, to re-review the piece-of-cake approach next door, in course of which he's been enjoying the extended shot of Mrs.'s bare boobs, not bad at all for her age, and her pantied butt, ditto, in the flickering light of their patio candle. Her skinny husband looks to be no great threat, though trim and fit-appearing for an old gent. The right way to've played it — the right way to *play* it, if the guy goes macho or gets his balls in an uproar like Mr. Seven . . .

Sam believes that he knows, now, the right way to play it, and although Supermom is hands down the sweeter score, he's tempted to clear his record, so to speak, by doing this couple without losing his cool or using more force than necessary. Now that Boobs has given up on the binoculars (seven-by-fifty "night glasses," Sam has observed, such as boaters use, quite able to resolve his crouching figure in the dim light if they're aimed his way), he edges closer through the cover of pines toward where the grade slopes up beside the deck, thinking that perhaps their conversation, if he can make it out, will tip the scales one way or the other. From his kit he fishes forth and dons the latex gloves and itchy ski mask.

Granted that life's cruelties and injustices are measureless, there is in it at least occasional justice too, however imperfect and sometimes accidental. Samuel Buffett's impending Spotted Fever, though severe, will do him less damage, alas, than he has doubtless done to any one of the targets of his operations past and to come. It will, however, be of a virulence sufficient to inflict upon him pneumonitis, uremia, and an extended general debilitation that will significantly increase the misery of his prison time after the resourceful victim of Operation Ten, a full year hence — another Claudia Tully, but with a literal vengeance — skillfully traps him into telephoning her, two weeks after her rape, for confidential therapy-referral, and holds him on the line long enough for Wilmington police to trace the call, reach the shopping-mall phone booth, and make the arrest. Ill and incarcerated, he will come to know something of his victims' pain and degradation, if never quite their terror. To hell, or one of its numerous terrestrial approximations, with him.

ॐ 6

"Time time time," Joan Pollard says now, and her husband guardedly replies, "Yes, well." The binoculars flat on the serving tray between them, they're both lying back now in their side-by-side lounge chairs, lightly holding hands across that space while waiting for their good-night Perseid meteor, and Frank's not sure whether what his wife has on her mind just now is bedtime, or their return to the city and what awaits them there, or (as the grim sigh in her tone suggests) both of the above plus evanescence and ephemerality in general, and in particular the brevity of even such an extended happy connection as theirs. He himself, now that he has retrieved the word *ephemerality*, sidetracks to a less voltaged association, as is his sometimes annoying habit:

"I've always liked the word *ephemerides*," he declares to her. "In the astronomical tables: upcoming celestial events and such. Ephemerides."

"Sounds like a minor Greek hero" to Joan, who is used to these deflections: "Epimenides, Ephemerides."

"The sons of Time?" Frank wonders, "Or 'children of the day,' maybe?"

"Of *a* day, like goddamn mayflies, and then good night. Who was it that ate his own children, anyhow?"

"Old Kronos?"

"It figures."

"*The true hero of every feast*," Frank remembers having seen Time somewhere called.

"The uninvited guest," in Joan's opinion, "who scarfs the canapés and guzzles the bubbly when nobody's looking, till before you know it the party's over."

"But he's the life of the party that he's also the death of, right? He's the fizz in the Codorníu — of which this is the end, by the way: fin du vin. Here's to Papa Time."

"Hell with that mother."

Frank turns his head herward. "Thirty years, her husband reminds his dearest friend: three-zero and counting."

"Freaking eyeblink." But she raises her flute to his.

"Yes. Well."

They sip.

"What was that?"

"Raccoon," Frank supposes. At moments lately it has almost seemed to him that he can not only feel but *hear* the tumor growing; yet he looks forward with all the more pleasure to embracing his sorrowed friend before dropping off into sweet sleep. Together now, at the same instant, they see a meteor directly overhead, streaking southwestward as if through the constellations. Sighs Frank: "There she blows. B-plus?"

"B-minus tops," in Joan's grade-book. She's trying to remember whether that Unitarian proto-hippie who married them in San Francisco in 1964 said *As long as you both shall live* or *Till death do you part*. "Maybe C-plus. Maybe we didn't even see the little sucker, so we can't go in yet."

"We saw it," her husband says gently.

∽ 7

Beginnings are exciting; middles are gratifying; but endings, boyoboy.

So here's our universe, reader, whatever its curvature. Somewhere or other in it is our galactic supercluster, almost unimaginably vast — ah, yes, here it is — from which a mighty close-up resolves our particular Local Cluster, and another just as mighty discovers our very own Milky Way galaxy, bless its unfathomable black hole of a heart: one more bright sand-grain on the dark beach of abyssal space. Zooming right in on it, we may just possibly find our dear solar system and its cozy inner belt of planets, including miscellaneous cometary debris. Sure enough, here's old Earth, complete with atmosphere — into which latter a fist-size lump of Comet Swift-Tuttle plunges, from our perspective, at 11:14 P.M. Eastern Daylight Savings Time on 13 August 1994, said plunge or anyhow collision effecting its prompt incineration in a meteoric streak over the eastern seaboard of North America, including the Atlantic coast of Delaware and Maryland's portion of Chesapeake Bay, where yours truly winds up a short story entitled "Ever After," having to do, on the human level, with Joan and Frank Pollard, among others. Here now some while later are the printed pages of that story, its several paragraphs, sentences, phrases. Look you now: See at its end the words *ever after*, their several letters, the *r* of *after* and the full stop after. Closer, closer, obliging reader: the millions of molecules of printer's ink composing that full stop; the several atoms of carbon in each of those molecules; the furious motion of subatomic particles in any one of those virtually immortal atoms, all but oblivious to time, raging on like so many separate universes since ours exploded into being: now here, now there, now briefly in this dot of ink until it crumble, fade, disperse; now on past the episode of human life on Earth to whatever comparably ephemeral next and next and next and on and on, neither happily nor un-, ever after.

Pillow Talk: Presently

... he goes on with the stories, on likewise with talking to her, agreeing and disagreeing, soothing, coaxing, distracting, beguiling them both as best he can with narrative possibilities still unforeclosed. There is no timetable, no hurry. The DO NOT DISTURB sign (in several languages) hangs on their outside doorknob. They have, as he has so often declared to her, all the time there is.

He remembers now that he forgot to tell her, back there when they were doing love and physics, about the sundry "multiverse" theories that have been popping up lately in scientific journals like ... well, alternative universes.

"Multiverses," she would have said, perhaps, eyes closed, musing back against their headboard or in her beach chair: "Sounds like a long poem."

I'll make it a short story, he'd have promised, and in fact does promise, in effect at least, and then amuses himself by imagining *her* this time replying, "No hurry, love: Things end soon enough in any case."

Now you're talking, he tells her, though the only voice in the room is his.

The not-so-short story begins:

I2.

Countdown: *Once Upon a Time*

⮟ 12 *Any line at all*

... can start a story. It doesn't have to be *Once upon* et cetera.

"Really."

Take the proposition just proposed, for example. Hang it between quotes like dialogue and tag it somewhere along the road, like this: "Any line at all," Sheila's new lover declared to her on the balcony of her parents' condo in Perdido Key, Florida, where the young pair had run off together for a long spring weekend and were currently lounging naked in mid-March forenoon sunlight, "can start a story." See what I mean?

"Maybe."

In fact, strictly speaking, the quotes and tag material aren't necessary.

"We suspected as much."

Throw me a line. Any line at all.

"You asked for it: Try this." Wherewith trim fortysomething Sarah, an amateur of physics who has taken up storywriting as a pastime and found in it what she now believes might be her real vocation, dashes off from memory (with a Delta Airlines ballpoint pen on a sheet of our hotel's stationery) Erwin Schrödinger's equation for the evolution over time of the wave functions of physical systems, an axiom of quantum mechanics:

$$i \, \frac{h}{2\pi} \, \frac{\partial}{\partial t} \, \Psi(x_1 \ldots x_{3N},t) = H\Psi(x_1 \ldots x_{3N},t)$$

"The ball," she then declares, rolling pertly onto her tum like an impish odalisque, "is in your court."

Nothing to it, replies her unfazed bed-companion. I'm going to use quotes again, although we understand et cetera:

"$i \, \frac{h}{2\pi} \, \frac{\partial}{\partial t} \, \Psi(x_1 \ldots x_{3N},t)$," Jerry scribbled across his half-dozing lover's tidy left buttock with a felt-tipped Kelly-green marking pen; on that young lady's equally appealing right he then added "$H\Psi(x_1 \ldots x_{3N},t)$," bridging her cleft and channeling its dainty semicolon with an elongated equal sign.

Sarah flexes her butt. "That tickles. What is it?"

It's Schrödinger's wave-function equation, which happens also to be the first element of Bohm's Alternative Theory, I believe, as well as the opening line of some other couple's story.

"No, I mean *that*."

Thanks to you, that is what it is. On with our story?

"Maybe. Is it Jerry talking now, or Joe or John or who?"

Your call.

"On with it, then, dear Fred. Where'd you learn physics, by the way?"

Relax just a quantum, and I'll tell you. Where'd you learn storytelling?

"Ah."

There we are. I picked up physics from my friendly. Local. Physics teacher. Okay?

"Easy does it."

Endings, on the other hand, not-so-young Frederick feels

obliged to recaution his not-so-young friend, physics coach, and narrative protégée, are another matter.

"Another story? Ouch."

Sorry. Better?

"Best."

Et cetera, one supposes.

     11 *From time to time*

. . . we talk like this, even now. One needs anyhow to imagine a couple so speaking: late-afternoon late-life lovers, post-coitally lassitudinous and sweat-wet, skin to skin. Pillow talk, however, you know . . . you really have to *be* there, in the ardent flesh. Joan and Frank Pollard are seasoned partners and old best friends: storms weathered, delights delighted in, ups downs ins outs, thousands of shared meals and matings under their still-trim belts. They've seen their several offspring through college, parents through their last age, professional careers through their gratifying peaks onto plateaus and thence into acceptably gentle decline and/or retirement, like their high-mileage bodies and sundry well-gratified appetites. Large surprises no longer either likely or hankered after, themby, at this stage of their game. Eros be praised, therefore and however, for certain small ones, such as their easeful making of love earlier today, at afternoon's end or evening's commencement, however one looks at it.

It's a rainy November Friday in Philadelphia, raw and wretched though not yet wintry, and, in its wet gray way, handsome. The couple have motored to the city from their Delaware Valley country seat for the opening of Joan's watercolor show this evening at her dealer's gallery in Society Hill. The artist herself drove their van, as she has come regularly to do this fall except for local errands; Frank is much weakened lately by his illness, belatedly diagnosed (his own procrastination) and found already to have metastasized. Prognosis grim indeed, but he has declined heroic measures in favor of palliatives while he considers how and when to end his story before it turns excruciating and/or undignified. The pair have discussed this subject both gravely and light-heartedly; they're in accord as to principle. Frank judges himself to have proceeded successfully, over the past months, right through "DABDA," the medical mnemonic for the stages of mourning as described by the psychiatrist Elisabeth Kübler-Ross: Denial, Anger, Bargaining, Depression, Acceptance. Having dwelt so long a while in the first of these, he likes to declare, he would readily have spent more time in the second and third, if there'd *been* more time, before arriving at the fourth and fifth. As for Joan, they agree that she's stalled in the neighborhood of B, with occasional relapses into Anger or even Denial and prolapses into Depression, but nary a smidgen yet of Acceptance of her partner's impending death.

After checking in at a favorite small hotel of theirs not far from the gallery, at Frank's insistence they strolled instead of driving or taxiing those few and handsome old brick blocks through the eased-off rain, to inspect Joan's dealer's mounting of the exhibition. *Water Watercolors*, it's being billed, although the series includes a number of pen-and-wash items as well: two dozen studies of that ubiquitous element in sundry modes and moods, from sun-fired rain-splatters on the windows of Joan's rural studio to a waterspout raging along the Atlantic horizon near their rented summer cottage. While his wife discussed with a gallery assistant some details of lighting and labeling as well as the program for the evening, Frank admiringly reviewed the works themselves, so intimately familiar to him and yet so splendidly official now, like one's children or students at graduation-time. It is the dozenth or so such opening that he has proudly attended over the years as Joan Pollard's stock rose slowly but steadily to its present comfortable level among collectors in the region; it will doubtless also be his last, as he has of necessity recognized many other recent things to have been, whether in retrospect or at the time: his last summer at their Fenwick Island cottage, last Perseid meteor shower, last set of tennis as his debilitation grew, last glorious October foliage-change in "their" valley, and now in all likelihood his final visit to this handsome city. Unthinkable, his still-Bargaining mate would insist if he spoke of it thus; but Frank's best evidence that he has attained DABDA's terminal A is that these recognitions, while inevitably saddening, afford him on balance these days as much gratification as dismay; that he has been blessed for so considerable a while (though less considerable than expected) if not with wealth or fame anyhow with the respect of his prep-school students and colleagues during his teaching years, the affection of his grown-up daughter and of Joan's grown-up son by each's previous marriage, and above all the loving companionship of his second life-partner, whose talent and belated recognition give him at least as much satisfaction as if they'd been his own.

In particular he paused before *Puddled Dew*, a study of that homely phenomenon in late-morning light on the deck of their seashore cottage. In the brochure of the exhibition, a critic-friend of Joan's has praised "certain dark suggestions between her bright lines, so to speak: turbulences on the verge of erupting through serene, even *pretty* surfaces." The critic instances specifically "the unnatural calm of *Waterspout Off Fenwick Island*, its surfless sea and insouciant bathers blithely unaware of or indifferent to the approaching funnel-cloud"; also "the disquietingly blood-like tints of *Puddled Dew*." Overdramatizings, in the Pollards' joint opinion: Squall lines and twisters don't normally approach East Coast beaches from offshore, for one thing, and so that waterspout will most likely have belonged to a storm already passed (Joan hadn't had heart to point out to her obliging critic-friend that, as anyone who knows beaches can see, the sunlit sand is still wet from a recent shower — an optical effect in which the artist justifiably takes pride); and while the critic herself is a Main Line blueblood, who ever saw the vital stuff in *lavender*? All the same, Frank thought now, the woman was onto something, as the literary critic Lionel Trilling had been in speaking of the "terror" lurking in Robert Frost's poetic rusticity: In retrospect, at least, *Waterspout* epitomizes the Pollards' "last summer" — a golden season of sweet work and play while Frank's late-detected cancer busily colonized his body. And although nothing sanguinary had been implied in the delicate wash of lavender light that *Puddled Dew*'s painter had taken such pleasure one August morning in capturing, that view from their sundeck happens to be toward the neighboring cottage, where — the very night after the picture was finished, perhaps while artist and spouse were watching Perseid meteors from that deck — a young divorced mother of two small children had been bound, raped, and robbed by the infamous "Duct-Tape Rapist" of Wilmington and environs, still at large. The Pollards had heard nothing until the courageous young woman, whom they'd befriended over the summer, woke them by telephone at 2 A.M., after her attacker had finally left the premises and she'd managed to cut through her bonds with a kitchen knife, to ask whether one of them would please baby-sit her still-sleeping children while the other drove her to the nearest police station and emergency room, so that she could report and be treated for her rape with minimal effect on the kids. The assault itself had drawn no blood, but in sawing awkwardly through her duct-tape manacles (behind her naked back) she had sliced the skin of one forearm with the serrated sandwich-knife, and so Frank had quietly cleaned up red spots and pudlets on the kitchen tiles while Joan chauffeured and comforted the victim through the rest of the night, and had played his grandfatherly part in next day's difficult charade of normalcy-for-the-children's-sake. Thus had there come indeed to be, though never consciously intended by the artist, "dark suggestions between her bright lines" and "turbulences on the verge of erupting" from the innocently puddled dew, as if some microscopic amplifier were picking up the roar of nuclear energy latent in placid molecules of the universal solvent. It is the same feeling that Frank gets these days from reviewing their photographs from that season: There's lively Marjorie on the beach, still inviolate and prettier even than his own daughter, with those two darling children; there he himself poses astride his bicycle, still not quite aware that his pancreas has set about to kill him in short order.

"Peg's one of those critics who like to think they've found an artist's secret key," Joan piffed when Frank spoke of this, en route back to their hotel. Meanings, she likes disingenuously to declare, bore her; artistry is what matters.

"I suppose they *do* find such keys now and then," her husband allowed — and leaned on her arm a bit as a spasm of his now-permanent gut ache threatened to double him over. "Secret ... ," he added in the most normal voice he could muster, "even from the artist herself."

"And sometimes there's no damn lock to be unlocked," stoutly maintained Joan Pollard, her heart constricting at his pain: "just a funky little key to hang on the critic's charm bracelet. Can you make it?"

"No problem. These things pass." But he stopped for a bit on the brick sidewalk, until the worst of it did. "*All passes*," he intoned meanwhile; "*art alone endures*. Matthew Arnold?"

"Chautauqua Institute," his wife reminded him — and Frank now remembered their having once shaken their heads, years ago, at that portentous inscription over the auditorium stage, on which a much-flawed production of a second-rate opera was in tedious progress. *For better or worse*, they had agreed should be added to the inscription.

By chance their pause was before a bookshop window featuring, among other displays, works on sundry linkages between science and art: Leonard Shlain's *Art & Physics: Parallel Visions in Space, Time & Light*; Susan Strehle's *Fiction in the Quantum Universe*; coffee-table albums of gorgeously intricate Mandelbrot fractals, both computer-generated and photographed in their many natural manifestations; and, mirabile dictu, a calendar for the upcoming year illustrated with da Vinci's drawings of turbulent water.

"Gotta have it," Frank decided on the spot, and notwithstanding Joan's mild complaint that beside Leonardo her *Puddled Dew* looks like piddled doo-doo (and the stabbing realization that she'll be a widow before that calendar has run), they went in and bought the thing to hang in Frank's study, used these days chiefly for family bookkeeping and medical-insurance paperwork.

On then to their hotel, in plenty of time to shower and change for the opening: a three-hour wine-and-cheeser, after which Joan's dealer has scheduled dinner with one of her principal Main Line collectors. It is in this leisurely interval of dishabille — Frank's gut-pain having subsided, but not Joan's soul-pain — that they found themselves agreeably aroused by the cozy ambiance, among other factors, and presently embracing, caressing, and making gentle but vigorous love. When they had been a new couple in her late twenties and his mid-thirties, the degree of their ardor and the proximity of their names (genders switched) to the "Frankie and Johnny" of Tin Pan Alley fame had made that old song a running tease between them. Oh lordy, how they could love! Belly-down on the mattress now with her spent friend full-length atop her, the woman half-growled, half-sighed into her pillow, "He done her *right*."

Alas, in their subsequent joint shower the man's abdominal cramp returned, with such severity that he was obliged to wrap himself in a bath towel and lie down before even drying himself, his knees clutched up toward his chest. "It'll pass; it'll pass," he insisted, dreading that this time it might not.

"Hospital," counterinsisted Joan. "Never mind Donato" — her dealer and the gallery owner — "I'll call for an ambulance."

But Frank wouldn't hear of that; they've agreed he'll have the final say in these matters for as long as he can, and he is resolved not to let things reach the point where he can't. He forbade her even to telephone Donato that they'll be late: If he's still out of action when get-dressed time comes, she'll show up as scheduled and he'll join her later. In the worst case, she'll go on from the gallery to dinner with the others and he'll order up something light from room service.

"Sexy small hotels don't have room service," Joan tearfully reminded him.

"So I'll diet, and you'll bring me a doggie bag from Le Bec Fin."

"Tiramisu?" — which they had become enamored of a dozen years past at a pleasant gay restaurant in Key West; pretended was the name of a Puccini aria; have found only inferior versions of in their subsequent travels, even in Italy.

"Chocolate Decadence," Frank counterproposed, "with raspberry sauce. Uh oh . . ." Just when his cramp seemed to be easing, he was seized by an urgent diarrhetic spasm and dashed half-doubled toiletward. Joan's legs went weak; she sat on the bed-edge, hearing him. "Are you managing?" she called in presently.

"Within the parameters. Bit of chocolate turbulence." He'd better sit this one out, so to speak, he decided and declared: "Get yourself dressed and out of here, s.v.p."

For his sake she did, and now dutifully has done, lord knows how. Three hours — two and a half, anyhow — of shmoozy small talk, her heart the whole time clenched fist-tight with concern. Donato, bless him, had kept the chitchat going and her wineglass filled, seeing to it she didn't get cornered overlong unless the cornerer was a likely customer. She had even managed to tease Peg, her critic-friend, with that "dark suggestions" business in the brochure (at the same time stroking her with Frank's comparison to the late eminent Professor Trilling), and Peg had cheerily responded, "Deny it till the cows come home, Joanie; Frost did the same thing, but the critics were right: 'Stopping by Woods on a Snowy Evening' is a poem about death."

Come restaurant-time, however, she could take it no longer, despite Frank's considerately phoning the gallery at six-thirty to tell her not to worry; he was in no pain and managing fine, but had decided to sit tight — "Sit loose," he had corrected himself — and let the trots run their course, excuse the expression and don't forget the tiramisu. She couldn't imagine that a collector's decision to buy or not to buy might hinge on the artist's physical presence at dinner (well, she could, actually, in Harry and Flo Perkins's creepy case), but if so, tant pis. Her husband was ill, and that was that; she told them as much, begged off dinner, and with some misgivings granted Donato's requested permission to confide "the truth" to the Perkinses once she was out of there. He was, after all, her dealer; had been so for years before his faith in her paid off, and she prays he'll remain so despite this evening's smallish turnout. If anything gets her through what lies ahead, it will be her work, and while she would no doubt paint even without a dealer to market the output, her professionality is at least as important to her as the income from her efforts.

Now she *is* out of there, by cab this time to make the short hop shorter yet. The driver's previous fare has left the evening *Inquirer* on the seat; Joan couldn't care less just now about dreadfulnesses in Bosnia, Rwanda, Haiti, but a more local headline catches her eye: DUCT-TAPE RAPIST SUSPECT ARRESTED. So brief is the ride, she has time to read only the lead paragraph by ambient street-light, to the effect that Delaware State Police have arrested a forty-nine-year old white plumbing and heating contractor in suburban Wilmington on suspicion of being the notorious serial "duct-tape rapist" of New Castle County and Delmarva beach resorts. Suspect declares innocence. She adds a quarter to her tip and takes the paper with her, to share the welcome news with Frank.

Having elevatored to their floor, she fumbles for but fails to find her room key in the clutter of her bag, then remembers that in her scattered exit from the hotel she dropped it into her pants-suit pocket. She must ask Frank sometime, her all-purpose infobase, why it is that whereas American hotel patrons customarily take their room keys with them on sorties from the premises, European hotel patrons customarily check theirs (with their massive pendants to reinforce the custom) at the front desk. She bets he'll know.

She is suddenly smitten with apprehension at what she'll find when she enters their room; actually closes her eyes for a moment, compresses her lips, then decisively turns key and doorknob and goes in. The space is dimly lit. Their bed's out of sight from the short entry-hall leading past the bathroom, but the television is turned on, its sound muted. Tropical reef-fish swim gorgeously across the silent screen; both Pollards are great fans of underwater cinematography. Lest her husband be sleeping, Joan suppresses her urge to call out to him.

Frank is, indeed, she finds, asleep: pajama'd, propped on his pillow against the headboard, looking altogether old and dead with his rumpled hair, closed eyes, and slacked-open mouth, the da Vinci calendar open on his blanketed, lamplit lap. So light is his respiration, it's the closed eyes that tell her he's merely sleeping after all; the day she finds him really dead, she supposes, his eyes will be open. The calendar, she sees now, is turned to February next, its graphic a meticulously rendered maelstrom. Leonardo, boyoboy. Which famous physicist was it, Joan hopes she'll remember to ask Frank along with the hotel-key question, who on his deathbed declared his intention to query God in Heaven on two matters, quantum electrodynamics and turbulence, and expressed his optimism that the Almighty might actually be able to shed some light on the former? Frank will know. Won't you, Frank.

Won't you, Frank.

Against Australia's Great Barrier Reef, where it must be midmorning now, the serried waves smash in from the Coral Sea. Viewed submarinely, each explodes in a chaos of bubbles, their swirls unpredictable though perhaps retrospectively explainable; they sweep the unalarmed tangs and wrasses brilliantly this way and that, alert but mindless and at home in their awesomely complex, vast and protean, utterly mindless element.

❧ 10 *He agrees to continue,*

. . . does our narrator, stipulating only that she do likewise, and he'll readily take her silence for assent.

"Agrees with whom?"

Aha: With the late Greek writer Nikos Kazantzakis, for one, author of *Zorba* et cetera, who, in a letter to his second wife, Eleni, expresses his hope that on his deathbed he'll have the opportunity to bid good-bye to, perhaps even *kiss* good-bye, the various fruits of the Mediterranean that he has so relished through his decades. It is a happily pagan wish, a sort of thanksgiving, altogether more life-affirming (if that's the proper adjective for a hypothetical dying wish) than extreme unction or even "setting one's affairs in order." One's dying wish, after all, so far from being a death-wish, may well be the wish for life, even where there is no further hope therefor. One imagines the old Cretan bussing a peach and exclaiming, "Good-bye, dear peaches!"; a pear: "Thank you, sweet pears!"; a plum: "Plump plums, *epharisto*!"; then a persimmon, a pomegranate, and he's still only in the P's, having kissed his way already from apples through oranges, and with quinces through zucchinis yet to go.

Not so, you'll say: Zucchini stretches the category Fruits in the direction of metaphor, as in "fruits of the earth," thence to fruits of the sea, fruits of knowledge, Fruit of the Loom underwear, etc. — no problem for *this* fareweller, who has in fact rather enjoyed a lifetimesworth of stepping into and out of undies both boxer and brief, the latter both flied and flyless, and of assisting love-partners out of and into theirs: *Mwah*, dear delicate deliciosas! Stretch away, say some of us — as, after all, old Zorba there may be said to be stretching *his* category the other way, letting one papaya stand poetically for the class Papayas, as if there weren't differences among individual specimens of each variety — between Joe Papaya and Fred Papaya, for example, not to mention Fred and Gladys — in some instances as significant as their Linnaean similarities. Would he, bidding sad adieu to only one of his several children (if several he had, if any he had, which, as it happens, Kazantzakis did not), say, "That does it for the fruit of my loins"? Or, last-embracing his dear Eleni, "That takes care of Human Beings"? Of course not, unless she were — as, come to think of it, would be the likely case — the last on his list (because the most important) in that category.

This point made, one might in fact lay down reasonable parameters of valediction: Among human beings, farewell to individuals as individuals, not as representatives of classes, although even here there will be not only categories but hierarchies — one's spouse or other most significant other, the rest of one's immediate family, one's closest friends and associates, one's extended family, and on to one's less close but still valued friends, neighbors, colleagues, and acquaintances as far as time permits. Among non-human animals, individual pets (excepting perhaps the egg-laying tropical fish in one's tropical-fish tank, which tend to come in anonymous schools of half a dozen or so, as opposed to the more individualized live-bearing couples) but class representatives of whatever other species one inclines to valedict: a single blue crab or monarch butterfly or black-capped chickadee for the lot, etc. Likewise trees except for certain much-prized specimens such as the spreading Kwanzan cherry and perfect Zumi that grace one's waterfront lawn; house plants ditto, and all other objects and artifacts, always allowing for separable bye-byes to both individuals *and* their classes where called for: good-bye, e.g., to particular poems but also to Poetry; to particular places but also to Geography, Terrain, Locale; to Swiss Army knives in general but in particular to the trusty Tinkerer in one's trouser-pocket. One cloud of each sort — cirrus, cumulus, cumulonimbus, and the rest — should do for all; likewise one sample of each weather — fine, showery, warm, cool, humid, dry, still, brisk (and their sundry combinations, fine-warm-dry-still, fine-warm-*humid*-still, etc.) for all individual days (and nights) of that weather, notwithstanding that a foggy mild still early morning is surely a pleasure differentiable from that of the same conditions at noon or Happy Hour.

And so forth. Having agreed on the "rules," however, one ought surely to feel free to take every legitimate advantage themof, as one does in preparing one's income-tax return. Granted that the orange enjoyed this morning is not the orange enjoyed the morning before, and further that in the nature of the case one cannot kiss good-bye the oranges enjoyed but only their memory as embodied in the orange one kisses and therefore has yet to enjoy except in nostalgic anticipation (or in nostalgia *tout court* if one be at this point no longer permitted to partake of what one has valedicted), it may nevertheless be argued that to let one orange stand for Oranges is to ignore not only Charles and Chiquita Orange, so to speak, but the distinguishable pleasures of the subset Jaffas versus Mandarins, Floridas, Californias, and the rest. Who would maintain that to bid adiós to the oranges of Seville is to do likewise to those of Valencia, or that Bloods are the same as Navels, kiss-good-byewise? As well deny the difference between navels themselves: those that one has once upon an excited time kissed hello and must tenderly now kiss good-bye as opposed to those that one has enjoyed the more-or-less-innocent mere sight of, live or photographed, on beach or movie-screen or *Playboy* centerfold or newspaper lingerie advertisement — and not forgetting, in the "hello there" category, the dear belly buttons of one's children, be they (the buttons) Innies or Outies, before they (the children) attain the age of parental-pipik-kissing protest. One dainty, tonguable, sea-salt- and sun-lotion-tasting navel stand for all? Just ask your current bedmate whether her/his may represent to you its serial predecessors!

To what end, a certain sort might ask, these protracted, fractalized, interminable addios, like the tubercular soprano's in *Traviata* or *Bohème*? To the end, it goes without saying, of postponing the end; and their ground-perspective on this matter divides good-byers into two camps, each calling for its own farewell though not necessarily on its own terms. Faced with the facts that all things end and that good-byes to life's pleasures have about them an inevitable component of sadness, there are those who would abbreviate or even avoid valediction; who, indeed, feel that what must end in any case (i.e., everything, even unto art) had as well be dispatched in short order, if even begun. We know of whom we speak, who would bid a curt good-bye to such bitter-sweet good-byes as Kazantzakis's, for example. And then there are those who, accepting the inevitable, are however in no rush to attain it; who on the contrary find that valediction hath its own mournful pleasures, and who therefore et cetera. Take as a thought-experiment the case of those Florentine assassins of whom Dante is reminded in Canto XIX of his *Inferno* (Circle VIII, Ditch iii, lines 49–51), executed by live burial trussed head-downward in a hole. Thus positioned for quietus, they are permitted their last confession to the priest, who must bend low to hear it as Dante bends to hear the simoniac Pope Nicholas III and, bending, is put in mind of those condemned assassins. Your former sort of valedictor in this pass would say simply, "*Nunc dimittis*; get it done with." Your latter, on the other hand — to which category belong the wretched Nicholas, also Kazantzakis, one imagines, and most certainly the present narrator — will draw his confession out, so to speak, simply so to speak, perhaps even fabricating a few peccadilloes to pad the catalogue and thus adding the sin of lying to the list of his factual lapses to be confessed.

Not that any one of those three aforespecified fictors, mind, might be taken as "standing for" the others, whether right-side up or upside down, and therefore kissed good-bye in their stead. Bear in mind our Rule of Individuals, not to mention the diplomacy of love: One is oneself, one prefers to believe, not the surrogate of one's analogs and forerunners, and would be kissed only as such. . . .

Unless, of course, it is one's *last* kiss, the kiss-good-bye-to-good-bye-kisses kiss, in which case by all means kiss one (*this* one, anyhow) not only as himself in propria persona but as each and every of his lucky avatars, real and fantasized, in every mood/mode/venue/weather, to the end of love and breath and language and beyond, the end of this story and of all stories, the end of this agreed-upon continuation and its attendant stipulation —

"No stipulations."

♠ 9 *Very well, then, damn it,*

. . . they'll play it *her* way: Nunc dimittis, whambamthankyoumaam. No proper close-out of their visit; no last reveling in the limpid light of their ultimate resort, no celebratory bye-bye breakfast of ultimate sesame-seed bagels on their seaside balcony, no final exercise laps in the pool, last set of tennis, last light lunch in the annex restaurant, last skinny-dip-snorkel out to the reef off their pet pocket-beach, no subsequent drowsy lounge-chair beach-out, last Jacuzzi, last late-afternoon retreat to make last love in love's last mode, snoozing off skin to skin in each other's arms; no final wake-up call therefrom, final hors d'oeuvres and fin du vin. They'll simply suitcase their stuff, maybe not even that, hell with it, just throw on their get-out-of-here duds, button buttons snap snaps zip zippers lock locks and drop their room key in the Express Check-Out slot, that's for them, all right, old Mr. and Ms. Pre-Paid, or not even that, just pop it into any letterbox down the line, return postage guaranteed, hell with it, time to go.

"No. He's jumping to conclusions."

Name of the game, yes?

"No. But Carrying On for Its Own Sake isn't the name of the game, either."

Tell him all about it; he has an infinite attention span.

"No. Anyhow, they can't lock locks drop key et cet yet."

No?

"No. They've *lost* their key."

Lost their key?

"No: mislaid it. Would he mind awfully searching high and low for it? She's pooped beyond pooped."

His pleasure. Is it here?

"No. Stop that."

Here?

"No no no no no no no. What part of No needs clarification?"

This part?

"Maybe."

Here.

"Here."

Hear hear.

"Story of their life."

On with it, then.

❧ 8 *What in this pass they dream,*

. . . this terminally playful pair, when presently they drowse, shall be passed over: Dream-sequences are a no-no in their house, be it only a rented resort-room on some Caribbean or Florida key, latest and last of a fortunately extended series over the hard-working decades of their coupled life-stories, or story of their coupled life. Let them sleep much-needed sleep now, rest as best they can in peace, while the author (but not narrator-in-chief) of this rhizomatic tale hunts randomly high and low among sundry other losses, his own included, for their missing key. As with any such search, we'll not be surprised if this turns up surprising items other than its object. Is it here? Nope. Here? Nah. Here, perhaps? Unh-unh — but hey, look what we've found instead:

A few blocks from where these words and I find each other like more or less predestined lovers, astronomers at the Space Telescope Science Institute search for the lost Dark Matter of the universe — no trifling loss, as it theoretically comprises some ninety percent of the whole shebang and is the key to whether that shebang goes on shebanging, achieves some equilibrium, or with a mighty sigh relapses into the Big Crunch. With the aid of the Hubble Space Telescope, they'd hoped to find what they're after in the form of plenteous Red Dwarf stars too dim to see with ground-based instruments; when however the mighty Hubble scanned likely large voids in our Milky Way galaxy, instead of revealing them to be red-peppered with the missing matter it showed them dark and empty as Mother Hubbard's cupboard or the pocket in which you're *sure* you put those keys, and by the way turned up another head-scratcher: evidence that the universe is several billion years *younger* than its oldest stars, as we're accustomed to measuring their respective ages. Go figure — and don't be surprised if, searching for a lost thread, you find instead the Lost Chord, the Lost Generation, the Lost Battalion of World War One, the ten lost tribes of Israel (toting in their backpacks the missing two books of the original Septateuch), the lost continent of Atlantis, Louis XVII (the Lost Dauphin) of France, the works of classical antiquity lost to the Christian Dark Ages, the lost cities of Africa, assorted lost sheep and illusions, opportunities and causes, lost youth and sleep, arts and languages, lost time never to be recaptured or made up for, and all the wax ever lost by Benvenuto Cellini while casting jewelry by the method called *cire perdu,* of which yours truly is irreverently reminded whenever he sees advertisements for the product of the Maryland poultry magnate Frank Perdue. When will all those *poules perdues* come home to roost?

Here one comes now, a-cluck from Memory's brooder or a-clink from the scattered treasury of lost coins: *le franc perdu* of the only literal key that I can recall ever having lost: In July 1983, my wife and I rented a funky little Renault wagon in Tangier, Morocco, whither we had flown for me to lecture on Scheherazade's menstrual calendar as a key to *The 1001 Nights*. From our lodgings in La Grand Hotel Villa de France, where Matisse had been inspired to paint his odalisques, in the city that had earlier inspired Rimsky-Korsakov to compose his *Scheherazade*, we had explored on foot the bustling, redolent Medina, the Saccos both Grand and Petit, and the Kasbah; preferring to lose ourselves without professional assistance, we had shaken off disagreeably sticky would-be guides and had shrugged off a startling anti-Semitic tirade from one such reject; we had been serenaded morningly by urban roosters and five times daily by the muezzin's amplified prayer-calls from the neighborhood mosque-minaret; and we had decided to extend down-coast our innocent first foray into Islam. Aficionados of shores and beaches, points and promontories, corniches and capes and coastlines, once I had mastered the Renault's exotic dashboard gearshift we drove on the last day of Ramadan through bougainvillea and dazzling sunshine east from Tangier to the cliffs of Cap Spartel, where the Strait of Gibraltar meets the Atlantic, thence alongshore southward through fish-rich Asilah to an off-road beach park called La Forêt Diplomatique, where we paused for a swim. At the djellaba'd beach-warden's direction, I·parked (and locked) our squat little wagon among the pines, and faute de mieux (or perhaps a touch OD'd on Arabiana: camels on the beach, a scattering of cabanas like nomads' tents, some of the older women black-veiled as well as -caftaned) dropped the keys into my swim-trunks pocket, whence in course of our romping in the surf they joined the vast inventory of the lost at sea.

Dismay; indeed, alarm, as we were a considerable way from anywhere, in a forêt sans telephones or helpful park rangers, on a plage sans lifeguards or other officials except the elderly, perhaps self-appointed director of parking, who was sternly sympathetic when in faulty French we reported our loss, but unable to assist us in any fashion. Few other picnickers/bathers about, and they by the look of them deeply local; no Arabic at our command beyond a naughty glossary picked up from Scheherazade, and while most Moroccan businessfolk speak French or Spanish or English, ordinary workfolk often don't. Anyhow, Tangier was several hours distant; even the main coastal highway (where there might be buses) was a few kilometers from the beach, and the afternoon was running, and we were scheduled for dinner back at the American School before my P.M. lecture — which, given the subject, I had to hope would at worst be merely lost on the Tangerians in my audience and not offensive to them.

A dozen years later, upstreet from the Hubble astronomers, I pen these words: Ergo, we are not still stranded in Morocco's Forêt Diplomatique, our infidel bones a-bleach in the Afric sand while our rented Renault rusts 'neath yonder pines. No matter the mechanics of our and the car's retrieval (helpful Brit motorcyclist to the highway; even more helpful Arab family, out for an end-of-Ramadan holiday drive, to Tangier with a pair of grateful middle-aged Yank tourists; helpful and well-tipped driver from the rental agency next day, who of course had copies of the keys; steadfast beach-warden, who with pained dignity let the agency-chap know that my eight-dirham tip was incommensurate with his having kept watch "all night" over our now finally unlocked wagonette, but that another two DH would do the trick); the point of this lost-key anecdote, which I had scarcely since thought of until this temporizing digression recalled it to me, is . . .

But in refinding the story, I find I've lost its point. Better to lose than to be lost? That depends. Better the key lost than the car? For sure, in this instance anyhow. But although a *roman à clef*, for example, ought to be at least reasonably intelligible without its clef, a code without its key is as meaningless as a key without its code. And if, moreover, as has elsewhere been proposed, the key to the treasure may *be* the treasure, then . . .

Well. Unlike Anton Chekhov, Ernest Hemingway, Ralph Ellison, and other scribblers too numerous to catalogue, I have never lost a manuscript (the Lost Original, or "Mother of the Book," is a tradition as old as writing, echoed in the East by the lost six-sevenths of the *Kathā Sarit Sāgara*, or Ocean of Story, and in the West by the aforenoted lost two-sevenths of what's since been the Pentateuch), neither my own nor any of my four decadesworth of students'. At age twelve or so I was myself once briefly lost in a funhouse, and a quarter-century later found a story in that loss, which however is in no respect a *conte à clef*. My first marriage proved a net loss, but the net that lost it holds still some valued souvenirs. To Caribbean condo-burglars I lost my journal of certain post-Moroccan travels, and later recovered it from, of all unlikely places, the bottom of a beachside Jacuzzi — but that, too, is a tale to be found in another once upon a time than this; ditto that of the loss of my favorite hat, a Basque boina, into the awesome Tajo de Ronda in Andalusia, and its improbable, consequential recovery. Life, I do not doubt, is a game that affords its players only different ways to lose; that being the case, vive la différence. Sometimes, Q.E.D., what we've lost we may refind, although we shall most surely lose it again, one way or another. Christian scripture teaches that one must lose one's life in order to find it, and that's no mere Lost & Found gospel sophistry, for in truth one may find what thitherto had not been one's to lose: a coin in the grass; a bottled message to whom it may concern; a perfectly satisfactory pair of women's sunglasses five meters deep on a coral reef and, lolling near it in the lazy current, a palimpsestic page from some novel or short story (more legible than intelligible, at least out of context, despite its immersion), as if some mermaid had been interrupted in mid-read; a splendid new life-partner; a narrative voice wherewith not only to commence but to go on, on, on with the surmisable story.

Or we may not, serendipitously, so find. "*Perdido*," sings persistently the old swing-band tune of that name: "*Perdido, perdido, perdido* [two, three, four], *perdido, perdido, perdido* . . ." et cet. ad lib. ad inf.

❧ 7 & 6 "*Waves explained*

. . . are not explained away," she presently declares; "likewise particles," and he's not inclined to argue. End-of-their-tether body-and-soulmates, still-ardent skin to skin, their meter ticking even as Time's taxi waits. Have they, for example — while brooding over hadrons and leptons, fermions and bosons, sparticles and photinos — sportively removed each other's underpants with their teeth?

"Goes without saying."

So it would've gone, anyhow, once upon a time.

"And so it went." Then, presently: "So what? Please?"

Ah, so, he ventures. Then, presently: *Complementarity* is the nub of it, wouldn't she say? The key to Father Time's cupboard?

"Not impossibly, once explained. Or possibly not."

Or possibly so *until* explained.

"So . . ."

So let's explain till the cows come home, understanding that what fails to account for those cows may nevertheless fetch 'em, no? What fails to explain away may anyhow explain into real presence.

"She's all ears, I guess."

By no means, but we have to start somewhere. They've made love, this couple of ours —

"Start there. Couple of hours?"

Couple of minutes here, couple of half-hours there. It adds up.

"Couple of decades, till the cows et cetera. But not ad infinitum. Never enough."

Because besides lovemaking, they've loved making: their life together; kids and connections, headway and leeway. . . .

"Better people of their students; better students of their people."

Meals and music, hay and whoopee, beds and voyages and decisions.

"A living, jointly and severally. Waves, trouble, and messes now and then."

They never enjoyed making those. But they did clean them up, best they could; we'll say that for them.

"Making sense and nonsense, he was saying . . ."

Even trans-sense, now and then. Despite or because of or notwithstanding which, here they are: last-resorted, at sixes and sevens. . . .

"He mentioned complementarity."

She mentioned waves and particles.

"On with their story, then, s.v.p., moving their bodies as little as possible. Don't make waves while we're riding one."

Wave*hood*, then, he'll presently remind her, and particle-

hood: In the microworld, those are as inescapably complementary as momentum and position — or momentum *versus*
position, one might as well say. Your innocent, minding-its-
own-business photon or electron has both until *we* mind its
business, whereupon, as has been demonstrated, its wavehood gives way to particality, and momentum to position,
or vice versa.

"Is he suggesting, maybe, that couplehood and individu-
ality are like that? Is he hinting that she has her herness and
he his hisness, but that then there's their theirness, in which
she partakes of his hisness, long may it wave —"

And he all but eats and drinks her herness. . . .

"What's this *all but?*"

Slip of his distracted tongue. The point just now is that
it's not only their theirness that's both complementary to and
comprised of her herness and his hisness. After so much skin-
talk, pillow talk, talk-talk, and busy cohabitation; so much
sturm und drang und fun and games, her herness comprises
a fair share of his hisness, and vice versa.

"Mi palapa es su palapa — all but."

Or as they say at our Institute for Narrative Physics, his
and her shared space-time equals their worldline, and here's
where things get dizzy-making.

"May the cows not come too soon. She's enjoying this,
more than not, under the circumstances."

He likewise — despite their being, as aforeremarked, at
sevens and sixes. Their particality is at critical odds with their
wavehood, let's say, and yet . . .

"Thanks be to the muse of physical narrative for that *and
yet* . . ."

And for the suspension points thereafter: their only hope.
Think of their life-stories, separate and joint, as an extended
though alas not infinite string of past such points, at any one
of which each of them might have done A instead of B, or

had X happen to them rather than Y. Their worldline — which we'll take the liberty of calling their storyline —

"Take."

— is the sum of all such points thus far.

"So few to go! Maybe only one more."

Or maybe more than one only. In any case, what he'd have the pair of them perpend is that in physics and fiction alike, at any of many of those waypoints in space-time, alternative worldlines are not only imaginable but evidently quite possible — some, of course, more consequential than others. It *seems*, at least, that she could've ordered the gambas a la plancha at lunch instead of the chiperones, or the vino tinto instead of the blanco —

"With chiperones? Not her! But she might very well have gone to Macy's instead of to Bloomingdale's on a certain afternoon twelve chapters ago, or to Macy's *before* Bloomingdale's, or straight to Bloomie's Bedding department without detouring through Housewares, and thus would never've re-met him there amid the Krups coffeemakers. *That*'s a scary one."

Indeed — always remembering, however, for perspective's sake, that the Rwandan and Bosnian disasters and the rest would no doubt have happened despite all the Butterfly Effects from that handshake among the Krupses. And yet the contingency of this couple's re-meeting is less sobering than the consideration that in at least as many storyworldlines as not, it *didn't* happen. B happened instead, or C or D, and he and she went on with their separate stories separately.

"Do we have to? Multiverses?"

We do: It all starts with neutron decay, I'm afraid.

"So is she! Too late in the day to start with the neutrons! Too late in their story!"

Not in *this* their-story. Any cows in sight?

"Only a couple of geckos cuddling on the wall up there. On with the neutrons, she supposes; she'll let him know."

The short version, then. Back at the Institute of Love Among the Quanta, when we watched for a neutron to decay into a proton or an electron or an antineutrino, our watch was nearly always in the neighborhood of twenty minutes, right? Give or take five or ten. On the other hand, once in a while the thing would pop off immediately, and now and then we had to wait for it fucking forever.

"Particle physics is such a turn-on."

One goes on to remind her that in the "multiverse" reading of quantum mechanics, for each moment at which that neutron *might* decay, there's a universe in which it does or did, and a fortiori there's a version of ourselves the observer who observes that decay of that particular neutron at that particular moment in that particular universe.

"Holding hands."

In some universes yes, in others no, tant pis.

"The bottom line, guys, is that whatever *can* happen, physically speaking, *does* happen, in some actual alternative version of 'our' universe. In this one, meanwhile (she quotes her erstwhile mentor skin to skin), 'Quantum theory is probabilistic in predicting the chance of a given outcome in some *particular* universe, but it's deterministic in prescribing the proportion of universes in which that particular outcome comes out.' Did any real lovers in the history of the world ever pillow-talk like this?"

In most universes no; in some yes, and brava. So to get right to it — but why hurry?

"Because their clock is running. So to get right to it, there are universes in which we never met, and others in which we met but didn't re-meet. Her and him."

And plenty more in which we met and re-met, but some crucial next plot-corner wasn't turned: no follow-through, no rising action.

"No Her introducing Him to sashimi and Erik Satie and mountain-biking."

No Him introducing her to X and Y and Z.

"Which she's been hooked on ever since."

Universes in which, even as you and I lie here now like a couple of burned-out geckos, *they* never became lovers.

"Universes in which they not only became lovers but married, in some cases happily, in others not. Had children; didn't have children . . ."

Had children whom they treasured and were treasured by at every stage of the kids' development and their own, including even American adolescence and middlescence, believe it or not, respectively.

"That's the universe for me."

Next time, for sure.

"There is no —"

Of course there is, maybe: Closed Timelike Loops, Spacetime Wormholes between scenarios. I'll loop back to those.

"Next time, maybe. Meanwhile, chez l'Institut . . ."

This just in: There are universes in which the best of all those possible worldlines comes to pass, but *only in some fiction within that universe*: a made-for-TV movie, maybe, or a stage play, or a novel or short story. In those universes, She and He are mere words on a page.

"Not words on a page!"

Well: not *mere*, for sure.

"This and this, words on a page? These?"

Hard to accept, but quite possibly so. Quite probably, even. *Necessarily*, in fact, we suppose, since such a thing can be imagined within the bounds of physical reality.

"Not by her. Speak for himself."

He's speaking for all those other selves of theirs: the other usses going on with our other stories in those other universes.

"Stories with better endings, is what he's thinking."

Let him think it. The point is, in the story they're in, up to its denouement he wouldn't change a word.

"Thanks for that. *She* might edit a couple here and there, she supposes. Not the couple-couple, though. Not the Him of them, anyhow."

He wouldn't even diddle the denouement, come to that —

"And they *have* come to that."

— he'd only postpone it, unspeakable as it is. The best of all worldlines that come to pass *does* come to pass — and then it passes.

"*Art alone endures.* Thomas Carlyle? Frank Lloyd Wright? But art passes, too."

For sure. Art passes to Mort —

"Who passes to Irving, who goes in for the score."

Seven-six Mort d'Art, in the bottom of the twelfth.

"What game *is* this?"

Till the Cows Come Home: A Love Story.

Presently: "Dearest friend, they're home. They never left, she suspects."

Cows Explained, then.

"But not explained away. Like quantum electrodynamic dramaturgy."

QED, muse be praised. Likewise love.

Presently: "Q.E.D."

❧ 5,4,3,2: "On

. . . with the story," he would have her insist, however spent the pair of them at this point in this version of their coupled worldline, were he its author instead of its provisional narrator: "Once upon a time ad infinitum," while we rest upon each other crown to sole.

"Hey: They're soixante-neufing?"

In some versions. But what he meant was brow brow arms arms chest chest belly belly thighs thighs et cet, she draped atop him doggo in the dark; not sixty-nining but five-four-three-twoing, except when some story puts their count on Hold. Once upon a time, he'd tell her . . .

Once upon a time, he *tells* her, there was this couple freeze-framed in spacetime, or *as if* freeze-framed, the way you and I would be if we were flying cross-country again, east to west at six hundred miles per hour while the USA zips under us west to east at a thousand per, carrying with it Earth's atmosphere and our DC-10 at a net speed of minus four hundred, while our planet chugs around the Sun at sixty-six thousand plus and our solar system laps the Milky Way at half a million mph and our galactic Local Group sprints en bloc toward the Great Attractor at maybe a million und so weiter, but the effect for us is as of sitting still in the dark with our plastic tumblers of Mendocino Chablis at thirty-two thousand feet over the Mississippi, let's say — which point like any point could be considered for us just then the *Stillpunkt* at the center of our universe and all others, their vertiginous motions and countermotions reckoned relatively therefrom. Ignoring the in-flight movie more or less in progress (appropriately freeze-framed just now in midst of a special-effect chase scene), we click glass-rims in the muted cabin light and toast our Story Thus Far, perhaps only just begun in consequence of each's noticing that her/his attractive seatmate happened to be scanning the same in-flight magazine photospread as her-/himself — "Island Hideaways," it's called, let's say — and discovering in bemused conversation that each in an earlier life-chapter had once sojourned in the other's favorite themof, almost though not quite at the same time but in fact at the same resort complex, Cayo Olvidado, and further — get this — that each in course of said romantic escapade (the one then-couple married but not honeymooning, the other honeymooning but not married) had found and retrieved, while snorkeling the coral reef just off the beach, a page torn or unglued or otherwise detached from some paperback novel and bottled like a message of distress, hers bone-dry on the sea-floor in a well-capped former rum-fifth inexplicably half-filled with pebbles to make it sink, his paradoxically afloat in a likewise well-capped wine-jug filled with sea water and perched high and dry on an exposed coral ledge. Quelle coïncidence! Quel cute meet, now that we've met! So what'd hers say?

"Hard to tell, 'cause it was just the closing words of some story and not even in complete sentences: *Bosnia, Haiti, Rwanda. The web of the world.* Rest of the page blank. Go figure. Yours?"

Some SF or semi-cyberpunk thing, as he remembers: *The Dream-Park Project*, let's call it, from which across the years bits still come back to him: *Alura, their shapely cave-guide, tugged at Fred's sleeve and cried, "Must go now!" Ariana, however, watched the approaching lava-flow with the practiced eye of one who has worked this Reality-Level before. "The missing key," Walt muttered,* dot dot dot et cetera.

"Got it," his seatmate says, and sips and chuckles, and permits herself to wonder whether those two pages mightn't constitute *their* passkey to a new and liberating connection, if joined like the sundered moieties of an old-time indenture bill.

"Sundered moieties?"

We talk like that now and then, pour le sport, sometimes even with our own last-lapped indentures postcoitally still snugged. Anyhow *they* used so to speak, she and he, once upon. Once upon another time, he tells her now, there was this chap alone in his shoreside digs, yet not alone in being alone there: great mother hurricane approaching, say; end of the world, maybe; hatches all battened, all storm-preps prepped, nothing left but to wait 'er out, maybe pop a cold one while there's still one cold to pop, tell himself a couple couple-stories in the dark: the one, e.g., about the youngish neighbor-lady every bit as independent as he, likewise battened down next door to ride out the blow with no company more interesting than her saddle-brown Chesapeake retriever. He spins out versions of their possible story as the wind off the bay begins to pipe in earnest: She he, he she, hi ho, ho hum, and then one day aha —

"The end," she'd say. No way, 'd say he: There're narrative options still unforeclosed, other storyworldlines wormholing through the multiverse. "Happy endings are all alike," she'd retort, were she the retorting sort, "but in *this* universe, at least, delta p times delta q equals or exceeds h-bar over two, and so while it may *seem* that Achilles can never reach the tortoise nor any tale its end, he does and theirs did, amen."

Maybe once upon a time it did, he grants, amending her amen, but that's another story: the one in which a terminal brace of longtime lovers checks into what they're grimly calling their Last Resort. There's a thing to be done, but they're in no rush. They've time yet. . . .

"No."

Time time time time; never enough, but some still yet . . .

"No."

No end-stops in *their* love-story; only semicolons, suspension points . . .

"No."

. . . between any one such which and the next, space-time to spare; still space, still time . . .

"No."

Tales unended, unmiddled, unbegun; untold tales untold; unnumbered once-upons-a —

"No."

☙ 1 *Check-out*

. . . time come and gone long since; she likewise, his without-whom-nothing.

There is (he nevertheless tells her presently) a narrative alternative universe, an alternative narrative universe in which by this time at this point in this particular wormholed worldline the pair of them are *laughing*, although what's come to pass is anything but a laughing matter. He had all but forgotten that *laugh* of hers, of theirs, ours — unbuckled and unabashed, merry beyond pain, beyond merriment, existential yet gut-deep — but he hears it now, all right: They're laughing freely, almost helplessly, the way they used so often to find themselves laughing, sometimes despite themselves even in circumstances grim or solemn, or anyhow wanting so to do, back in the beginning: their so-fortuitous, staggeringly contingent, richly consequential once upon.

T-zero.